AF573702

Doomsday Contract

by the same author

THE CONNECTOR
COUNTERSTRIKE ENTEBBE

Tony Williamson

Doomsday Contract

COLLINS
St James's Place, London
1977

William Collins Sons & Co Ltd
London · Glasgow · Sydney · Auckland
Toronto · Johannesburg

First published 1977

ISBN 0 00 222153 5

Set in Linotype Times
Made and Printed in Great Britain by
William Collins Sons & Co. Ltd, Glasgow

FOR RAYA

Whoever and Wherever she may be

Chapter 1

The four men sat in miserable silence, sweating in the white Cougar that shimmered in the Nevada air. Ahead, the black tarmac road wound between sandstone cliffs that gave the name to Stonewall Pass, before falling away to the barren wastes of the desert below. It was noon, hotter than the dungeons of hell, and death was only a whisper away.

'Here comes the chopper,' said the driver, squinting up into the harsh light.

The others made no move, content to wait until the chattering of rotor blades enveloped them. The man beside the driver was tall and thin, his face pinched, glistening with a sheen of perspiration that gave his features a coppery cast. In the rear were two who might have been brothers, except that they had never met before this day. They were squat, heavily-muscled men, with small eyes and flat, empty faces. Their hair was brown, thick and untidy, and they each wore PVC overalls with a coating of a silver, metallic substance. The trousers were tucked into short rubber boots, and at the wrists the garments were tightly fastened. The two men sat in stolid silence, the heat beating at them, broiling them unmercifully in their heavy suits.

A small sandstorm blew around the car, spattering it with grit and pebbles. The driver stretched and opened the door, collecting the Walther PPK from the seat before climbing out and moving towards the helicopter which had settled beside the road. He was a tall, lean, agile man with fair hair, strongly moulded features and penetrating blue eyes. The mouth was wide, firm, and the lines around it suggested an easy-going and cheerful nature. But at this moment, in this place, Lee Corey was in no mood for laughter.

The helicopter was a small, fast 206 Jetranger, and as Corey approached a man in a black flying suit stepped out and stood waiting for him. The rotors whispered softly above his head, but he paid them no heed. He was a tall, lithe man with large, powerful hands and black hair beginning to recede at the temples. A scar ran from his left cheekbone to the corner of a wide mouth, twisting it slightly so that he seemed to have a permanent smile on his face. But by far the most distinctive feature was the stillness which enveloped him. Even in motion each move was precise, unhurried, using a minimum of effort before lapsing once more into stillness.

'You're Slade,' said Corey.

He nodded, his dark eyes flicking briefly to the gun held casually in Lee's hand. 'Are your people ready?'

'As they'll ever be.'

Slade pressed the button on his gold Omega and watched the seconds flick away before speaking. 'The convoy is five miles back, nothing in between except our own people. It will pass you in six minutes.'

'Check. How about the other end of the pass?'

'Bottled up tight. You just worry about this end.'

Lee shrugged. 'No sweat. Just so long as you're ready to take the stuff when we bring it out. And this chopper of yours has got the power to lift it.'

Slade moved back to the helicopter without bothering to reply. Lee smiled to himself, then turned and strolled back to the car. Behind him the Jetranger whined into life and rose into a steel blue sky.

It was three minutes past noon, and the convoy was just five minutes away.

In another desert, some eight thousand miles away, it was night and a golden moon was painting harsh shadows along the gleaming pipeline that wound its way towards the pumping station at Al Qatif. The thick steel pipe trembled in the night as a thousand barrels of oil measured each minute, hurtling on towards the waiting tankers in the Arabian Gulf.

Raya Dassan lay on the ridge of a sand dune that looked down upon the gaunt white skeleton of the pumping station. The pipeline came out of the desert below the dune, passing through barbed wire and a high steel fence to disappear into the maw of the building. Other pipelines curved into the station, from north and south, passing under and over each other like sleek black worms. Beyond the building, which throbbed softly in the still air, twin pipes emerged and headed towards the distant port.

The girl rose to her knees, a shielded torch flickering briefly in the night before she moved along the ridge to the first of the five dark figures stretched out in the sand. His eyes gleamed briefly as he glanced towards her.

'One minute,' she said.

He nodded, nestling his shoulder into the mounting of the RPG rocket launcher, checking the calibrations for the tenth time. She pressed a button on the black steel timepiece on her wrist, watching the seconds glow like fireflies in the night.

'Thirty seconds,' she said, flashing the shielded torch along the ridge.

Raya Dassan felt no emotion, a fact which vaguely surprised her. Less than an hour ago they had stepped out of the Rockwell Commander ten thousand feet above the Saudi Arabian desert, falling in tight formation towards the dropping zone. Their parachutes had automatic releases set for two thousand feet, and once deployed they had guided themselves to a landing less than two hundred yards from the Gawar Field pipeline. There had been a fierce exhilaration in soaring through the night, an exultant triumph in knowing that even the coastal radar could not detect their presence. The attack itself already seemed an anti-climax.

She was a tall, slim girl with thick, chestnut hair, presently wound tightly into one of the black woollen caps they all wore. Her eyes were hazel, flecked with gold, and her mouth wide and full, reflecting only a quiet assurance. She wore a black jumpsuit, crossed with webbing which held a brace of grenades and a Uzi machine pistol. She had no awareness of danger, only a firm resolve to carry out this mission for the honour of Irgun Zvai Leumi, the Israeli extremist organization dedicated to the elimination of Arab power in the world.

'Now!' she said sharply, flashing the torch for a full second.

Along the ridge five missiles fired with a crackling roar, arcing with burning tails towards the pumping station. Each launcher held his finger down hard, keeping the cross-hairs steady on the target. It took less than five seconds, and then the night erupted into incandescent fury.

Three of the five missiles struck the pumping station, blowing it apart like a fragile house of cards. The remaining missiles struck at the main terminal of pipes, rupturing steel and igniting the oil that spewed out on to the sand. Within seconds an awesome mushroom of fire was climbing up into the sky, bathing the desert and the distant town of Al Qatif in a crimson glow.

But long before the hastily assembled fleet of military vehicles came roaring down the road towards the inferno, Raya and her group were running through the night, hugging sand dunes, heading due east for a rendezvous with the powerful launch which had been waiting all night on the deserted coast below Bahrein.

In Beirut it was also night, but Calad Farik had no thoughts of sleep. His eyes were fixed on the television screen before him, his heavily jowled features gleaming with perspiration as he watched the two girls moving rhythmically on the large, fat American. The girls were beautiful and enthusiastic, qualities which Farik always insisted upon. The blonde, Birgit, was Swedish and an outstanding discovery in a city noted for its profusion of beautiful women. Her natural curiosity, coupled with an insatiable appetite for sex, made her an ideal subject for Farik's rather special diversions.

The second girl was Lebanese, small, dark and sensual with wide hips and full, round buttocks. Fellatio was her forte and, as she avidly sucked the American, the Swedish girl was caressing her with growing intimacy.

For Walter Matheson it was the realization of his wildest fantasies. Again and again, the Lebanese girl would bring him to the point of climax and then, sensing the approaching ejaculation, pull him back from the brink with tantalizing touches of mouth and fingers. It had been that way for almost an hour, with every nerve in his body vibrating like steel wires, the blood pounding in his ears, the perspiration running from him like warm rain. He moaned, an animal in pain, as the silken mouth closed over him again and the blonde pressed urgently against him, spreading her thighs.

'Jesus, baby,' he gasped. 'You're too much.'

In the room above Farik began to laugh in a shrill, high-pitched voice. Beside him the video-tape machine hummed softly, recording the scene through the wide-angle lens positioned above the bed. A file lay open beside the machine, the front bearing the American's name. Inside was a detailed dossier on Matheson, listing his occupation as production engineer for a major oil company. It included details of his home in Dallas, Texas, of his wife, Betty, and his two daughters who were almost as old as the two girls currently occupying his attentions. There was also a medical report which went into some considerable detail on the 53-year-old American's physical condition. A recent cardiac report indicated a slight murmur of the heart attributed to a deterioration of the right ventricle, a condition which had caused Matheson's doctor to order a drastic cut-back on smoking and drinking. It had not occurred to him that his patient had a proclivity for sexual gymnastics.

Farik leaned forward, his small, black eyes fixed avidly on the screen as the American began to gasp and moan. He touched a switch in front of him, speaking into a microphone.

'Now,' he said in a thin, brittle voice.

The Swedish girl reached beneath the bed and produced a small glass phial of Amyl Nitrite. Crushing it expertly between her fingers, she held it in front of the American's face as he began to gasp and jerk into a violent climax. The powerful stimulant had an immediate effect. The American's eyes opened wide, he cried out in a strangled voice, the flabby muscles around his neck bulging with the intensity of the ejaculation. His face became purple, his eyes distended as though about to burst from their sockets. And then, just as suddenly, the contortions froze and the blood drained from his face. His chest heaved twice, his lungs in spasm, but that was all. A curious stillness came over the bulky figure on the bed and the Lebanese girl lifted her head with a puzzled, slightly disappointed expression.

Birgit bent down to his chest, listened for a moment, then looked up towards the camera with a shocked expression.

'He's dead,' she said, the fear beginning to tremble in her voice.

Farik's words came down to them through the speaker. They were calm and matter of fact.

'Very well, Birgit, you can call an ambulance in a minute or two, there is obviously no need to hurry. Oh, and Aysha,' he said, almost as an afterthought. 'You can bring me his briefcase from the hall.

The convoy was made up of two patrol cars and a five-ton armoured truck bearing the insignia of the Atomic Energy Commission. The vehicle was fully refrigerated and shielded, the five one hundred megaton devices nestling in their cocoons. Only the cab was hot and the two drivers had done little but complain since leaving the nuclear warehouse in San Jose, California.

Each man wore the obligatory film badges on their coveralls, but any radiation hazard in this vehicle would trigger a klaxon horn long before the badges turned black. There were also weapons in the driving compartment, a heavy Colt Commander automatic in a spring clip beside the gear shift, and a 12 bore Savage pump gun standing upright in a slot between the twin driving seats. On the ceiling of the compartment was a radio transmitter on a fixed frequency constantly monitored by the San Jose special security division and the FBI Bureau in Sacramento.

Lee Corey watched the heavy truck enter the pass, noting that both patrol cars had their windows down. He was slumped in his seat behind the wheel, a magazine propped in front of him, and received only a cursory glance from the men in the patrol cars. As it moved beyond his line of vision he lifted the microphone cupped in his hand and pressed the transmit switch.

'Unit One to Black Leader. Entering pass now.'

'Check,' replied Slade crisply. 'All units on red. Unit One in thirty seconds. Units two and three are go on contact. Unit Four now clear to head back along the highway. Report any oncoming traffic.'

'Check.' The voice was quick and cheerful, and Lee had the feeling that the driver a quarter of a mile behind them was glad to be out and away.

The other men in the car were getting up from the floor now. The man beside him was donning a pair of goggles, whilst the two in the rear were pulling on the bulky PVC helmets.

Slade's voice crackled over the radio. 'Go, Unit One.'

Lee pressed down on the accelerator and lunged out on to the road, going fast through the gears so that he was in top and pushing seventy as the walls of the pass closed in on them. Remmick, the thin-faced man beside him, lifted a C.E. canister from the bag between his feet, winding the window down.

'Make sure you get close,' he said bleakly.

'I'll let you blow in his ear.'

The road wound through the pass in a series of gradual bends, the air shimmering with the heat. A haze of dust ahead marked the progress of the convoy, the grinding roar of the truck echoing between the pale sandstone walls.

'Here we go,' said Lee, pressing the switch of the microphone. 'Unit One in contact.'

The patrol car was occupying the crest of the road a hundred yards behind the truck, when the Cougar came up on the inside. Braking sharply, Lee matched speeds, catching a brief glimpse of the driver's startled face before the C.E. canister landed on his lap and filled the interior of the patrol car with a billowing cloud of nauseating gas. The policeman at the wheel strove to keep control, but in seconds he was retching uncontrollably and the car was lurching off the road.

Corey slid the car neatly behind the truck, watching for some sign that the driver had seen the incident in his side mirror. There was no slackening of speed, and a moment later they were turning a bend in the pass, effectively losing the wrecked patrol car.

'Unit One to Black Leader. We are go for phase two.'

'Check. We have sight contact now.'

Corey nodded to the man beside him who picked up another C.E. canister and gripped the tab. They were rounding the final bend which led into a narrow stretch of road at the southern end of the pass. Here the sandstone cliffs leaned towards each other, squeezing out light, amplifying sound so that the walls vibrated with the thundering roar of the truck ahead. Only now there was an answering roar as a large van entered the pass, swinging wide to the crown of the road.

The leading patrol car flashed its lights, signalling the van to pull away. Obediently the driver began to swing over, but at the last moment braked hard and swung wide across the road, effectively blocking both lanes. The pass exploded into a cacophony of sound as the armoured truck blared its horn, the patrol car slammed on the brakes, tyres screaming, in an attempt to avoid the van. Corey was already pulling around the side of the truck as the patrol car slammed into the van, the windscreen shattering with the force of the impact.

'Take him!' shouted Corey, standing on the brakes and spinning the wheel so that the Cougar slid broadside against the patrol car, enabling Remmick to toss the C.E. canister through the shattered windscreen.

Even as the canister exploded in the car, the rear of the van was bursting open and four hooded men lunged out, each carrying 9mm Ingram machine pistols. Beyond the van a Ford station wagon could now be seen, reversing back along the side of the road, the tailgate hanging open to give the two men with riot guns an uninterrupted line of fire.

The driver of the armoured truck was Jim Fenshaw, a big, red-faced man in his early forties. It had taken him the best part of ten years to get a full security clearance with the Nuclear Engineering Division at San Jose, and for most of those years he had been telling his wife, Millie, just how crazy they were for not giving it to him sooner. He ascribed this lunatic caution to a system which automatically rejected the kind of man who enjoyed speaking his mind and who made no attempt to conceal a basically aggressive nature. Such a man, Jim frequently declared, was just the type of person they would need in a violent situation. The fact that he was given to heavy drinking sessions on a Saturday night, had twice been involved in savage brawls, and was currently having an affair with a married waitress was none of their damned business. What really mattered, he was often heard to say, was where you stood when the chips were down.

The chips were down for Big Jim Fenshaw on a hot July day in Stonewall Pass, Nevada. He was suddenly faced with the wrong ends of two riot guns and four machine pistols. The sight dried out his mouth in seconds and brought a cold numbness to his limbs. For some unaccountable reason a muscle in his cheek began tying itself into knots and there was a singing in his ears. He was dimly aware of his partner, Pete Berry, pulling the lever which dropped steel shutters over the windscreen and side windows of the cab, but the ensuing darkness only increased the terror which seemed to be bubbling out of a bottomless pit where his stomach should have been.

'For Christ's sake, Jim, get us out of here,' shouted his co-driver, checking the load of the twelve bore Savage.

'Shit,' croaked Big Jim, 'we ain't got no kind of chance.'

Pete Berry looked at him in astonishment. 'We got guns, an armour-plated truck . . . Let's get the hell out of here!'

The co-driver was reaching for the radio microphone when a shotgun blasted the antenna from the roof of the cab. It was followed a moment later by a series of heavy blows on the door and a cold, uncompromising voice that left not the slightest doubt in their minds that its owner was not given to exaggeration.

'You guys in there better listen, and listen good. You got two choices, and I don't give much of a damn which one you take. You either sit tight and keep your noses clean, or you go for broke with that riot gun. Do the first and we take what we came for and call it a day. Do the second and we'll just blow your cab apart with a couple of pounds of plastic!'

With a disgusted sigh, Pete Berry began to eject the shells from the pump gun. Jim Fenshaw sat behind the wheel, gripping it tightly to stop his hands from shaking. After a moment he managed a voice that trembled with relief.

'It's all we could do, Pete. We had no chance.'

'Sure, Jim. As long as you didn't move the fucking truck, we had no chance at all!'

Lee Corey stood beside the Cougar watching as the two patrolmen, still vomiting from the effects of the gas, were blindfolded and handcuffed to the fender of their car. The two men in silver PVC suits were crouching by the roadside, waiting for the explosive charge to be fixed to the rear of the truck. Barely two minutes had passed since the heavy van had straddled the road, yet the situation was already under control and the station wagon ready to move the moment the truck doors were opened.

The explosives man waved his arms, then lit the short fuse and ran for cover. Corey grimaced and lit a cigarette. Every step of the operation so far had shown pin-point accuracy and perfect timing. Twenty-four hours ago he had not known one single man in the group, and yet for three months he had been checked and briefed again and again until every facet of the operation had been stamped on his mind – except the location. That had been given to him this morning when he met the rest of his unit.

The explosives detonated with a thunderous roar, filling the pass with a chorus of echoes. A cloud of dust obscured the rear of the truck, but the station wagon was already reversing until it was level with the doors. The explosives man ran forward, was lost briefly in the dust, and then, as it cleared, could be seen pulling at the buckled edge of the door. Two other men moved forward, crowbars in their hands, and together they wrenched the heavy armour-plated doors apart.

The tall, black figure of Slade seemed to step out of nowhere, gesturing for the men to get back. The dark interior of the truck gaped open, the steel spheres glinting in the dim light. The two men in PVC stepped forward, climbing awkwardly into the truck, moving to the first of the spheres until they could see the triangular emblem and black stencilled legend – Operation Plowshare. Slowly, with great care, they began to lift the cobalt steel ball with its deadly cargo of 5.5 kilos of plutonium.

Corey glanced at his watch, leaning casually beside the open door of the Cougar. Elapsed time was now four minutes. It would take precisely four minutes to transfer the bombs from the truck to the station wagon, and a further two to drive them to the helicopter waiting at the head of the pass. With mounting tension he realized that time was running out.

Almost with the thought he heard the whine of the helicopters, building rapidly until the sky above was full of the clattering of rotors and the scream of jets. They were large 212 Bell helicopters, each capable of carrying fourteen fully equipped policemen, and there were five of them hovering above the pass.

Even as the group around the truck scattered for the cars, Corey was slipping behind the wheel and starting the engine. Above, an amplified voice boomed down into the pass, advising them all to drop their weapons and lay face down on the ground. Nobody did. One of the men by the station wagon raised his machine pistol and fired a short burst towards the helicopter. It was immediately answered by a fusillade of shots which riddled the station wagon and wounded two of the three men who crouched beside it.

Corey didn't wait to see the outcome of the battle. He was already accelerating down the pass, flashing past the startled group around the armoured truck, catching the briefest glimpse of Slade gesturing frantically at him. Then he was round the first bend and racing through the pass. The clatter of rotors above informed him that one of the helicopters was following, but he was more concerned about the two patrolmen who would still be with their wrecked car.

Holding the wheel with one hand he spun the dial of the radio transmitter clamped beneath the dashboard, finding the wavelength he wanted as he approached the centre of the pass.

'Calling police chopper, do you read me?'

'Yeah, buddy, we read.' The voice that came through the receiver was heavy with suspicion.

'This is Blue Eagle. Now will you get that busted patrol car out of my way?'

The receiver crackled for a moment. Corey took his foot off the accelerator, slowing down as he approached the last bend before reaching the patrol car.

'Blue Eagle?' It was a different voice this time.

'Go ahead.'

'We got problems with the patrol car. We can't raise it on radio. Maybe they blew a valve.'

'Can you see them?'

'Sure we can. They're getting themselves set to blast you all the way back up the pass.'

'You're such a comfort,' Corey said, dryly.

'You'd better pull over and wait until we send one of our own cars in.'

'No way, friend. I've got about two minutes to get clear. After that, nobody's going to believe it was an accident.'

'You go round that bend, Blue Eagle, and there's going to be one hell of an accident.'

Corey sighed. 'So book me!'

He pressed hard on the accelerator, leaping round the bend with the seven litre engine howling. The patrolmen had pushed the battered car into the centre of the road, effectively blocking both lanes, and were now crouched behind it with the twelve bore pump guns aimed and ready.

For a split second he considered spinning the car round and heading back, but just as quickly discarded the idea. Turning now would give them clear shots at his tyres and side windows. With grim features he took a firm grip on the handbrake, gauging distance until he was within fifty feet of the patrol car. The two policemen behind were easing up for their shots when he pulled hard on the handbrake and spun the car broadside, sliding towards them on screaming tyres. Even as they fired he was lunging down along the seat, waiting for the impact.

The patrolmen got off one shot each, then as the Cougar

hurtled at them, dived for cover at the side of the road. The impact smashed the patrol car to one side, leaving one lane open. Corey took it, stamping down on the accelerator, racing through the gap on spinning wheels and was away down the pass before either of the patrolmen could get off a second shot.

'Jesus, friend,' said the voice from the helicopter. 'When you got to go – you sure as hell do go.'

Chapter 2

The distinctive shape of Pigeon Rocks jutted from a deep blue bay like some ancient triumphal arch eroded by wind and sea, as the '707' descended towards Beirut. Beyond the rocks, perhaps the city's most well-known landmark, stretched the ultra-modern and eminently fashionable Raouche quarter – an imposing skyline of glass and concrete expressing all the power and vigour of one of the world's great trading centres. Unfortunately the effect was somewhat marred by a series of large black craters and tattered holes in the elegant façade; a reminder that only recently this city, noted for compromise and acumen, had been busily blowing itself apart.

Raya Dassan sat beside the window of the Boeing, watching the wide boulevards and gleaming white buildings float by. It had taken slightly less than three hours to cross the arid lands of Saudi Arabia and it was difficult for her to comprehend the vista below when her mind was still seething with memories of the exploding oil terminal at Al Qatif and the race across the desert for the rendezvous at Ad Dammam. One of their group had died in that race. A stupid, senseless death that still filled her with a bitter anger.

His name had been Jehad Kassif, the son of a tailor in Tel Aviv. At twenty-two he was dark and handsome, a smile never far from his lips, and he had all the arrogance of youth, the brashness of immaturity. Running through a strange desert in darkness was just a game to Jehad, and it would always have been had he not stepped on a black horned viper. The snake bit deep just above the ankle, injecting venom directly into the femoral artery. By the time they could slash the wound and suck at the venom, it was already making its deadly journey around his body. And, of course, no one had thought to bring an anti-viper serum.

They carried him for three miles, using a tourniquet at ten-minute intervals, but it had been hopeless from the start. The leg began to swell at an alarming rate and he soon lapsed into delirium. They were five miles from Ad Dammam and time was running out when they took the vote.

There was no solace in the fact that had the venom not penetrated the artery he could have walked for at least four hours, that with proper care and an injection of serum he would have fully recovered in two weeks. All that mattered was reaching the rendezvous before the net closed in and daylight made them vulnerable.

And so they shot young Jehad. A man who had known him all his life held him down as he raved deliriously and Raya, as group leader, put the gun to his head and pulled the trigger.

An hour later they had flashed a light from the beach at Ad Dammam, bringing in the powerful launch that was to take them to Qatar. By dawn they had been safe in the independent sheikdom, eating enormous quantities of pacha, the succulent dish of sheep's head and trotters, and congratulating each other on striking a massive blow for freedom. Then they slept for a day, and the message came for Raya to fly to Beirut.

Beirut International Airport is a streamlined affair of glass, steel and concrete, managing to convey the finest elements of modern architecture whilst retaining a subtle Moorish quality. Both customs and immigration are noted for their understanding, but there was still an edge of tension in Raya as she handed the passport to the immigration officer. He flicked over the pages with disinterest, noting that she had been born in Algiers and was a naturalized citizen of France. He also noted the chestnut hair and full, wide mouth; the golden skin that glowed with vitality and, inevitably, the slim legs and rounded hips. There was no way he could have known that she was a highly trained Israeli commando who had fought in the Yom Kippur war at the age of nineteen, no way he could tell that she had killed five times without hate and without pity. Instead he stamped her passport with a flourish and spoke in French, wishing her a pleasant stay. Raya gave him a warm smile and moved on to collect her bags, aware that his eyes were on her all the way across the concourse.

The white Mercedes that took her across the city was driven by a slim, fair-haired Dane who told her that his name was Troy. He did not appear to be prepared to offer any further information, and the subtle odour of musk-laden perfume that wafted across from him did not fill her with any great desire to press the matter. Instead they drove in silence, turning down the Boulevard de Mazraa towards the Corniche Chouran. Everywhere there were signs of destruction, from the blackened structures of famous hotels to the scaffolding outside the Iranian Embassy where workmen painstakingly plastered over the bullet holes.

Driving south along the Corniche they came to a large white villa set behind high walls and perched on the edge of the cliffs overlooking Pigeon Rocks Bay. Troy turned the Mercedes through high, wrought-iron gates into a drive that wound through funereal cypress and sweet-scented orange trees. The villa itself was a long, split-level structure with a loggia extending down its southern side, overlooking a wide patio and pool.

Troy drove to the front of the villa, getting out of the car and opening the door with an expression of studied disinterest. She left him to carry the bags and went into the house, finding herself in a wide, airy hall with a green-tiled floor. The double doors to her left were of glass with elegant gold handles, and beyond was a long, luxuriously furnished room with marble-topped tables, white leather furniture and deep, black fur rugs. She entered the room, gazing at the original Bosch which dominated one wall with a ponderous finality, the grotesque figures entwined against a macabre landscape. The painting gave the room a surrealistic air and this was heightened by a bronze bust of Janus set in a mirrored alcove so that the twin faces gazed out from a hundred different angles.

Troy appeared in the doorway, having deposited her bags in the hall.

'Do you want a drink or some food?'

'No, but I could do with some information.'

'Mr Farik will provide you with that.' He smiled with measured malice. 'When he finds it convenient.'

'In that case,' she said, sweetly, 'you might as well feed the goats.'

His mouth went small and hard. 'Don't get bitchy with me. I watch your kind come and go all the time.'

She let the remark pass, but after he had left began to wonder what kind of guest he thought she was. Her orders had been vague, but there was nothing unusual in that. There were at least a dozen shadowy organizations operating in the Middle East for the preservation of Israel. Some of them – like Unit Nine – received a grudging recognition from the government, others held such extreme views that they were only slightly more popular than the Black September. Groups like the Israeli Black Panthers, the Irgun Zvai Leumi and cells of the old Stern Gang, operated in such secrecy that the chain of command soon vanished into a labyrinth of cyphers and code names.

Her direct commander was Joshe Boran in Jerusalem, and she assumed that ultimately his orders would come from Rabbi Kahane, the Head of the Jewish Defence League, but it could just as easily have been some other Israeli extremist group which had decided that she was the right person for this particular assignment. She pushed the thought aside, disturbed by its implications. It was too late to query now.

She crossed the room and went out on to the loggia, relaxing in the perfume-laden air. Gradually she became aware of muffled sounds coming from a partially open door at the end of the terrace. She went towards it, feeling a chill of apprehension as the sounds sharpened into small cries and gasps, interspersed with deeper grunts and exclamations. Looking into the dimly-lit room, she saw a television screen glowing. Someone sat close to the door, watching the screen and, as though sensing her presence, suddenly turned to gaze at her.

He was a large, muscular man with heavy jowls and bright, patent-leather eyes. Giving her the briefest of glances, he turned back to the television set which she now saw was connected to a video-tape machine.

'If you're Raya Dassan,' he said, 'you'd better take a seat.'

But she was already looking beyond him to the screen where two large negroes were performing with a small, plump, blonde girl. From the speakers came the harsh rasping of breath, the rhythmic moans of the girl who was staring into the camera with glazed, unseeing eyes. Even as Raya took in the scene, the men changed positions, one of them moving to the girl's head whilst his companion knelt between her legs and thrust savagely into her. The girl cried out, trying to push him away, but the other man gripped both her wrists in one huge hand, holding her easily.

'I'll wait upstairs, Mr Farik,' Raya said coldly, turning towards the door.

'You'll sit down and watch,' he answered sharply, his voice strangely shrill.

She hesitated briefly, then shrugged and took a seat, her face reflecting none of the contempt she felt.

Farik had turned back to the screen, leaning forward now with an intent expression. The sounds had subtly changed, the girl's breath suddenly sharp and terrified. Reluctantly, Raya glanced at the trio on the screen, only then realizing that this was something more than a blue movie. With horrified eyes she watched the girl struggle with pathetic terror between the two men, her eyes bulging, her face contorting as the man kneeling beside her slowly and deliberately strangled her. It was over in a moment. The two negroes, their bodies gleaming with perspiration, stepped away from the bed and the camera slowly zoomed in on the still, lifeless body of the girl.

Raya stared at the screen until the film ran out, revulsion vying with disbelief. The lights came on, flooding the room, and she turned to Farik, more nauseated by the sheen of perspiration on his face than by his slack, sadistic smile.

'That girl,' she said. 'She couldn't really have been . . . ?'

He nodded, his small, black eyes fixed on her with a kind of remote curiosity.

'It's called a snuff movie. The ultimate theatre of realism in which the leading lady gives her greatest, and final, performance.' He smiled, amused by her revulsion. 'I thought you were used to death.'

'Death, not that kind of perverted crap.'

Farik laughed, and again she was startled by the shrillness of his voice. 'I must confess it does lack subtlety, but very shortly such a film may have its uses. Who knows, you may have a part to play in it!'

She rose slowly to her feet, no longer making any attempt to conceal her loathing for the man. 'I think it's time I went back to Israel.'

She had reached the door before he spoke again, only now his voice was soft, the deadliest of sounds. 'Leave this house and you will never leave Beirut. That I guarantee.'

The small Beretta was in her hand when she turned to

face him, and he knew from her expression that she was fully prepared to use it. But there was no fear in him, only a wry amusement. Rising from the chair he gestured mockingly to the door.

'Will you go first, or shall I?'

She contemplated him in silence for a moment, disturbed by the forces that seemed to play against each other in the man. Facing her now he seemed completely at ease, but the cream silk shirt he wore above dark brown slacks was stretched tight across a powerful chest and thick muscular arms. Although he was well into his forties, there was no suggestion of fat except in his face. Here the thick lips and sagging jowls suggested dissipation and self-indulgence, an impression completely contradicted by the man's superb physique.

'I think you had better tell me precisely what is going on, Mr Farik,' she said finally. 'Otherwise our relationship is going to be terminated – whichever way you prefer.'

He smiled coolly as she made the smallest gesture with the gun, then spoke in a matter-of-fact voice. 'You are here to assist me in a venture which will destroy, once and for all, Arab influence in the Western world.'

She stared at him incredulously, then shook her head, at a loss for words to describe the man's arrogance. Farik nodded, unperturbed, as though expecting her reaction.

'I'm quite serious. There is a way, and the people who sent you to me know some of the details. But for the moment you will have to take my word for it.'

He moved towards the door, ignoring the gun. 'Now let's get some fresh air.'

He led her out through the loggia to a table beside the pool. A young Lebanese girl, no more than fifteen, moved to him from the shade of an olive tree.

'You can bring me an ouzo, Samir,' he said, glancing enquiringly at Raya.

'Something cold,' she said. 'An iced lemon will be fine.'

Farik nodded to the girl who smiled nervously at Raya and then moved towards the house. They sat down at the table, the colourful awning above shading them from the sun that beat down on the patio. The pool looked cool, inviting and, seeing her glance, Farik gestured at the water.

'Why don't we swim? It's a pity to waste it.'

'In a moment,' she replied. 'But first I'd like to know a little more about this operation. To begin with, who will I be working with?'

His face tightened and she was aware of the anger in him, although it was not directed at her.

'If things had gone according to plan some of your colleagues would already be here. Unfortunately we now have to fall back on an alternative which will take considerably longer to execute.'

'How much longer?'

He shrugged. 'Two weeks. A month.'

'And then?'

'And then you will be given instructions and a target. At that time you will begin to realize that I am not given to exaggeration.'

She considered him silently for a moment, far from convinced, yet reluctant to create any further hostility between them. Her instructions had made it clear that she was to take her orders from Calad Farik, yet what little information she had been able to gather before leaving Qatar suggested that the Lebanese was renowned for his opportunism rather than his idealism.

'Mr Farik,' she said, choosing her words with care. 'I am here because I want to fight for Israel. But that is the only reason.'

He steepled short, stubby fingers and regarded her coolly. When he spoke it was in a tone of mild curiosity.

'Would you kill for Israel?'

'Of course,' she said promptly.

'Die for it?'

Her mouth twisted. The question was in itself an insult.

He nodded, his black eyes boring into her now. 'Would you fuck for Israel?'

Her eyes flashed angrily, but before she could reply Samir had returned with the drinks and a plate of cheese and olives. She placed them on the table, then returned silently to the house. Farik was still waiting for a reply.

'With you?' she asked, cynically.

He laughed, his voice a shrill, almost girlish sound. It went on for a long time, as though the idea amused him enormously, but the laughter never touched his eyes and she sensed the malevolence in him. The laughter stopped abruptly.

'Answer me.'

'Perhaps,' she said, warily. 'But I would need to be convinced it was necessary. At the moment nothing I know about you convinces me that you are anything more than a —— Lebanese.' She let an edge of scorn underlie the word.

He smiled bleakly. 'So you wonder why I should fight the Arabs and help the Jews?'

She nodded, watching him warily. He rose to his feet and strolled to the edge of the pool, staring into the water for some minutes before turning back to her. His face was dark and remote, his eyes telling her nothing.

'It's time we had that swim,' he said.

She shrugged and rose to her feet. 'All right. Is there somewhere I can change?'

His mouth twisted briefly. 'Here will do.'

She considered him without expression for a moment, then unzipped her dress and stepped out of it. The only other garment she wore was a pair of simple white briefs which enhanced the golden tan of her slim, firm body. Ignoring Farik's appraising look, she stepped to the edge of the pool, preparing to dive in.

'We can do without those,' he murmured, flicking a hand at the briefs.

This time she gazed directly at him with frozen features, her eyes holding his as she slid the briefs off and placed them on the chair.

'Satisfied?' she asked him, coldly.

He let his gaze move over her slowly and deliberately before nodding, with grudging admiration, then unbuttoned his shirt and took it off. Raya plunged into the pool, swimming to the far side before surfacing. The water was cool and refreshing and she let herself relax before turning to glance across the pool towards Farik. He was standing by the edge, as though waiting, and now that he saw he had her attention he unzipped his slacks and stepped out of them.

The icy shock was so intense that for a moment she could not comprehend what she was really seeing. As though aware of this Farik continued to stand naked by the edge of the pool, legs spread, hands on hips, his face dark and unreadable. The shock dissolved into a mixture of horror and revulsion whilst in a corner of her mind she was beginning to understand why there were so many contradictions in the man.

Why, also, his voice was unnaturally high. The final emotion that came was pity. Standing there in the sun he was a superbly proportioned figure with wide, powerful shoulders and strong legs. His stomach was flat, hard, and the hips narrow. What was dreadfully missing was the very roots of his masculinity. All that remained was a large, ugly scar that covered most of his groin. At some time in his life, Calad Farik had been brutally, and totally, castrated.

He remained standing there until she swam across the pool and gazed up at him with white, strained features. 'How?' she asked, in a small voice.

'Arabs. Four drunken Arabs on patrol in Syria. They caught me with a truck full of stolen supplies. This was their idea of a little fun.'

'I'm sorry.' It was the only thing she could say.

His laugh was cold and malevolent. 'Not half as sorry as the Arabs are going to be!'

Chapter 3

The White House glowed softly like a pink, candyfloss castle in the setting sun, the less romantic Washington skyline dissolving into a purple haze above the Potomac. It was a scene that never failed to move Lee Corey, representing as it did so much of his life and so many of the ideals which had first brought him to the capital. Looking down from the tenth floor of the soaring steel and glass building that housed the Special Services Division of the Department of Justice, he could just see the green park of the Mall with the Washington Monument beyond.

It had been just such a day, so very long ago, when he had first walked in that park. With him had been the slender, laughing blonde who had so recently become his wife. It had been an idyllic week which culminated in his appointment as an agent in the FBI after days of tests and interviews. Paula had been waiting in the park, serene and confident, knowing long before he reached her that he had won.

The familiar sadness rose up as the memories flooded back. The small apartment they took in Arlington, Virginia, and the long summer months exploring gentle towns with gentle names like Sleepy Hollow, Columbia Pines, Indian Springs and Wilton Woods. It had been a time of laughter, of sharing every thought and every dream. Even his trips on FBI assignments were so routine that he had been able to take Paula with him. He never lost the glow of pride that came each time they checked into some new hotel, never ceased to marvel that this golden girl was now a prefix to his name.

But his stature with the bureau quickly grew and soon the assignments were no longer routine. There were the stake-outs that exploded into violence in the night, the days of surveillance and the split-second timing of the arrest. There were long nights in cheap motels, listening through the thin walls with suction mikes and needle bugs. And then there had been Dallas and the death of a President.

The images came then, refusing to be blocked out. Paula

in Washington, refusing to stay behind for the months the Dallas investigation would take. Paula in Dallas, seeing only the gleaming façade of a city that seethed and smouldered with prejudice and hate. Paula collecting his car keys, walking out into the sun with her golden hair bouncing on slim shoulders, smiling happily at the world even as she turned the key that blew her to pieces in the street.

'Mr Corey, we're ready for you now.'

The images dissolved and he found that he was gripping the steel sill of the window, his eyes blurred with emotions that time would never dull. The girl was beginning to look concerned, but her face cleared as he flashed her an easy grin and put just the right intonation on: 'You've gotta be kidding.'

Chapter 4

Max Weller was a small, lean, grey-haired man who once told J. Edgar Hoover that he owed it to himself and the nation to walk across the Potomac and that he, Max Weller, would be the first to touch his cloak when he got to the other side. Hoover's reply was lost to posterity, having been erased from the tapes that same day, but in spite of it the wiry little man who looked more like a harassed accountant than a senior operative of the FBI went on to become the chief executive of C-2.

The original brief for the department had been to co-ordinate the work of agents operating outside the United States, ostensibly as legal attachés at major embassies in Europe and the Mid East, and to act as a liaison office with Interpol I – the Washington arm of that world police network. In practice C-2 became much more. Max Weller quickly built an elite force of undercover agents to carry out clandestine operations against organized crime throughout the world. He justified this with simple logic: the United States was the ultimate target of all international operators, whether in the field of direct armed robbery or the more devious methods of counterfeit currency and narcotics. Sooner or later, all roads led to Rome, only in this instance it was a room on the tenth floor of a modern skyscraper office block in Washington.

The office itself had certain features people tended not to talk about. The floor was composed of nine-inch cubes of rubber, insulating it completely from the remainder of the building, which was just as well for the walls carried a constant electrical charge, as did the ceiling. It was, in effect, a bug-proof cage where even the windows were laminated with a fine filigree of wires capable of detecting the delicate touch of a laser probe.

Lee walked across the resilient floor of the office and dropped into a chair, waiting patiently for Max to finish the report he was reading. It was a room he had come to know well in the years he had been with C-2, a room that the FBI agents in the grey stone building across the Mall referred to as *'Mission Control'*. In spite of the sarcasm it was an apt description, for there was only one man who knew precisely where and what C-2 was up to at any given moment, and rumour had it that ever since Watergate the last thing he did each night was to erase all tapes and shred Sight-Only communications.

The man in question finally put the report aside and leaned back in his deep leather chair, pushing up his spectacles and pinching the bridge of his nose with a tired grimace.

'Nevada was good,' he said, his eyes still closed. 'But one of these days you'll drive yourself into a very expensive funeral . . . and on the budgets we're getting these days we just can't afford expensive funerals.'

'I'll keep it in mind. Maybe something at sea?'

Max gave him a long, bleak look then tossed over a file. It was heavy, sealed in a grey plastic security pouch with a Class Four rating and Sight-Only embossed on each corner. Lee slid the file out of the pouch and leafed through it with barely concealed disinterest. It concerned Operation Plowshare, the Atomic Energy Commission's programme for peaceful uses of nuclear energy, although there seemed to be a certain contradiction in the aims of the programme and the red 'secret' emblems on every page.

Max let him scan a dozen pages before suggesting he turn to page thirty-four.

'Thanks,' Lee said, dryly. 'Do you have any particular line in mind?'

'You might try Operation Gasbuggy, the 1967 tests in San Juan. It goes on to describe the new tests planned for Nevada next week.'

Lee quickly read the page in question, finding much of the information technical and beyond his understanding. The report did, however, give a detailed specification of a newly developed one hundred kiloton device which was only a fifth of the size of the bombs used ten years ago in New Mexico. The report pointed out at some length that the new device was highly mobile and incorporated a simple mechanical detonator, rather than the sophisticated electronic detonators used in the past.

'I take it these are the bombs Slade and his team were after?' he said finally, putting the file back into its pouch and handing it to Max.

'Yes, and we're getting nowhere with Slade.'

'Did you expect to?' Lee was mildly astonished.

'The Bureau was cautiously optimistic. They put Ganton and Masters on to it.'

'They're good men, but Slade is a pro. He told us nothing we didn't need to know, and even that was the bare bones. You'll never break him.'

'We knew that yesterday,' Max agreed. 'But somebody needed those bombs pretty badly, and that means they'll try again.'

'Who?'

Max considered him without expression, then unlocked a drawer in his desk. Taking out a file he studied the contents for a moment before glancing across at Lee.

'A good deal of this is supposition,' he said, gesturing at the file. 'Any attorney worth his salt would rip it to shreds.'

'But you believe it?'

'I don't know. There's a gut reaction that tells me there has to be something in this. It goes back twelve years, Lee . . . opens old wounds.'

Lee leaned forward, his face suddenly pale and strained. 'Texas?'

Max nodded, making no attempt to hide his concern now. 'When I put you on this assignment we only had one lead to go on. We knew that Slade was recruiting a team, but we didn't know why. You had a heavy rating on the Continent, and you were clean over here, so we let him put together a file on you and take it from there.'

'Texas, Max? Where the hell does Texas come in?'

'Slade did a lot of travelling during the last three months. He bought equipment on the West Coast and took it to the East Coast. He spent a week checking you out in Chicago before setting up the meeting with his front man. It was the same with all the others. He was under surveillance every step of the way, and never knew it, yet at no time did we get a lead on the target or the date. Without you in his team they'd have pulled it off cold.'

'For Christ's sake, Max, get to it!'

'All right. Every trip he made, except three, could be accounted for. Men, equipment, information. But twice he went to Dallas, and we don't know why.'

The air-conditioned office breathed softly around them. The air was cool and fresh, but the beads of perspiration stood out on Lee's forehead. 'There's got to be more than that, Max?'

He nodded. 'The Plowshare Project was switched from New Mexico to the Nevada Proving Grounds following pressure from Texas. About the same time there was a big push to keep the Bureau out of any investigations connected with national security. The usual crap, Defence Department and Secret Service autonomy, our role to be confined to those criminal activities covered by the statute books. By that time C-2 was involved and you were part of the team.'

'But who in Texas? Who was twisting arms?'

'We don't know. The people who made all the noise were just doing their job, but every instinct tells me it didn't happen by chance. It took power and influence, and at the end of the day a hand-picked group of men were all set to deliver five one hundred kiloton atom bombs.'

Lee gazed at him in disbelief. 'That's it?'

Max nodded with weary resignation. 'That's all. Just a pattern, a web of power and influence that seems to emanate from the mid-west. Nobody kicks any doors down, nobody starts a campaign. Just pressures. I call it the Texas Connection, because every time it happens all hell breaks loose.'

Max rose to his feet, stretched with a grimace, then moved to the window. He stood gazing out towards Capitol Hill, shrouded now in gathering gloom, the 258 foot high dome of the Capitol suddenly brilliant white against the sky as the floodlights came on.

Lee reached across the desk and took the file, the tension knotting his stomach as he read the entries that began with Dallas and the death of a President. After five minutes he felt like a blind man in the centre of a maze, trying to remember the route he took when he came in. There were cross references to such books as *Six Seconds in Dallas** and *Whitewash*†, to the Rockefeller Commission on the activities of the CIA. There were dossiers on Jack Ruby and Lee Harvey Oswald that answered nothing, but posed more ques-

* *Six Seconds In Dallas* by Josiah Thompson (1967, Random House)

† *Whitewash* by Harold Weisberg (1967, Dell)

tions. There were obscure directives with coded origins, a pattern of obstruction, of information lost, distorted or passed to other agencies where it was classified and condemned to lay forever in forgotten archives. There were references to the murders and inexplicable deaths of people who were all connected, in some way, with the Dallas assassination – and one of those names was Paula Corey, killed by mistake in the car her husband should have driven.

But the file didn't confine itself to Dallas. There were other assassinations, from Martin Luther King to Joseph 'the Baron' Barboza, a trail of anarchy and murder that stretched from California to Alabama and South Carolina. And far too many times papers went astray, witnesses vanished, evidence was mysteriously lost. Much of the information in the report could be explained by local prejudice, misguided political expediency, but at the same time it hinted at a sinister and shadowy web of intrigue that seemed to sprawl across the mid-western states.

It took an hour to absorb the contents of the file, and throughout Max waited patiently at his desk. Occasionally Lee would pause to ask a question, the lines of his face deepening into a bitter expression of defeat as all too frequently the reply was vague and negative. When he finally put the file aside his mouth was a tight, angry line.

'Why didn't you show me this before?'

'It wasn't necessary, and you can see the trail leads nowhere.'

'It starts in Texas, Max. That's clear.'

'But with whom? What group? I've spent ten years putting that file together and still I don't know. But if all the pieces ever do fall into place we still won't be able to do anything. It'll need a congressional enquiry and the Supreme Court, you know that.'

'So why show me now?'

'Because now you need to know. Whoever is behind Slade is big, very big, and he needs five atomic bombs. I want to know why.'

'Slade?'

'It's the only way.'

Lee nodded without emotion, he had known as much for more than an hour. Max was putting him on the firing line and the bait he was holding out was that somewhere along that line was the man who caused Paula's death.

'Where is he now?'

'Carson City. They moved him into the State Prison this morning.'

'So where do you pick me up?'

Max smiled a mirthless smile. 'You were caught an hour ago in Las Vegas. Agents Orsini and Purvis are taking you to Carson City by helicopter. Your flight leaves in ninety minutes for Sacramento. They'll be waiting for you.'

'You know something, Max? At times you can be one hell of a pain!'

'You know me, Lee, I like my people to make up their own minds!'

Lee gave him a disgusted look and started for the door. He was about to open it when a thought struck him. He turned back.

'You said that Slade made three trips you couldn't account for? Which was the third?'

Max beamed across the room. 'I thought you'd never ask. He went to Beirut where he saw a man called Calad Farik.'

'So where does he fit in?'

'We don't know yet – but he's just killed one of our top oilmen!'

The full implication of Max's words were shattering.

'Oil?' he croaked.

Max couldn't resist a wolfish grin. 'Yes. Odd, isn't it?'

Chapter 5

Nevada State Prison is a drab, grey building constructed at the turn of the century on what is now 5th Street in Carson City. The prison is divided into two very specific areas: one for medium security prisoners, the other a series of bleak, inhospitable corridors lined with self-locking steel doors. It was here, in the maximum security block, that Lee Corey arrived in the afternoon of the following day.

The guard who marched him down to the last cell on the second level was a short, squat, ugly man who looked as though he had been hewn out of rotting wood with a blunt axe. The only words he uttered were a grating 'open' into the communicator attached to his dark blue tunic. There was a series of clicks from the door and it widened to reveal a long, narrow room containing two bunks and the usual conveniences. He gestured, his lips compressed, his bushy brows knotted with concentration. Lee threw him a mocking grin and strolled into the cell, standing in the centre of the room, unmoving, until the steel bolts slid back into place and the guard's footsteps receded down the corridor.

'Next time you take off like that,' Slade said bleakly, 'I'll put a bullet in you myself.'

Lee sat down on the bunk facing him with an expression of injured innocence. 'You mean you wanted a lift somewhere?'

Slade swung his legs off the bed and leaned across until his face was less than a foot away. His eyes were still, searching for signals. Lee held his casual demeanour, but alarm bells were beginning to sound in the corners of his mind.

'You had time,' Slade said softly. 'You swung past me, no more than six feet. You could have stopped.'

'That's right, Slade. I could have picked you up – and Remmick, and Jacko, and Harris, Yancy, Boris. We could all have gone hareing out of that pass, easy as hell . . . only at the time I didn't think of it!'

Slade's face went pale and his hands, placed flat on his

knees, stiffened into blades of bone and muscle. Lee waited for him to strike, knowing that if he did then his assignment was over before it had begun. At the least they would be separated, at worst they would both be placed in solitary. But his immediate problem was none of those things. It was survival, for the stillness in Slade told him that he was a deadly adversary. When he struck it would be fast, accurate and savage. Instead Slade relaxed. There was no movement in him, but the light went out of his eyes and he began to breathe again. After a moment he nodded, as though surprised at his own decision, then swung his legs back on the bed and stretched out.

'Okay, hot shot. So how come you fouled it up?'

'You win some, you lose some,' Lee replied. 'I had to choose between Death Valley and Vegas. It wasn't that difficult.'

Slade allowed himself a small grin. 'You could always have taken the scenic route into Arizona.'

'You know, I thought of that,' agreed Lee, 'but I've got this terrible weakness for bright lights and cool chicks. Now I know you'd have gone straight into Death Valley, settled down with the snakes and the gilas for a month if necessary. Probably made it, too.'

'Maybe,' said Slade, without conviction.

He was silent for a full five minutes, frowning at the ceiling. Lee stretched out on the bed, tension easing from him for the first time since he had been marched into the governor's office. The FBI agents who delivered him had produced a court order stating that he was to be held in maximum security until his arraignment the following week. As far as he knew, the entire prison staff were quite convinced that he was as guilty as Slade.

'Any idea why they put you in here?' Slade asked quietly.

'You mean you didn't ask for me?'

Slade glanced at him without amusement. 'We're probably bugged.'

'Funny you should say that.'

'Not that it matters. Somebody set us up, so that means they've got all they need to put us away.'

'I'll settle for three to five.'

Slade sat up, his laughter echoing derisively around the white-walled cell. 'Try telling that to the judge!'

The day dragged on with the heat diminishing in almost

direct proportion to the conversation. Slade seemed to lie on his bed and stare up at the ceiling, responding with definitives to Lee's attempts at conversation. Their meal trays were brought at 5.45, the guard standing back in the corridor whilst a trustie brought them into the cell. It was an adequate meal consisting of a meaty, wholesome soup, fried chicken and french fries with coleslaw on the side, and a portion of cheese with one dry biscuit.

They ate in silence, the food a welcome respite from the creeping boredom. At six o'clock the guard and trustie returned, collecting the trays and leaving a carton of steaming coffee with two plastic cups. At six thirty the light came on in the cell. It was a day just full of surprises.

'Did you have a medical when you came in?' Slade asked some time later.

Lee tore his gaze from the spider which had been working diligently on its web in the corner of the cell directly above his head.

'No. Just the usual coffee and cookies with the governor.'

Slade nodded and contemplated the ceiling for a full minute before adding: 'They'll do it tonight.'

'What?'

'Medical.'

'So what's wrong with tomorrow morning? I'm always fitter in the morning.'

'Tomorrow's Saturday. They'll have to check us over tonight.'

'I'm busy tonight.'

Slade lapsed into silence again and Lee went back to studying the absorbing habits of *tegenaria domestica,* the orb-weaving house spider who was doing quite nicely some six feet above his head. Slade wasn't exactly the loquacious type and Lee Corey's health was hardly likely to be high on his list of worries for the day, so his sudden reference to a medical clearly had some significance. Glancing idly across to the tall, lean figure stretched out on the opposite bed, he tried to assess that significance against what he now knew of the man.

Before leaving C-2 in Washington he had studied the preliminary report and FBI file on Slade. The contents had been disturbing.

Born in Boston, Mass., some thirty-eight years ago, James

Arthur Slade had taken an easy ride through college by excelling at both basketball and tennis. His parents, both in their sixties, died in a car crash during his sophomore year, and this double blow took the edge off his aspirations. By the time he left college he was a confirmed cynic with a burning contempt for all the disciplines, in particular those which sought to channel his energies into any useful pursuit.

He dodged the draft by selling the family home and taking an extended holiday in Canada, but a year later he was selling cars in Montreal and in his spare time trying to find the girl who had run off with his money less than a month after moving into his apartment. He found her on a winter's night in 1961, hustling a convention at the Mount Royal Hotel. Other people found her the following morning, naked and frozen on the south bank of the St Lawrence, and from the tyre tracks on the ice it seemed that her boy friend had driven out across the frozen river and left her to walk home the hard way. The inquest verdict was death by misadventure with a rider that premeditation by a person or persons unknown could not be ruled out.

By that time Slade was back in the United States, having surrendered himself to the draft board who were more than delighted with his contrition and preference for overseas service with the Marines. He spent two years in Vietnam, where he earned his commission through two citations and the medal of honour, and was then detached from his unit and flown to Thailand for special training. The FBI report, without specifically stating so, clearly suggested that during this period Slade was attached to the CIA. During the next year Slade rose to the rank of Captain, heading a shadowy unit of men who operated independently along the Laotian border. They were known as the 'Hit Squad', a highly trained team who were completely at home in the jungle and could spend months stalking the gangs of Communist guerrillas attempting to infiltrate Thailand and Cambodia. Their mission was death, to kill as silently and effectively as possible, to take no prisoners and to mutilate all bodies in an attempt to undermine enemy morale.

When James Slade returned to the United States in the spring of '65, he was a lean, humourless man with hostile eyes. He spoke rarely, as though conversation was an excess, and between periods of movement he was totally still, like a lizard in the sun. He was clearly wasted as a car salesman.

The remainder of the report had been exasperatingly vague. For five years Slade appeared to have no steady source of income, yet was never short of money. He called himself a business consultant, but there was no record of any business being consulted. It was only in the early seventies that the Bureau began to take a closer interest in him. An investigation on the West Coast yielded his name, then an Eastern syndicate specializing in hijacking and protection was found to have a J. Slade on its books as consultant. An informer revealed that Slade specialized in finding personnel – the kind you couldn't get from an employment agency.

The bolts slid back with a metallic clang and the door opened to admit the squat, hand-hewn guard who gestured curtly towards the corridor.

'Outside. Both of you.'

Lee considered him with mild irritation. 'I was just about to drop off. It's been a very long day.'

'Move it, and cut the crap!'

Lee grimaced and rose wearily to his feet, noting that Slade was gazing at him with a curiously intent expression. As he turned to step into the corridor he made a vague gesture with his hand. 'Cool it, Corey.'

Lee gave him an amused look. 'So when did you join the parole board?'

Slade glanced back, his eyes stabbing at him with both menace and, strangely, a warning. With mounting interest Lee followed him through the door and along the corridor.

The prison clinic was located on the ground floor of the west wing, a medium security area which encompassed the library, television room and chapel. An orderly was waiting for them when they entered, pointing to a cubicle and telling them to strip. The guard, after beetling his brows with indecision, took up a position facing the cubicle, his hand resting pointedly on his gun.

'You've got one minute. After that I want you bare-assed against the wall.'

'Did anyone ever tell you that you have a personality defect?' Lee asked, in a conversational tone.

'Crap!' grated the guard.

'Couldn't have put it better myself,' replied Lee, and followed Slade into the cubicle.

As soon as he entered Slade closed the sliding door and gestured for silence. Moving quickly across the narrow cubicle he bent down and pulled out a plastic package which had been taped beneath the bench seat. Opening it he took out two pairs of goggles and gauze masks. There was also a small, flat Mauser automatic and a glass phial filled with a colourless liquid.

'Looks like they want you to come along,' whispered Slade, gesturing at the extra mask and goggles.

'Nice of them,' Lee murmured. 'But if that's the best they could do I'm not exactly brimming over with enthusiasm.'

Slade's gaze was cool, the stillness settling over him like a shroud. 'In or out, it's all the same to me.'

Lee grinned and took the mask and goggles. 'Which guard do I take?'

'Just follow me.'

Slipping on the mask and goggles, Slade glanced at Lee to check he had followed suit, then tossed the glass phial over the wooden partition of the cubicle. It exploded in the room beyond with a dull plop, spraying liquid which vapourized into a dense white gas on contact with air. In seconds the guard and orderly were on their knees, vomiting uncontrollably, their eyes streaming. Slade stepped out into the clinic ahead of Corey, crossing swiftly to the guard and putting him out of his misery with an efficient blow behind the ear. The orderly was crawling towards the window, retching but determined, when Lee reached him and tapped him gently into nirvana.

When he turned round Slade was already at the door leading into an office at the end of the clinic. Lee followed, holding his breath now as some of the gas began to filter through the mask, twisting his stomach into a nauseous ball. Fortunately little of the gas had seeped into the office and he was able to breathe more easily. Slade was opening a leather holdall placed just inside the door, passing one of the dark blue uniforms it contained to Lee. They changed quickly, putting their prison greys into the holdall which Slade then pushed behind a filing cabinet. Crossing to the window he opened it slightly, gazing out for a moment before turning back and removing his mask and goggles.

'We've got two minutes, three at the outside.'

'To do what?'

'To stroll across the exercise yard and out of the main gate.'

Lee stared at him incredulously. 'You've got to be kidding.'

'Look in your top pocket.'

Lee unfastened the flap of the blouse pocket, taking out the plastic-coated identity card inside. The face that stared back at him was his own, complete with prison grading, the name of Steven Howard, and the signature of the governor.

'That's impossible. I didn't even know I was coming here myself until this morning.'

Slade gave a thin smile. 'A pass like that only takes five minutes if you know the right people.'

'Like the governor!'

Slade shrugged, expressionless once more, and motioned towards the light switch. 'Switch off.'

With the room in darkness they dropped from the window to the exercise yard, crouching in the deep shadows beside the wall until their eyes adjusted to the night. Slade tapped him on the shoulder, then together they stepped out and began strolling across the sandy surface towards the squat silhouette of the gatehouse. They were halfway across when a door opened in the main block, spilling out light and uniformed figures.

'Keep moving,' Slade said softly. 'It's the second roster men finishing.'

They reached the path which ran along the side of the exercise yard, pausing to light cigarettes as three guards walked briskly by towards the gate. Other guards were emerging from the main block behind them, their voices relaxed and cheerful.

'No sweat,' murmured Slade. 'Just follow them through.'

They strolled up to the main gate where a guard was opening a side door. The three uniformed men ahead waved their passes at him, one of them calling out: 'Come on, Charlie, let's move it.'

Charlie opened the side door, giving the passes only a cursory glance, then Slade was stepping forward, holding the pass low so that the guard had to look down at it, then moving on as though he did this every night of the week. There were bright lights on the gate, a lamp directly above the side door which they had to step through. From this position two other guards in the gatehouse could watch through a window. Lee kept his face expressionless, flashing the pass briefly, then stepping forward.

'What's your hurry?' grunted Charlie irritably.

Lee stopped and turned back, giving him an easy, relaxed smile. 'Sorry, Charlie.'

He took the pass and studied the picture, then stared intently at Lee. A group of four guards were moving up behind them as, with growing tension, he watched the needle of doubt come into the guard's face.

'You're new?' he asked, his eyes narrowing.

Lee shrugged. 'Not that you'd notice. Just changed shifts, that's all.'

Charlie hesitated, doubt nagging at the corners of his mind. He started a turn towards the gatehouse, probably to call out one of the other guards, when a heavily-built man in a dark blue prison raincoat stepped into the light on the other side of the gate.

'Come on, Steve, we haven't got all night.'

Charlie glanced towards him, then back at Lee. Behind him one of the guards moved forward restlessly.

'For Christ's sake, Charlie!'

The indecision faded and he handed the pass back to Lee, nodding towards the gate with a grudging apology. A moment later Lee was through the door and beyond the lights, walking briskly beside the stranger towards the black Lincoln Continental parked a few yards beyond the prison gates.

'Any second now they're going to start blowing sirens,' Lee commented.

'Relax, friend. The doc is busy in the west wing. Until he goes back to the clinic, no one's going to know.'

He opened the door, smiling calmly. Slade was already in the rear, his steady gaze on Lee as he got in beside him. There was a slim, dark-haired man in his mid-twenties at the wheel and as his companion took the seat next to him he pulled out into the traffic on 5th Street, heading downtown.

'That was neat,' said Lee, as the grey prison buildings disappeared into the night. 'But it beats me how you got organized so quick.'

'Our business, friend. All you have to do is sit back and enjoy the ride.'

The ride was smooth and uneventful, taking them across

the city to U.S. 395 where they quickly picked up speed on the freeway, heading north towards Reno. They had travelled some ten miles along the route when a persistent bleep sounded in the car. The heavily-built man in the front opened the glove compartment and took out a radio mike, flicking a switch.

'Mallory, come in.'

The voice that answered was cool and laconic. 'We just had word that they're blowing the whistle along boulevard and 5th. You clear of Washoe Lake yet?'

'Just about.'

'Check. We'll lay on a back-up in case the State boys get ambitious.'

'They won't. Monitor their transmissions and let me know if there's an all points.'

'Will do. You got airport clearance and everything's clean at Reno.'

'I read you. Out.'

Lee watched Mallory return the microphone to its compartment with increasing concern. This was no hastily conceived escape plan – it was the product of a highly efficient organization which clearly had access to state departments and radio frequencies. If anything it was as efficient as the FBI, yet there was no criminal organization in this part of the country capable of sustaining such an operation. Unless the Bureau had been going to sleep and the State Police were walking around with blinkers, it just didn't exist.

He glanced at Slade and found the man watching him with a thoughtful expression. 'You any idea where this mystery tour ends?'

Slade shrugged. 'Does it matter?'

'I'm the nostalgic type. I like to know where I've been before I get back.'

'If you get back.'

Lee allowed his lips to compress into a thin, hard line. 'Don't get cute, Slade. I'm still very interested in finding out which one of your goons was a fink!'

Mallory turned round and shook his head at them. 'You'll be wasting your time. It was an FBI operation, set up in Washington and co-ordinated by San Jose security. We're working on it, but it's top drawer. You're best out of it.'

Lee felt the perspiration on the palms of his hands. It was

all getting too close for comfort.

'That suits me,' said Slade. 'How about you, Corey? You still on the payroll?'

'You mean I've got a choice?'

The man in the front laughed softly, without humour. 'Right now you've got a ticket to New York. Whether you stick with Slade is your business.'

Lee glanced at Slade who was studying the back of his hand as though he'd never seen it before.

'I don't work blind. So far I'm impressed, but now it's question time. How much? How long? How far?'

Slade sighed and nodded, accepting it. 'The money's the same as before, five hundred a week until you're operational. After that it depends on the target and the split.'

'That's never-never land, Slade. What target? What split?'

The eyes went reptilian, gleaming in the night. 'That's one question too many.'

Lee stared at him with tight features, matching his anger. 'In that case I'll settle for New York. You better find someone else to play games with.'

There was silence in the car for a full five minutes until the lights of Reno appeared ahead. The radio bleeped and Mallory answered it briefly, confirming that they would be entering the airport in five minutes. Switching off, he exchanged a look with Slade before turning to Lee.

'Suppose we make it a grand a week, guarantee of six weeks, bonus of fifty grand if everything works?'

'I'll buy that, but I still want to know where.'

'You know something, Corey?' Slade said savagely. 'You're beginning to get up my nostril!'

'You're so far up mine I've got tears in my eyes!'

'Look, Slade,' the man in front interjected with a note of impatience in his voice. 'Either you need him or you don't. Let's cut the crap and get on with it.'

Slade controlled his anger with an effort, his mouth ugly. 'Just one word, Corey. If that isn't enough you can screw off!'

'Let's hear the word then.'

'Beirut.'

Lee's face betrayed none of the emotions that leapt with the word. So Max had been right. Somehow Nevada and Beirut were connected, and the common denominator appeared to be a brace of atom bombs. Slade was watching him intently, so he threw him a mocking grin and nodded his head.

'That's not a bad town. I'm told it's even more fun than Vegas.'

Slade relaxed and the quick glance he gave Mallory was tinged with relief. With some surprise, Lee realized that his acceptance was important to Slade. The knowledge gave him a slight advantage, and the best time to test it was now.

'You've still got to get us on that plane, Mallory,' he said in a conversational tone. 'That's not going to be easy.'

Mallory gave a short, barking laugh and waved a contemptuous hand. 'Relax, that's the easiest part of all.'

They were approaching the municipal airport, flashing signs directing traffic into the arrival and departure lanes. Glancing at Slade, Lee was even more puzzled by his apparent lack of concern. The terminal, like any other major airport in the country, would have a strong contingent of municipal police and security men. The fact that they were both still wearing the uniform of prison guards didn't exactly improve their chances.

The answer began to emerge before he could voice the question. The Lincoln Continental slid out of the approach lanes on to a service road which curved away from the terminal complex to an entrance marked 'Airport Personnel Only'. One of the two uniformed security men manning the barrier approached the car, but before he could look inside Mallory was leaning out of his window and waving a leather-bound pass at him. The guard took one glance at the pass, then stiffened with respect and motioned to his colleague who tilted up the barrier.

'What have you got there, Mallory?' said Lee, as they swept through the gate. 'A letter from the President?'

Mallory chuckled. 'Just about.'

With reluctant admiration, Lee watched as they drove swiftly around the cargo bays, through an underpass which brought them up on to the main perimeter where a blue and white chequered security car was waiting to whisk them past the loading piers to a Boeing 727 parked on the apron. The aircraft was wearing the livery of Sun Vista Charters, and even as they stepped out of the car the jets were growling into life. A senior security officer stepped out of the car and crossed to them, saluting Mallory respectfully before glancing at the pass. He handed it back almost immediately, his expression a mixture of pride and prejudice.

'Whenever you're ready, sir.'

They got out of the car, neither the security officer or the maintenance crew around the aircraft showing the slightest interest in the fact that two of the party were prison guards. If anything, they studiously avoided looking at either of them.

Mallory led them to the steps, then turned to the security men who seemed about to go on board with them.

'I take it we're fully cleared?'

He nodded. 'You're listed as a domestic flight in accordance with the directive from Washington.'

'Fine. I'll just go on board, then follow you back.'

The security officer hesitated, not quite sure of his ground. 'Does that mean you won't be travelling with them?'

'It does.'

Lee was halfway up the steps when the man's next words stopped him in his tracks.

'Can I assume they are also CIA operatives?'

'You can, although we naturally expect you to treat that information as classified.'

Lee was still trying to come to terms with the shattering revelation when Mallory came on board, grinning cheerfully and waving a magnanimous hand at the 132 empty seats. 'Take your pick, friends. It's all yours.'

'Is it?' Lee stared at him coldly. 'Just what kind of crap are you handing around, Mallory? If you're CIA then I'm on the wrong plane!'

Mallory gazed back, unperturbed. Slade, after an amused glance at Lee, dropped into a seat and began fastening his belt. Outside the whine of the engines rose to a howl, then diminished again.

'Listen, Corey, you got this far because you've got a sharp track record and you lived up to it in Stonewall Pass. Slade thinks you're useful, so we do too, but only as long as you keep us happy. Okay?'

Without waiting for a reply he turned and went forward to the flight deck. Lee sat beside Slade with an exasperated sigh.

'You really mean to tell me that the CIA is pulling prison breaks?'

Slade gave him a glassy smile. 'Crazy world, isn't it!'

'Yeah, so crazy I'm wondering what the hell I'm getting into.'

The smile dissolved into a stoney silence. When Slade finally spoke it was a flat, emotionless statement of fact.

'The big one, hot shot. You're into the biggest caper of them all.'

Mallory returned after a few minutes, accompanied by the co-pilot who remained by the door, ready to close it when he left. The CIA man leaned over them, waving a casual hand towards the flight deck.

'Everything's cool. You got a flight plan to Miami, but somewhere along the way it's going to get switched to a flight from New York. You should touch down in Cuba round about dawn.'

'Check,' said Slade, as though everyone who went to Miami touched down in Cuba.

'Whatever happened to Beirut?' Lee asked, dryly.

Mallory beamed at him and patted his shoulder. 'Relax, friend. This plane's got to refuel somewhere . . . so why not Havana.'

'How stupid of me,' murmured Lee. 'It's the obvious place.'

Mallory chuckled and headed for the door. Within minutes they were jolting across the tarmac towards the runway, the voice of the captain cheerfully telling them that once they were airborne they could help themselves to food and drinks from the galley. But there were other things on Corey's mind. He was wondering just how long it would take the CIA to run down the Nevada operation to an undercover agent from C-2. And then how long it would take before someone discovered that, almost ten years ago, there was a Lee Corey in the FBI.

Chapter 6

They touched down at Beirut exactly thirty-six hours after leaving Reno, acquiring along the way some fifty hard-eyed members of Castro's elite commando force. The men, all in jungle green and carrying Russian automatic weapons, were being taken to Mozambique in exchange for fuel and landing facilities at Havana. For the most part they kept to themselves, regarding Slade and Corey with sullen disinterest, but to Lee it was further evidence, if any had been needed, that this was the work of a large and highly efficient organization.

In addition to a complete set of clothes, all of which fitted to perfection, they were each provided with passports, papers, currency and traveller's cheques. Considering that the entire operation must have been planned and executed within forty-eight hours, it was a masterpiece of organization and clearly bore the stamp of the CIA. Yet in spite of that agency's devious record, Lee found it difficult to believe that they could be part of a plan to steal atom bombs from the USAEC. Slade had begun to relax now that they were on the final leg of the journey, so Lee took the opportunity to voice his doubts.

'The only time I met Mallory before yesterday was in Dallas,' Slade revealed. 'It was his job to get me and those Plowshare bombs out of Reno.'

'And that's why this plane was laid on?'

'All the way to Beirut. When things got fouled up, they must have switched the schedule and used the flight to get us both out.'

Lee gave him a baffled look. 'But why? What the hell are we doing working with the CIA.'

'Who says we are?' Slade grinned when he saw his bewilderment. 'Look, make no mistake about it, this is a caper. The front money – and I don't think there'll be much change out of a million bucks – comes from Texas. Maybe part of that money comes from the CIA, maybe not, but I'm pretty sure that they want us to pull it off.'

'Then it's political?'

Slade considered him warily. 'Why should that bother you?'

Lee shrugged. 'It wouldn't, except that things like that are usually messy. It's a different league and once you're in you end up with an early retirement in places like Cuba or Libya, or on the wrong end of a firing squad.'

'Not this one, it's far too big for that. When you start tossing A-bombs around, everybody listens.'

'Is that what we'll be doing?'

Slade stared out of the window at the Atlantic twenty thousand feet below, weighing his words carefully. When he spoke it was in a voice made all the more menacing by its total lack of concern.

'We're living in the age of terrorism, Corey. It's not what you want that matters, it's how far you're prepared to go to get it. Do you think governments really give a damn if you're Black September, Red Army or IRA? Half the time they don't even know what crazy idea you stand for. No, what makes them get down on their knees and beg to pay-off is terror. And by the time we're through we'll put the fear of God into half the western world.'

'Aren't you forgetting something? We didn't get the bombs.'

Slade grinned, supremely confident. 'Oh, we'll get them. Calad Farik will tell us how to get them.'

Lee wanted to ask more, particularly about the Texas Connection, but there was a finality in Slade's voice that told him any further questions would only arouse his suspicions. Lee's immediate problem was to find a way of letting C-2 know where he was, and this was now made doubly difficult by the CIA's involvement. His normal channel of communication was through the local Embassy, but in Beirut – a hotbed of international intrigue – any official messages were bound to be monitored by an agency operative.

Calad Farik met them in the cool, vaulted hall of the villa that sprawled along the hillside overlooking Pigeon Rock Bay. He was not at all what Lee had expected, from the fine tooled Italian shoes to the French silk shirt and elegantly flared trousers. He was a thick, muscular man with a disturbing air of effeminacy about him, and this was enhanced by the curiously shrill voice which was in such sharp contrast to the heavy features and bulging biceps. His eyes were dark, unreadable, pausing briefly on Corey as Slade introduced him.

'Do make yourself comfortable, Mr Corey. I'm sure I can answer all your questions later, but for now there are questions of my own that need to be answered.'

He moved off into the depths of the house without waiting for a response, already asking Slade about Nevada with barely concealed irritation. Lee went out on to the loggia where vines hung down, heavy with fruit. Across the patio a pool gleamed in the sunlight. He strolled towards it, his gaze already fixed on the dark, slender girl who lay there. She let him stand looking at her for a full thirty seconds before tipping sunglasses off the top of her head and gazing up at him.

'Are you Slade?' she asked in a cool, mellow voice.

'No, I'm Corey.'

Her white teeth gleamed in the sun and then she closed her eyes and slid the glasses back on to her hair. 'You just missed out.'

Lee tossed his jacket on to a chair and squatted down beside her. 'Why don't we run through that again?'

Her mouth twitched. 'Are you Slade?'

'Sure I am.'

'The man I'm supposed to meet?'

'The very same.'

She sat up slowly, considering him with hazel eyes speckled with liquid gold. 'Then you better give me the password.'

Lee pursed his lips, looking thoughtful. She waited. 'God but you're beautiful,' he pronounced, finally.

'Is that the password?'

'It should be.'

'Wrong,' she said, and pushed him deliberately into the pool.

When he surfaced the girl was lying back in the sun as though she frequently threw total strangers into swimming pools. Lee climbed out and stood over her, dripping water on to the smooth, flat stomach.

'I'll bet you're a smash with the Girl Guides.'

She rose to her feet in a single, fluid movement, and considered him with growing annoyance. There was a subtle arrogance in her manner, a poise that had nothing to do with sophistication, more a state of mind and body. 'You're becoming a nuisance, Mr Corey.'

'Good,' he said, his eyes mocking her. 'It's the very least I can do.'

'You'd better go and change your clothes,' she said, waspishly.

'That's just the point,' he replied. 'I didn't bring any.'

She shrugged, unperturbed. He let his anger come and go, noting the alertness in her, an almost instinctive awareness of his intention. When he reached for her it was with a lazy indifference, giving her ample time to knock his hand aside.

'I wouldn't advise that,' she said, warningly.

He smiled, his gaze moving over her with deliberate slowness. Her eyes flashed angrily, but she had completely misunderstood the purpose of the glance. He had the measure of her now. The legs, placed precisely two feet apart, heels raised slightly to balance her on the balls of her feet, allowing each to act as pivot for a kick. The hands, flat blades, each moving in relation to the other so that one was always a natural feint. Even as he started the sequence of moves he was wondering what she did that made it necessary to be this good at karate.

He allowed her to read the first move in his eyes, then as she slashed at his forearm, reversed and stepped to one side, chopping her lightly above the elbow. The blow never landed. She twisted, agile as a cat, then pivoted a full 180 degrees to kick at his midriff. This was precisely what he had expected. Swaying back he caught her foot in one hand, then stepped forward as she tried to turn back. It was an impossible position, already off balance, still facing away from him, she was incapable of movement.

'You really must have more respect for the opposite sex,' murmured Lee, and gave her a stinging slap on the bottom before catapulting her into the pool.

She surfaced on the far side and ignored him completely. Grinning, he picked up his jacket and turned towards the house, finding Farik watching him with a smile of approval.

'I see you've introduced yourself,' he said. 'I'm afraid Miss Dassan is not the most sociable of people.'

'She is a bit on the aggressive side,' replied Lee in a voice that carried across the pool. 'It's a wonder she's lasted this long.'

Farik gave a shrill laugh. 'It is indeed. Now what are we going to do about those clothes? I could offer you my wardrobe, but . . .' He gestured apologetically at the considerable disparity in chest measurements.

'That's okay, I needed a couple of outfits anyway. I'll dry these off, then take a stroll round the shops.'

'Of course,' Farik agreed smoothly. 'I'll see that Miss Dassan takes you to the most suitable places.'

'I can manage,' Lee said casually, hoping that he was not going to insist. The wet clothes were a perfect excuse to get out into the city and work out some method of contacting C-2. The hope died as he saw the wary gleam come into Farik's eyes.

'You're a stranger to Beirut,' he said smoothly. 'I absolutely insist that she accompanies you. After all,' he beamed towards the girl who was watching with tight features, 'you might as well get used to working together.'

Lee gave him a disgusted look. 'You know, I had a feeling that things had been going too well lately!'

When he had gone into the house Raya moved angrily to Farik. 'He can go alone. I've got better things to do.'

'Don't argue. Do it.'

'Listen to me, Farik. I didn't come here to sit around a pool all day and take stupid Americans to the shops!'

Farik's neck became thick, bulging cords of muscle and his heavy jowled face contorted with anger. Staring at her with glittering eyes he spaced each word with contempt. 'You will do precisely what I say, without question, or take yourself back to your kibbutz!'

A cool breeze was coming off the sea when they left the villa and walked along the Corniche into Rue Chouran, past the elegant walls of the Carlton Hotel and the gleaming modern structure of the Beirut International. Turning left into Rue de Berlin, Raya led him at a brisk pace to Jeb el-Nakhel, a prominent shopping district in which many of the buildings were still undergoing repairs, their walls speckled with the graffiti of war. She was still simmering with indignation and made no secret of the fact that his company was only slightly more preferable to that of one of the local scorpions. She waited outside each of the shops he visited, her mouth compressed with impatience as he deliberately took his time over each purchase. After the third shop she was ready to explode.

'How much more do you need?' she fumed. 'Already you

have enough to make a gigolo blush!'

'You'd know more about that than I would,' said Lee, handing her another package.

'What the hell is that supposed to mean?'

He raised a shocked eyebrow. 'Well, you obviously know all about their wardrobe!'

For a moment he was sure she was going to fling the package at him.

'Did you know that your nose twitches when you're mad?' he asked in a conversational tone.

'It is none of your concern.'

'I just thought you ought to know, seeing as how it turns me on no end!'

She glared at him, about to make a cutting retort when a dark-haired girl walking briskly and blindly down the street collided with Lee and sent the rest of his packages in every direction.

'My God, I'm sorry!' she exclaimed, with a stricken expression. 'I was miles away.'

'You could have fooled me,' Lee replied, then took the edge off it with a grin.

They began to gather up the packages, Raya watching aloofly. The girl handed him the last package, smiling nervously. 'I'm not normally so clumsy. Do forgive me.'

'Nothing to forgive. It was just an accident.'

The girl nodded, looking relieved, then moved on with a quick, wary glance at Raya. Lee watched her continue down the street and enter a café. She had a small, neat figure which was interesting without being striking. Her hair was cut short, giving her a boyish appearance which was enhanced by the blue jeans and plain white shirt. He knew she had deliberately collided with him – the question was: Why?

'Whenever you're ready,' Raya said, the edge of sarcasm not entirely lost on him.

'I've just had a great idea,' said Lee. 'Why don't we have a cup of coffee?'

Raya's look was right out of the deep freeze, but Lee only grinned and led her along the street and into the café. The girl was sitting at a table by the window, the waiter already taking down her order as they entered. Lee chose a table on the far side of the room, making a point of sitting Raya with her back to the window.

'French, Turkish or expresso?'

'Tea,' she said, and deliberately moved her chair so that she could see the girl.

Lee gave the order to the waiter, then leaned back and considered her with a thoughtful expression. Raya quickly became impatient under his gaze.

'Well?'

'I'm just wondering what makes you so uptight. Most girls I know would rather shop than eat.'

'I am not most girls, especially of the kind you would know.'

'That's true,' Lee agreed cheerfully. 'I don't usually go for the aggressive type.'

Her eyes flashed dangerously, but before she could think of a suitable reply Lee was glancing towards the window and smiling warmly at the girl there. Raya's mouth compressed. The fact that the girl across the room was smiling back didn't help matters. The waiter brought thick Turkish coffee and iced mint tea, enabling Raya to spend the next five minutes studying the glass as though she expected to find it booby-trapped. Lee smoked a cigarette, his gaze moving frequently to the girl in the window.

'Do you have to make it so obvious?' Raya said finally, in a brittle voice.

'Sorry,' said Lee, 'but the vibrations are pretty strong. I don't suppose you'd happen to know who she is?'

The atmosphere between them went sub-zero. 'I'm sure you could find out.'

Lee grinned and stood up. 'It's worth a try.'

He crossed the room to the table in the window, the girl watching him with a quiet smile as he approached. Even before he reached her she was gesturing to the other chair. He grinned and dropped into it.

'I just had to say hello.'

'I thought you might. My name is Freddy, by the way. Freddy Stone.'

'It doesn't suit you, but I guess I can live with it. I don't really need to introduce myself, do I?'

The question hung between them for a moment, then she smiled, the amusement reaching up into her eyes. She shook her head. 'I have a blue index on you. I spent a full twenty-four hours drinking coffee at the airport until I picked you out.'

Lee began to relax for the first time in days. Max had been on his toes, as usual, alerting all possible destinations the moment he knew that Lee had broken out of Carson City.

'What's your station?'

'Detached from the bureau in Paris. I've been here for three months.'

'Okay, how's your recall?'

'Total.' She was quiet and matter of fact.

'Check. Person to person only. No relays and no copies. Tell Max Weller in C-2, Washington, that I'm with Farik and active. There may be a CIA trace on the Nevada operation so I want a total clamp, tell him to set up a decoy source, then to check out a CIA group in Nevada headed by a man called Mallory. You got that?'

She had been gazing at him with a gentle smile, but her eyes were intent. She nodded. 'How about here?'

'I want a four-man team, round the clock. Find a bar near to Farik's villa and man it day and night. Tell Max that the target seems to be this end of the line, but he could be right about the Mid East. It's a big contract, maybe the biggest one of all, so I've got to stay with it until I know where, when and how.'

He stood up and held her hand. She smiled back at him warmly. 'I have it, Lee. But I should bring in my bureau chief.'

'Screw him. If the agency gets wind of this I could find myself with some very unfriendly people. File a routine negative on the blue index and leave the rest to Max.'

'All right,' she said softly, her eyes holding his. 'Take care.'

He returned to Raya, amused by the aura of hostility emanating from her. 'I'm in luck. She's free all day tomorrow.'

'Really?' Raya rose to her feet, looking like the cat with the proverbial cream. 'That's too bad, I've a feeling you'll be a long way from Beirut by this time tomorrow.'

Chapter 7

The island of Corfu is a vivid splash of green against the deep blue of the Ionian Sea. Its terraced hills are cloaked with olive trees and cypress, and from the higher ridges you can look out over the Straits of Otranto to the arid hills of Albania. It is a friendly island, made famous by both the Durrells, and nowhere is more than an hour away from Corfu Town.

Lee arrived shortly after noon of the following day, accompanied by Slade and a surprisingly radiant Raya. Her attitude had changed noticeably since they left Beirut, but he wasn't sure whether this was due to the journey itself or the prospect of action after the enforced idleness at the villa. In any event she was gay and amusing, chattering enthusiastically about Israel, her parents who ran a hotel in Haifa, her brother who was too young to fight but already chasing girls.

From the airport they drove to Benitses in the rented Fiat which had been waiting for them, and even Slade began to mellow as they travelled along the picturesque coastline, the air redolent with lemon and olive.

'Maybe this is one assignment you ought to foul up, hot shot,' he said with a grin, indicating the ski boat below them. 'There's plenty to keep Raya and I occupied!'

'What makes you so sure I can pull the chick anyway?'

'You're only the first string, fella. After you it's Raya's turn with the old man.'

'And if she strikes out?'

'I don't think you need to worry about that,' Raya said confidently. 'When I put my mind to it I can be very persuasive.'

'Oh, I know,' Lee said, fervently. 'I only hope he's got a change of clothes with him when you say hello!'

She laughed at his reference to their first meeting. A moment later they turned a bend to look down on Benitses, a wide bay dotted with fishing boats and a few private yachts. One of them, a gleaming white cruiser, was anchored off a narrow point above the town. It was easily the largest boat in sight.

'There she is,' said Slade, quietly. 'All ready and waiting.'

Lee stopped the car and they gazed down the hillside, the laughter gone now as the presence of the motor yacht brought home to them the more sinister purpose of their visit. Slade had taken binoculars from a case in the back of the car and was studying the hillside above the town. After a moment he grunted with satisfaction, passing them to Lee.

'Halfway up the hill, beside the olive grove.'

Lee lifted the glasses and found the neat white villa with a red tiled roof and dark, shuttered windows. There was a verandah running the length of the building, jutting out from the hillside to look down on the sea. Even as he watched a girl came out of the villa and leaned over the parapet. He lowered the glasses, searching the olive grove below. After a moment he found a tall, grey-haired man in shorts and open shirt. He was moving through the trees, following a narrow path up to the house.

'They're both there now,' he said.

Raya took the binoculars and studied the scene silently for a moment before handing them to Slade.

'So we're in business,' she said.

Lee nodded, his features betraying none of the frustration and concern he had felt since Farik first broke the news to them over dinner the previous night. He had been in an expansive mood, his shrill voice vibrating with excitement as he outlined the plan.

'It's simplicity itself,' he declared. 'The Paxtons are staying at a villa just above Benitses. They keep very much to themselves, going for occasional walks, a little sunbathing. By the time you get there Troy will have sailed my yacht over from Athens, and he'll be cleared to anchor off Corfu before sailing on to Beirut where the yacht is due for a refit.'

He beamed at them across the table, his gaze finally coming to rest on Lee. 'It will be your task to make the acquaintance of Julia Paxton, the daughter, then invite both her and her father on board the yacht. At that point Slade will take over and you will all set sail for Beirut.'

'How important are they?' Lee asked.

'Vital. Quite vital.'

'You mean they're part of the main operation?'

Farik's eyes hooded over and for a full minute he appeared to consider the long-stemmed crystal glass containing a vintage Mouton Cadet. When he spoke it was to Slade, his voice thin and cold.

'How long have you known me, Slade?'

'Long enough.'

'How have I survived that long?'

'Need to know.'

'Indeed.' He turned back to Lee. 'If you need to know any specific fact, Mr Corey, you can be sure that I will tell you. Other than that you are obliged to be told nothing at all.'

Lee gazed back with equal coldness. 'I'm not one of your houseboys, Farik. My price is high, and it's not all in dollars. I need to know what I'm getting into, or I catch the next plane back to the States.'

'I wouldn't advise that.' He smiled, but it was no more than a movement of the mouth. 'You are on my ground, Mr Corey, and that gives me certain advantages!'

Slade stirred restlessly, flicking a warning glance at Lee across the table. 'I'm sure that Lee is only really concerned about the money end of it, Calad.'

Farik gave a short, contemptuous laugh. 'He will be paid well.'

'How well?' persisted Lee. 'And who are the Paxtons?'

Slade sighed and closed his eyes. Raya, who had been watching disdainfully, pushed back her chair and rose to her feet.

'If you'll excuse me, Senor Farik.'

'Of course.'

She left, ignoring Lee, who continued to regard Farik with bland assurance. Slade was a still, distant figure, no longer a part of the conversation. A fan revolved above them, swirling the sluggish air. The Lebanese rose abruptly and crossed to a carved oak bureau. Unlocking a drawer he took out a wad of notes and returned to the table, dropping them in front of Lee.

'Five thousand dollars, Corey. That's what you're worth to me if you bring the Paxtons back, secretly and unharmed.'

Lee took the money and slipped it into his pocket. 'That's a good price. You'll have them.'

Farik nodded, his eyes intent, a thin film of perspiration on his forehead the only outward sign of the anger that was burning in him. Lee waited, knowing there was more.

'Tread lightly, American. I tolerate your presence here because I am assured that you are a good man in a difficult situation. However, if I find you lacking, I can very quickly decide that you are more trouble than you are worth.'

Lee gave a lazy grin and waved a hand towards Slade. 'He gave me the same spiel in Nevada, so I go into a job without knowing what it's all about. Next thing I know it's disaster time, so all I can do is get out.'

Slade had opened his eyes and was now staring intently at Lee. Nothing moved, he barely breathed. 'You complaining, Corey?'

Lee nodded. 'Dead right I am. If I know what I'm into I've got some chance of weighing up the odds, or maybe changing them.'

'You're just a regular hot shot, aren't you,' Slade sneered.

Farik silenced them with a gesture, considering Lee with grudging approval. 'If I told you what Paxton does,' he said, slowly, 'would that improve your chances?'

'It might.'

'Very well, but before I do, I should warn you that only three other people know. They are all above suspicion, so if I find that there has been any leak – even a whisper of our purpose – we will know it has come from you.'

'You don't need to lose any sleep over that.'

Farik smiled a death's head smile. 'Perish the thought, Mr Corey.'

He patted him gently on the shoulder, then crossed the room to the door. He paused there and looked back, his eyes black and unreadable. 'Donald Paxton is a nuclear chemist. They're not easy to find, especially with attractive daughters.'

A cold wind of fear swept through Lee, and it took all his control to keep the alarm from showing. Slade was watching him closely, searching for some reaction, some deeper awareness. He was disappointed and a moment later left the room with a cursory good night. Lee remained at the table until Samir, the Lebanese girl, began to hover in the shadows. He rose and went out on to the patio, gazing up at the stars for a long time until he had put it all together.

Farik had failed to get his bombs in Nevada, so now he was planning to make his own. The fact that he needed a chemist rather than a physicist suggested that he planned to use conventional nuclear fuel, probably plutonium, and build a very basic device. The principles were already widely known, and only the previous year the FBI had been in a panic when a college student designed a perfectly feasible atomic bomb. What had made it all the more horrifying was the fact that the bomb could be carried in the average suitcase, yet had the capacity to unleash the explosive force of one hundred thousand tons of TNT.

It was midnight before he went back into the villa, but by then he knew that there was no way he could save the Paxtons. They were the key to Farik's plan, and only through them could he hope to answer the most terrifying question of all – how the bombs were going to be used?

Troy was lounging on the shingle beach with a vaguely bored expression when they arrived. Lee parked the car, then followed Slade and Raya down to the water's edge. The young Dane rose and waved a languid hand towards the cruiser anchored in the centre of the bay.

'She's ready when you are.'

'What about the crew?' asked Slade.

'Spiros and Felipe, the usual ones. They're all right.'

Slade gave him a hard look. 'So you told them all about it!'

'That's right.' Troy grinned. 'Then we held a Press Conference.'

Slade gave him a sour glance and turned away. Troy was considering Corey, making a point of ignoring Raya completely. Lee found his gaze vaguely irritating, and this quickly crystallized into dislike when the Dane spoke.

'You're the one who's going to pull her.' There was an edge of scorn to the words that hovered somewhere between contempt and envy.

Lee gave him a long, level look, watching the way his thin lips tightened and the eyes fell away. He had pale, almost sallow features with straw-coloured hair and a fine down that covered his cheeks and his chin. The too-tight jeans and shirt, knotted just above the waist, said all that needed to be said about the youth. He tossed his bag into the dinghy, then helped to push it out into deeper water. As Troy began to row them out to the yacht, Slade gestured up towards the villa on the hillside.

'How do you want to play it?'

'As though it isn't even our game. We pick the taverna closest to them, then enjoy ourselves. If they show, we ignore them.'

'And if they don't?' Raya was curious.

'We try again tomorrow.'

Chapter 8

Julia Paxton rubbed a handful of suntan oil over her arms and shoulders, then lay back on the sand and listened to the murmur of the sea. It was hotter than yesterday, the sky cloudless and still. A seagull wheeled overhead, inspecting the fishing boats and, finding them already picked clean, headed listlessly out to sea. The girl breathed deeply of the warm, fragrant air, smiling happily to herself. Every day her father seemed to grow stronger. The hollowness around the eyes that had been there since her mother died some six months ago, had almost gone. His hair, though iron grey, was no longer dull. His voice had begun to sound the way it did in the old days, when they walked the fells of Cumbria and watched Coniston turn from silver to gold in the setting sun.

A shadow fell across her and she looked up, shielding her eyes from the sun. A tall, lean man with fair hair was smiling down at her. She smiled back. She had seen him the night before at the taverna when Fernando, the waiter, had made a point of telling her that he was one of the people from the yacht in the bay.

'You've got to be English,' he said, in a mellow American voice.

'I don't see why.'

He sat down beside her without waiting to be asked. 'You've got freckles. I was brought up to believe that all the nicest English girls have freckles.'

She smiled. 'Then I'd better not tell you what I was brought up to believe about Americans.'

He winced. 'I daren't even ask. The name's Corey, by the way. Lee Corey.'

She sat up and began to smooth oil on her legs. He watched, waiting. She smiled to herself, wondering if the meeting was accidental. She doubted it. He seemed to be the kind of man who left nothing to chance.

'If you put any more on you'll fry.'

She laughed. 'It's either that or burn.'

'You were at the taverna last night.'

She gazed steadily at him for a moment. 'That's right. With my father.'

'Ah. I was hoping he was your father.'

'Why?' Again the level gaze.

'It simplifies things.'

'What kind of things?'

'Taking you out to dinner tonight.'

She smiled, a little wistfully, and shook her head. 'I shall be eating with Father.'

'They can still get three chairs round a table.'

She laughed, liking his directness. 'It would take more than that to get my father into one of them. He's an introvert at the best of times and, at the moment, he's – well, he's not quite himself.'

'Okay. But if we just happen to be in the same taverna . . . ?'

'We usually eat there.'

'Then maybe I'll see you. In fact, if I knew your name, I could even say hello.'

She was immediately apologetic. 'I'm sorry, it's Julia Paxton.'

'Mind if I call you Jules?'

She thought about it, then shook her head. 'Not particularly. Why?'

'It's my favourite name, and it suits you.'

His clear blue eyes seemed to look right into her and suddenly she was aware of breathing, of a pulse that was beating far too quickly in her throat. Her cheeks were beginning to burn and she desperately hoped he wouldn't notice, but he was already turning away, waving a casual hand, walking off along the beach. She watched until he reached the path leading up the hillside to the road above, then lay back, closed her eyes and wondered about him for the rest of a hot afternoon.

Julia Paxton was a realist, and although barely eighteen had long since come to terms with the more basic facts that quickly became apparent in any full length mirror. Her black, shoulder-length hair and brown eyes could not be faulted. Her face, although too sharply planed, was enhanced by a wide, full mouth and flawless white teeth. It was below the neck that the disappointment began to appear.

Her shoulders were broad, too broad as far as she was

concerned, and her breasts tended to go with gravity unless assisted by the most expensive bras. Her waist was narrow, but her legs were definitely on the thin side and only served to exaggerate hips that were too wide and square. An obnoxious cousin she had detested for years, and who had grown into a slim, lissom blonde with the bitchiest tongue in the western hemisphere, once reduced her to tears by remarking that she looked as though she had been put together by a drunken gynaecologist. Like all effective insults, it cut deep because it held a grain of truth.

If this was true, she reasoned with reluctant logic, what on earth was an apparently rich, handsome, sophisticated man like Lee Corey doing chatting up a girl like her?

The answer would have been clear to her if she had been one of the flotilla of seagulls hovering above the yacht at that moment. Slade was waiting impatiently for Lee to climb on deck from the tender which had brought him out from the beach.

Beyond him, on the foredeck, Raya was stretched out soaking up the last of the sun. Above them, on the flying bridge, Troy was trying not to look interested.

'Well?' snapped Slade.

'I could do with a beer.'

'Screw the beer! Did you set it up?'

Lee gave him a disgusted look. 'Who am I? Casanova? It's going to take time.'

The scar that ran from the corner of Slade's mouth stood out like white bone against the tan of his face. He made a short chopping motion with his hand. 'We've run out of time.'

'What?' Lee's tone was incredulous. 'We've only been here two days.'

'Farik was on the radio telephone. We've got to be back the day after tomorrow. It has to be wrapped up tonight.'

'Then you wrap it up, genius, because there's no way I can work it that fast.'

Slade became very still, anger stretching his face into a gaunt mask. 'I said it has to be tonight.'

'Why? Because Farik is getting bored?'

'There's a change in the schedule, that's all I know.'

'So what's the plan? Do we just amble along to the taverna and lay them out with a couple of chair legs? For Christ's sake, we won't even get time to weigh anchor.'

Slade took a long, deep breath, his eyes polished stone. Raya had come up behind them and was now listening with a worried expression.

'Can you get the girl on her own?' she asked.

'No chance, she sticks to the old man like a leech.'

'But do you know her enough to stay with them?'

Lee nodded grudgingly. 'Just about.'

She turned to Slade. 'There's no way we can get an extra day?'

'If we leave around midnight we can just make it. According to Farik we have an important rendezvous the following day.'

Lee and Raya exchanged baffled looks. Slade gestured impatiently. 'We'll be briefed when we get back, the point is that without the Paxtons it's a wipe out.'

'Then wipe it out!' Lee said harshly. 'If we start a heavy scene around here it won't be like Nevada. If we manage to get as far as a Greek jail they'll throw the key away.'

Raya was looking doubtfully at Slade, the logic inescapable.

'Nobody's going to jail,' he said. 'Not as long as the locals are kept out of it.'

'And how the hell do you expect to do that?'

'Listen, Corey, if you don't learn to take orders I'm going to put you down.' He glared at him, the large hands flat and deadly. 'Any time, all you've got to do is say the word.'

Lee gave him a tight grin. 'Farik!'

Raya stepped between them, her eyes flashing angrily. 'This gets us nowhere. There's a risk, a big risk, but we have to have the Paxtons.'

'I'm still waiting to be convinced about that,' Lee said.

Slade stabbed a finger towards the villa on the hill. 'Men like Paxton aren't easy to find. In Europe there's maybe fifty, and most of those never go abroad because they're considered a security risk. Of the rest, perhaps a couple have the kind of family that makes them vulnerable. You with me? You can't buy a man like Paxton, not even for a million – and this deal is worth ten times that.'

He stared at them, weighing his words with care. 'We loused up Nevada, which was the easy way. Now the bombs have got to be made, and we don't even start without Paxton.'

A purple haze was lifting off the water, the dying sun etching it here and there with crimson. The yacht rode gently on the swell, the air still. Raya had moved to the rail, a slim figure, hunched a little against the first chill of evening. She spoke without looking back.

'My orders to join Farik came from Haifa. My loyalties are with Israel.' She turned, gazing at them with impenetrable eyes. 'My people are not concerned with money, no matter how many millions are involved.'

'That's your problem, honey,' Slade replied mockingly. 'Some of us like to get paid.'

'Including the Arabs?' she said sharply.

He smiled. 'Especially the Arabs. Only they won't like the price.'

She nodded, satisfied, and turned to Lee. 'There is a way to get them to the dinghy.'

The taverna was no different from the majority on Corfu. The basic tables and chairs were laid out on open ground beneath vine-covered beams supported by wooden pillars, roughly hewn from olive trees. Woven reed panels along the windward side kept out the sea breezes, and over the years a spreading tide of clematis and gardenia had turned them into a profusion of perfumed colour. Music was supplied by a battered juke box beside a small paved dance floor which was a constant challenge to tourists determined to master the art of Greek dancing.

For the past hour the floor had been dominated by one very drunken American, and the waiters he persistently pulled back were beginning to lose their patient smiles. Zorba's Dance concluded its fourth encore before he finally bowed to the delighted customers and weaved his way unsteadily to a corner table where Julia Paxton and her father were trying hard to look amused.

'Hi, Jules,' Lee said, managing to focus briefly on her before slumping into the unoccupied seat. 'Now don't tell me . . . this . . . this has got to be your father.'

He stuck a hand in the direction of the elderly man, almost knocking over a bottle of wine in the process. He stared at it owlishly, then tried to look apologetic. Julia giggled.

'What on earth have you been drinking?'

'That's a good question.' He considered it, noting that Donald Paxton appeared resigned to coping with him for a while at least. 'I think they called it excema.'

'That's a disease. You mean retsina.'

'You got it.' He swayed back in his chair and signalled to a waiter. 'Three bottles of excema!'

'That's a rather potent brew, Mister . . . ?' Paxton began diffidently.

'Corey,' Lee supplied helpfully.

'Mister Corey, my daughter is perfectly content with a glass of wine.'

'Okay, but at least you'll join me?'

Paxton's mouth tightened briefly and he glanced at Julia who was trying not to laugh. Lee appeared ready to slide from his chair at any moment.

'I'd no idea you had such . . . gregarious friends.'

'Daddy, we only met today. He's nice . . . when he's sober.'

A waiter had arrived at the table and was looking anxiously at Paxton. The older man shook his head and with some relief the man moved away. Lee was absorbed in a crumpled pack of cigarettes, succeeding in fishing out the last survivor. He bent towards the candle in the centre of the table, and Julia quickly moved it towards him before he ignited an ear.

'Thanks,' he said, staring intently along his nose, 'you're a pal.'

'Are you here on vacation, Mr Corey?' Paxton asked, in an effort to be polite.

'Jusht . . . Jusht cruising around,' Lee slurred. 'Say, have you seen the boat?'

'You mean the one in the bay?'

'That's it.' He began to laugh, lurching in his chair. 'I just hope I can find it tonight.'

Julia looked concerned. 'Aren't your friends coming for you?'

Lee frowned at her as though it was a completely new idea. 'I think they came down with excema.'

'Then how will you get out to the boat?'

Lee's head had begun to droop. He pulled it up with some effort and gave her a look of owlish cunning. 'No problem, Jules. No problem at all. I just flash my little old . . . my little old . . .' he pulled a small, powerful torch from his pocket and frowned at it for a moment. 'Anyway, I just flash this and out they come.' Julia gazed appealingly at her father. 'We'll have to take him. He'll never manage on his own.'

'He's not our responsibility,' Paxton said. 'Let one of the

waiters look after him.'

'In that condition?' Julia picked up the torch he had dropped on the table. 'It's not really out of our way. We can go around the bay and signal the boat. It's not that much trouble.'

Paxton gave her an irritated look. 'It isn't our business. We don't even know the man.'

'I know him,' she said firmly.

Paxton sighed and got to his feet, taking one of Lee's arms and gesturing for her to do the same. With a series of grunts he lurched to his feet and regarded them with benign affection.

'Don't tell me – we're going to have a party?'

'That's right, Mr Corey,' Paxton said coldly. 'It's a beach party.'

'Fan-tastic!'

They took him down the road and through the village to the grey stone quay, negotiating the steps down to the shingle beach with some difficulty as Lee persisted in demonstrating Zorba's Dance for most of the way. Julia was laughing helplessly by the time they reached the water's edge, and even her father was unable to hide a smile as Lee, arms outstretched, executed a complicated series of steps which deposited him in a heap on the sand. They were moving forward to pick him up when Slade stepped out of the darkness.

'You do exactly what I say and nobody gets hurt,' he said softly. 'But any fun and games and I put a bullet in the girl.'

They looked at him in astonishment, the blue steel automatic in his hand gleaming with a shocking menace. Julia looked at Lee, at first bewildered, and then as she saw the harsh, sober lines on his face, she began to understand.

'The boat's over here,' said Slade.

'Why?' asked Paxton. 'What possible reason can you have?'

'Just move.'

They walked to the boat, seeing now a third figure waiting there. This one was a woman, slim and dark in the night. Lee helped to push it into the water as Slade covered the Paxtons, then he turned to the girl and offered his hand.

'I'm sorry, Jules, but sometimes that's the way it is.'

She ignored the hand, gazing at him with pale, taut features. There was no mistaking the loathing in her eyes.

Chapter 9

The voyage to Beirut took two days, and for most of the time the Paxtons were confined to a small cabin in the bow of the yacht. Between this cabin and the companionway to the deck was a large saloon where they ate in the evenings. There was always someone in the saloon, either Corey or the girl, but the lean, dark-haired man with the scar running away from his mouth tended to stay on deck.

For Donald Paxton it was a confusing journey. The days were hot, the nights sultry, and although they were treated with a degree of consideration, his repeated questions were never answered, rarely acknowledged. He was left to reach his own conclusions and these ranged from the more obvious ones involving the KGB and sinister Oriental plots, to flights of fancy in which he and his daughter were being held as hostages in some political game of chess. Ultimately he was forced to conclude that his work as a nuclear chemist with British Nuclear Fuels provided the most likely motive, but this was hard to believe. In a field rich in research and government-backed projects clouded with secrecy, he was a quite insignificant chemist who, in recent years, had been occupying a very ordinary desk job with the technical journals division. The work was routine to the point of boredom and, with retirement less than three years away, he knew that he was being gently phased out. In a way he was quite content with this, but it meant that as far as modern developments in nuclear technology were concerned he was out of the picture. He knew only what he read, and this was normally available in journals widely distributed throughout the world.

In fact, try as he might, Donald Paxton could not think of one single secret.

And then there were the kidnappers themselves. The girl, Dassan, was pleasant enough, though coldly aloof when he tried to extract information from her. She had old eyes in a young face and she liked to stop her mouth from smiling. Sometimes she looked at Julia with pity, at other times with envy. But always there was a quiet strength in her that told him she would do what she must.

The tall, dark man they called Slade was undoubtedly the hardest, but without malice as far as they were concerned. He had told them bluntly, without emotion, that if they did as they were told no harm would come to either of them. The alternative was clearly a violent one and Paxton had quickly assured him that this would not be necessary.

The bewildering one was Corey. On two occasions he had made a point of speaking to them alone. The first time was simply to ask if they were comfortable and had all they needed. His eyes had been deep and sympathetic, although Julia had left no doubt in his mind that she would have much preferred the company of a snake. The next occasion Corey visited them was in the evening of the second day. This had been the most puzzling meeting of all, for in spite of their open dislike he had persisted.

'You've got to listen, both of you,' he had told them, his gaze probing Paxton. 'The man you'll be meeting in Beirut will want certain things. Answer his questions and do what he asks. That way nobody gets hurt.'

'What things?' Paxton wanted to know. 'What can I possibly do for him?'

Corey was evasive. 'It's too soon to go into details. All you've got to do is make sure he gets what he wants, no matter what it is.'

'Or else what?'

Corey looked at them unhappily. 'Or else he gets nasty, probably with Julia. Nobody wants that, and in the end you'll do it anyway.'

Julia confronted him with angry features, her face so pale that the freckles burned against the skin. 'You don't frighten us, Mr Corey. Sooner or later we're going to the police, and then you'll get exactly what you deserve!'

He smiled sadly at her and looked at Paxton. 'You'd better make sure she doesn't come out with any of that in Beirut. If you handle this right you can get out, once you've served your purpose. But that,' and he gestured at Julia, 'won't do any good at all.'

Paxton nodded grimly. 'All right, but I still want to know what it is I'm expected to do.'

'It doesn't matter. Whatever it is, you do it.'

After Corey had left, Paxton sat beside the narrow window looking out over the foredeck. The sun was beginning to set on a flat, oily sea, and the horizon was broken by the purple mountains of the Lebanon. A chill swept through him with the realization that soon they would be in Beirut, that he would be given a choice which would surely involve his daughter. For the hundredth time he wondered what it might be. He racked his brain and came up with only one possibility. It was a terrifying one which, once thought of, he realized had been lurking in the corners of his mind since they were bundled on to the yacht. If these people were terrorists then there was something he could do for them. It was an ugly, evil thing, but the more he thought of it the surer he became that this was what they would want.

Julia came and sat beside him, stroking the back of his hand the way she had since she was a little girl with skinny legs and Mickey Mouse teeth. Her wide brown eyes searched until they found his, then held them with a question.

He forced a smile. 'Don't worry.'

'Do you know what they want?'

He shrugged and tried to keep the fear from his voice. 'I think so.'

'You won't do it if it's something bad?'

'I don't know. I may have no choice.'

'Of course you will.' She held his hand tightly. 'What can they do? Sooner or later they'll have to let us go.'

Her innocence was a knife in his heart.

Chapter 10

The yacht hove to a quarter of a mile off Pigeon Rock Bay shortly after midnight and everyone assembled on the fore-deck whilst Troy flashed a shielded torch towards the shore. Some fifteen minutes later a launch came out of the darkness and bumped gently against the side of the yacht. Slade caught the rope that furled through the night and a moment later they were helping the Paxtons over the side, then dropping into the launch beside them.

The man at the helm was a dark, swarthy Lebanese with oily hair and a moustache that he sucked noisily between his teeth. It was the only sound he made during the journey to the shore, cutting the motor for the last two hundred yards so that they drifted in on a gentle swell to ground on the sand. The lights of a car flashed briefly from the cliffs and they set off across the beach, finding the steps hewn from rock immediately below the car. They climbed slowly to the Corniche, Paxton pausing frequently for breath, enjoying Slade's impatience.

When they were almost at the top of the cliff, Lee turned and looked back over the bay. The lights of the yacht were already a mile out to sea, heading north. He pointed it out to Slade who gave him an irritated glance. 'So?'

'So the harbour's the other way.'

'What are you, Corey? The goddam coastguard?'

'I'm one of the helpful type. I feel someone ought to let the Viking Queen know he's got nothing in front of him until he hits Sicily.'

Slade gave a short, explosive laugh. 'Viking Queen! I like that. You think he is?'

'Well if he isn't he's got one hell of a problem.' They climbed a few more steps, Slade still chuckling at the thought, then as they reached the top. 'How about that, though? Where could he be heading?'

'You really want to know?'

'Not really, but it passes the time.'

'Then I'll tell you. He's gone looking for sailors!'

Slade laughed himself all the way to the car where another Lebanese waited with a blank expression. Raya got in the back with the Paxtons, Lee and Slade squeezing into the front beside the driver. It was only a short drive to the villa, the streets almost deserted at this hour. The Paxtons were still, tense figures in the dim light, looking through the windows with hopeful expressions, as though praying for a police block at every corner.

Farik's greeting to them was short and brutal. 'You're here as my guests or my prisoners, it doesn't matter to me which way you want it!'

Julia pushed in front of her father, eyes flashing angrily as she confronted the Lebanese. 'If you have any sense at all you'll let us go this minute. You and your thugs can't get away with this for long.'

Farik laughed a soft, shrill laugh, the strangeness of the sound making it all the more menacing. Reaching out, he imprisoned both her hands in his, preventing her from pulling away. She went pale, but gazed at him defiantly.

'I think you should be told the facts of life, my dear,' he said. 'I am in touch with Corfu and, so far, no one has even noticed your disappearance. By the time they begin to wonder where you have gone, to inform police and your embassy in Athens, there will be no possibility of connecting you with either my yacht or this villa.' He paused, his black eyes boring into her. 'You do understand? You no longer exist!'

He bowed mockingly and released her, then turned to Donald Paxton who had been watching with gaunt features. 'You will occupy separate rooms and if either of you attempt to leave, or communicate with anyone outside this house, then the other person will suffer. Is that clear, Mr Paxton?'

Paxton licked lips suddenly dry and nodded his head. 'It's clear, but you had better understand that if any harm comes to my daughter then you'll get nothing from me.'

Farik grinned and nodded. 'Of course.'

He dismissed them with a gesture, the Lebanese driver taking them up the stairs. Slade waited until they were out of earshot, then said: 'It wasn't as neat as it could have been. There are people who could put two and two together.'

'A small risk. Anyway, the next time the yacht is sighted it will be off Algiers.' He dismissed the thought, beaming at them. 'You've all done extremely well, so now we can proceed to more interesting things.'

'You mean plutonium?' Lee asked coolly.

Farık's eyes narrowed, flicking at Slade who gave a brief noncommittal shrug. Raya was sitting in one of the wide leather chairs, looking very bored.

'Knowledge can be a dangerous thing, Mr Corey.'

'So can plutonium.'

Farik breathed noisily through wide nostrils, glancing at the Israeli girl before turning back to Lee. 'Of course. We are not fools. You will be fully briefed tomorrow night.'

'What's wrong with now?'

'Others will be present.' Farik was beginning to lose patience. 'Also it is late, and I'm sure our charming colleague would welcome sleep.'

Raya nodded and rose to her feet. 'I would. But I would sleep easier if I knew what we're getting into.'

Lee grinned. 'She's not just a pretty face.'

Farik sighed and shook his head as though astounded by their curiosity. 'The operation will involve four others in addition to yourselves. It will take place in two days' time with the minimum of risk to you all.' He paused, suddenly concerned that they should believe him. 'That part is most important because the plutonium is merely a step towards our final objective. Tomorrow night I will explain more fully, but until then rest assured that it will be as simple and effective as borrowing the Paxtons from Corfu.'

Farik clearly had no intention of enlarging on this, so Lee waved a casual good night and followed Raya out of the room. Slade remained in his chair, and as he closed the door Farik was already beginning to talk rapidly in his sharp treble-toned voice. He caught the word 'mercenaries' and a reference to them being the best on the market, before he reluctantly moved on into the hall.

They climbed the stairs and walked along the white-walled corridor, lit dimly by glowing amber lamps. At the door to her room, Raya turned to Lee and gazed thoughtfully at him until he grinned and held out his hand, palm up. 'Maybe you should read this too?'

She smiled and shook her head. 'I think not. You are a strange man, too strange for palmistry.'

'We could try phrenology?'

The smile widened. 'Not at two o'clock in the morning. Suddenly she was serious. 'What is it with you? Why are you here?'

'The smell of money.'

She looked dubious, disappointed. 'Only that?'

'I'm not fighting a holy war, if that's what you mean. I came because I was invited, and because staying behind meant a cell block with all the wrong kind of people.'

'Your kind?'

'I meant the screws. Next time they'll throw the key away and invite their friends around for coffee and Corey!'

The doubt was still in her voice. 'It doesn't show. If you were that kind it would be there.'

Her gaze had a disturbing quality that made him quickly change the subject. 'How about you? I always thought this was Black September country?'

She shrugged. 'I have false papers. Anyway, under the new regime Beirut is more enlightened. The PLO are no longer welcome here.'

'Is that it, then?' he asked. 'A blow for Israel?'

'What else? I have no interest in money, or Farik, or you Americans.'

'But plutonium fascinates you?'

She looked uncertain. 'I know very little. I'm not even sure I want to know any more.'

'Until it happens?'

She gave the Jewish *Ei* and looked unhappy. After a moment, when Lee was beginning to think she would go, she spoke again in a voice that was almost inaudible. 'You must be careful of Farik. He is not like other men. He has been warped into something that seeks only revenge, hungers only for death.'

'Is that in his hand, or do you have a better source?'

She looked at him, the brown eyes flecked with concern and, strangely, pity. 'He was castrated,' she said quietly. 'By the Arabs.'

'Jesus!'

She nodded. 'He hates us all.'

She left him with the thought and he walked slowly to his room, ticking off the facts and coming up with atom bombs and Arabs. It was a terrifying thought. He wondered what Henry Kissinger was doing tonight.

The following morning Lee announced that he needed fresh air, a new shirt, and the prettiest girl in Beirut. Farik considered him patiently across the breakfast table and told him he would send out for the shirt, that the patio was full of fresh air, and girls were not included in the terms of his contract.

'You mean I should have read the small print?'

'Between the lines would have been sufficient.'

Lee let it pass. For the rest of the morning he sat by the pool, watching Raya improving on an already perfect tan. Slade spent the morning closeted with Farik in his study, but there was little chance of getting close to the door or window with Samir constantly padding around the house. For most of the time he soaked up sun, and tried to come up with a legitimate excuse to get away for an hour. It was now essential that he made contact with Freddy Stone, who should have the surveillance team in position somewhere close. The solution came from the most unexpected quarter. During lunch the phone rang and Farik took it in his study, emerging a few minutes later with barely concealed annoyance.

'You're all going to have to take a stroll,' he said. 'I have a visitor and I don't want him aware that I have guests.'

'Suits me,' Lee said, casually. 'I could do with stretching my legs.'

'Just as long as you stretch them in the same direction as the others,' Farik said smoothly. 'Beirut is still a very dangerous city. I would hate you to get lost.'

'We could go to St George's Bay,' Raya suggested. 'It's a good beach.'

Lee shrugged, feeling Slade's cold gaze on him. 'Why not?'

They walked to the Corniche from the villa, turning south towards the hotel district and the Bay of St George. Many of the hotels were still in the process of rebuilding shattered floors and roofs, and most of them showed the strains of war in smoke-streaked towers and bullet-scarred walls. The St George's Hotel, once the most distinguished hostelry in the Middle East, was trying to put on a brave face in spite of gaping holes in the upper floors. The lounge decks overlooking the golden sand were unchanged, although the sunbathers were few and far between.

They changed in cabins on the beach, then stretched out on the sand. Across the bay the snow-capped peak of Mount

Sannin gleamed in the sun. A ski-boat weaved its way towards Long Beach, the twin skiers behind throwing curtains of spray at one another. Lee closed his eyes and waited, the clock that ticked in the corner of his mind counting off the minutes. He estimated it would take no more than five before Freddy appeared. She had been sitting outside the last bar they passed before turning on to the Corniche. He was thirty seconds out.

After half an hour Slade was getting bored with the sun. He squirmed in the sand, then rose and moved to a parasol where he squatted in the shade. Lee waited until Raya was looking drowsy, then rose lethargically to his feet and went down to the water. It was cool and crystal clear, and after wading the first few feet he plunged in and struck out for one of the yellow rafts floating some two hundred yards away from the shore. When he had covered half the distance he rolled over and gazed back towards the beach. Neither Slade or Raya had moved, but the girl in the white bikini who had been sitting on the lounge deck was no longer there. He turned and continued, reaching the raft and moving round to the far side. She surfaced from nowhere a moment later, shaking water from her short black hair and grinning like a Cheshire cat.

'Hi. Thought we'd lost you,' she said cheerfully.

'We went hunting.'

'Anyone I know?'

'Paxton. Donald. Nuclear chemist. Recently on holiday in Corfu with daughter Julia. You'll find them listed as missing persons, but right now they're very reluctant guests at Farik's villa.'

'Nuclear chemist?' She pulled a face. 'Your Mr Weller isn't going to like that.'

'I'm not mad about the idea myself. You've got the team?'

She nodded quickly, flicking a hand towards the hotel. 'Two of them are at the bar right now. Bevis and Young.'

He didn't know them. She watched him intently, the smile still hovering around her mouth.

'Anything from Max?'

'Not much. The CIA angle threw him a bit. It makes communications difficult through the Embassy here, but he's arranging a hook-up with the Reuters office. They've got a clear line.'

'No dice,' Lee said firmly. 'Tell him it gets bigger all the time. Everything has got to be sight only.'

He pulled himself out of the water and settled down on the raft so that he could be seen from the beach. She waited, clinging to the float.

'You all set?'

'Fire away.'

'Raya Dassan, Israeli girl, probably tied in with one of their fringe groups. Calad Farik is not the top, I'm sure of that, but he's pulling all the strings at this end. He's after plutonium and that's why he needs Paxton. He's also got it in for the Arabs in a big way.'

She interrupted him. 'How big?'

'They took away his lollipop!'

There was a splutter in the water beside him and he grinned, waiting until she surfaced before continuing. 'The target looks like this end, rather than the States, but he's playing it all close to the chest. We get briefed tonight on the plutonium job. Four mercenaries are coming in for muscle, but so far there's nothing on where we go and when. I'd guess at Europe. Either Germany, France or Britain. But there's plenty of other places in striking range with modern reactors and stocks of plutonium.'

'You want a blue index through Interpol?'

'That's up to Max. The first priority is to get the Paxtons away from Farik. Without them he can't put his bombs together, and without those he's not even a starter. The time to hit will be when we leave. Maybe tomorrow.'

'Check. I'll get this to him right away. Anything else?'

'No. But tell those guys to stay loose. Slade will only have to see them once.'

'I'll let them buy me a drink. Take care.'

He turned towards her at the words, but she had already sunk beneath the waves. She surfaced briefly fifty yards away, then vanished again. He soaked up a further ten minutes of the scorching sun before rolling off the raft and swimming lazily back to the beach.

A cool wind had begun to come off the sea by four o'clock and Slade, who had been showing increasing signs of impatience, suggested it was time they returned to the villa. Raya was disappointed, pointing out that there were still a few hours of sun. Slade gave her a look of studied indifference, so they changed and started back along the beach, deciding to cut across the promontory to Pigeon Rock Bay rather than use the Corniche.

'Any idea what time our friends are due to arrive?' Lee asked, as they picked their way across the rocky outcrop.

'Sometime tonight,' Slade replied. 'They're coming in on separate flights, just in case people get nosey.'

'I thought Farik had this town in his pocket?'

'Since the war nobody has that. The Christian and Muslim parties are still at each other's throats and if you've got one official as a friend, you've got another as an enemy.'

They walked on in silence, Raya leading the way. They passed two deserted villas, one of them long since gutted by fire, then descended into the wide, curving bay dominated by the weathered arches of the Pigeon Rocks. The beach was narrow, occasionally strewn with a tangle of boulders which at some time had detached themselves from the craggy cliffs above. Raya was enjoying herself, scrambling over rocks, finding a high vantage point and standing there, letting the breeze ruffle her hair. Watching her, Lee was struck by the firm, slim lines of her body. For all her beauty, she had the poise and physique of an athlete. A modern Diana, glowing in the sun.

Suddenly the laughter went out of her face and she slid quickly from the rock, gesturing as she came towards them.

'Two men. Europeans, I think. They're following us.'

'How far behind?' Slade asked quietly.

'The first one about three hundred yards, the other about the same distance further back.'

Inwardly Lee cursed the luck that had made her choose that rock, at that moment, and then just as quickly he was furious with Bevis and Young for trailing them along the beach. By taking the Corniche they could have watched them all the way without any chance of discovery.

'Any idea who they might be?' he asked in a casual tone.

Slade shook his head, the stillness in him as he glanced back, gauging distance, weighing possibilities. After a moment he made up his mind.

'You two go on along the beach, keep near the water so that you're in full view.'

'And you?' Lee asked, his expression betraying none of the alarm he felt.

'Oh, I'll just hang around. Maybe have a little chat.'

'Even if they're tailing us it's no problem. We're clean in Beirut.'

'You're doing it again, Corey,' Slade said tightly. 'One of these days you're going to keep your mouth shut, then we'll all be surprised.'

'I just don't see any point in making trouble.'

'Then do what I say,' he said harshly. 'Now!'

Lee walked on ahead with the girl, furiously trying to work out some way of warning the FBI men. Slade was capable of the most extreme violence if the situation warranted, and the moment he realized the men were American he would see them as a threat to the entire operation. Although Bevis and Young should be able to look after themselves, they would be no match for a man of Slade's calibre if he was able to take them on separately. He stopped and turned back again, aware that Raya was watching him now, her face clouded with doubt.

'You look worried, Lee,' she said slowly. 'Don't you think Slade can handle it?'

'Oh, he can handle it, all right. It's *how* that bothers me.'

She shrugged. 'It's his neck.'

'Ours too. If he fouls it up everything hits the fan.' He paused, searching her face and finding only a puzzled surprise. He reached a decision, not caring what she thought.

'I'm going back.'

'He won't like it.'

'So he can cry a little!'

He gave her no time to argue, leaving her on the beach and heading back towards the rocks at the trot. If the first of the FBI men had been three hundred yards behind he should be into the boulders by now, but as some of them were ten to fifteen feet high it was impossible to pick him out. Lee made for the centre where a great mass of rock and rubble made it necessary to squeeze through a narrow passage between two huge boulders. It was the obvious place for Slade to wait, yet there was no sign of him. He looked round, knowing he must be somewhere close.

There was a whisper of sound, almost a sigh, and he turned quickly towards a mound of boulders. He caught a flicker of movement and went towards it, crouching low, realizing long before he rounded the rocks that he was too late. But the scene which confronted him was more horrifying than anything he had envisaged. Slade was crouching over a body already beyond recognition. Even as shock and nausea engulfed him, a blood-stained knife was sinking into the lifeless figure again and again. Rage exploded and he lunged at Slade, pulling him round, finding only blank, staring eyes with no more comprehension than those of a dumb animal. He was taking quick, shallow breaths as though he had run for a long way, and the eyes were only beginning to focus as Lee smashed a savage fist into his face.

The blow sent him sprawling away from the body, but his reactions were fast and as Lee came at him again he was rolling, coming up off the sand with the knife weaving menacingly before him.

'You bastard,' said Lee. 'You filthy animal bastard!'

He kicked at the knife, but Slade avoided it, his eyes fixed on Lee with a kind of bewilderment.

'He asked for it,' he said, his voice thick and ugly. 'He's FBI.'

'You didn't have to do that. Christ! Only a mad dog does that!'

Blood darkened Slade's sallow features and he glanced instinctively towards the body. Lee moved instantly, stepping forward and chopping at the wrist, then slamming a fist into his stomach. Iron hard muscles contracted, took the impact, then Slade was stabbing a stiff hand into his side, his other hand slicing up for the throat. Lee blocked the deadly blow then feinted and turned, kicking high to take him in the chest. The force lifted Slade from his feet and flung him back into a pile of jagged rock, his face contorting with pain as he slammed into them. Lee was about to move towards him when a voice stopped him in his tracks.

'Hold it right there, friend.'

He turned to find the second FBI man behind him, a Browning automatic in his hand. As their eyes met he tried to convey a question, clearly concerned about his partner and puzzled by the situation. His position was such that he had not yet seen the mutilated body. Lee let him see it now, glancing deliberately to the side. The man followed his gaze, then as the shock hit him swung back with horrified eyes. But Lee was already moving, chopping the gun from his hand and striking for a point just below the ear. The blow connected and he went down with glazing eyes.

By the time he turned round, Slade was clawing himself to his feet, reaching for the knife that lay in the sand. Lee got to it first, then moved back to the FBI man and knelt over him. Glancing back he found Slade watching, his eyes fixed hungrily on the knife. There were some ten feet between them, but at any moment he could move closer. Quickly he turned back and slid the knife through the unconscious man's shirt and along his ribs, deep enough to cause a flow of blood, but no more. Pulling the knife free he pressed the shirt against the wound until the blood had soaked through. The man's eyes flickered open, his mouth tightening as he felt the pain.

'Play dead,' Lee hissed, 'then get out of here.'

Somehow the words got through and he let his head roll limply to one side. Lee rose to his feet, stepping away from the body so that Slade could now see the stab wound. He glanced at it, then gave a short nod.

'Let's go.'

Lee gave him a contemptuous look and tossed the knife to him. 'That's all it needed, Slade. Clean and simple . . . not a piece of goddam butchery!'

'You want out, Corey, just say the word.' He was in control again, the blood-stained knife held with casual menace. He nodded towards the body by the rocks. 'Sometimes it happens that way.'

'Not with me it doesn't. That's a sickness, Slade!'

Slade took the words without emotion, but his eyes were small and ugly. He glanced up at the sky, towards the sea, then finally back at Lee. His face was calm now. Bending down he cleaned the knife in the sand, then slipped it into a scabbard beneath his shirt. When he spoke it was in a flat, empty voice, but the words were the closest he ever came to an explanation or an apology.

'Some things you learn in Vietnam don't go away. Maybe it's a sickness now, but then it was routine . . . a way of killing that left its mark on the living as well as the dead. After a while it became a habit.'

'Then you better break that habit, Slade, because when they find those bodies all hell is going to break loose.'

Slade's mouth tightened angrily and he seemed about to argue, but the words died and he turned, moving away through the rocks. Lee waited until he was out of sight, then went back to the wounded FBI man.

'You heard all that?'

The eyes opened and he nodded.

'I got here too late to save your partner.'

'Then take Slade!'

'We'll take him,' said Lee, 'but not yet. Get the facts to Max Weller and no one else.'

The FBI man lifted himself painfully, holding his side. 'You play rough, Corey. Are you quite sure you know which side you're on?'

'You're alive,' he replied pointedly. He left him with the thought, catching up with Slade as he walked along the beach to the waiting figure of Raya. The sun was tipping towards the sea, spilling a crimson glow in the west that poured through the granite arch of Pigeon Rock. It reminded him of a river of blood.

Chapter 11

'Kill! Kill! Kill!' screamed Farik. 'What kind of blind, stupid animals have I got? Are your minds full of shit, your mouths overflowing with vomit, your eyes blinded by the festering sores of your own imbecility? Do you know that this city hangs on the precipice, that it will be a hundred years before the Muslims and the Christians forget what has been done to each other? I survive – I profit – because I cause no ripples, throw no stones. Go out and cut a Muslim's throat, there are ten thousand who deserve it and all that will happen is that the next day two Christians will die. But Americans . . . FBI agents . . . only in Arabic can I describe what you are.'

He paused, breathing heavily, then spoke rapidly in Arabic. The muscles of his neck bulged like gnarled wood, his eyes gleamed with the light of madness. His large, cruel hands thrust at them, clawed at the air, rending and striking the empty spaces between them. His rage was incandescent. The only sign that Raya understood was in the rush of blood to her cheeks as the words poured out. Even Slade stood in sullen silence when he had finished his tirade.

He gazed at them with contempt. 'You do not understand, so I will do my best to translate, although you appreciate that it will lose a good deal of flavour and subtlety in the process. You are dogs. Not just ordinary dogs, because they have some intelligence and understand obedience. You were sired by the vilest of dogs. You understand me? Your mothers were the scum of the gutter, copulating with dogs because nothing else would go near them. And out of that copulation came such as you. Blind, senseless jackals who kill in the afternoon on a public beach because your brains are composed of shit. Not ordinary shit. The shit of dogs!'

His voice had risen to a shrill scream, the perspiration running off his jowls in rivulets of hate. Now he waited, his hands still, his eyes boring into Slade.

'You've made your point,' Slade said in an uncompromising

voice. 'Now I'll make mine. We were being followed by two guys, and when I moved in on one he tried to get clever. If we'd walked away from it they'd be outside now, and you know as well as I do that you can't afford any delay. You're running out of time, Farik. I just bought you a few more hours.'

'And if they know you're here, what does that buy me then?' Farik asked savagely. 'Trouble at levels I cannot control. Embassy officials, government ministers, protests from Washington. And then what happens to us? What happens when your friends from the CIA learn that you are killing agents of the FBI? What happens when our American masters discover that there is blood on the carpet? Official American blood?'

Lee hung on every word, realizing that at this moment Farik was incapable of caution. It was an incredible display from a man who had previously shown such iron control. Clearly there was a timetable, a vital sequence being laid down not here, but in the United States. But why? For what purpose? It was a dangerous moment to provoke the Lebanese, but until he had the answers there could be no direct action against him.

Slade was stubbornly refusing to give ground, claiming that federal jurisdiction meant nothing in the Lebanon. Lee let him finish, then spoke before Farik had a chance to reply.

'Maybe it's all too much for you,' he said, his voice edged with contempt. 'As far as I'm concerned I've had a bellyful of this mystery tour. You're supposed to know the score, but you can't even tell us why we're being followed. What the hell do you expect us to do if we don't even know the name of the game you're playing!'

He turned deliberately towards the door, aware that Farik's face had paled with fury. He came round the desk at him, grabbing his arm before he had taken two steps, rage turning his voice into a reed-thin falsetto that would have been comical had it not been for the bull-like physique that went with it.

'Do you want death, Corey?' he screeched. 'I have it for you wherever you go. I lift one finger and it is done, either here or any place you try to hide!'

'You let go of my arm, or I'm going to kick you right in the balls!'

Farik's teeth gleamed in a malevolent grin. 'Try it,

American,' he suggested.

Slade, who had been watching Lee with reluctant admiration, stepped between them. 'That proves nothing.'

A sand lizard came in from the patio and considered them with diamond eyes, its tongue tasting the vibrations in the air and then, as though conscious of the venom in the room, it turned and scuttled for the sun. Lee made no move, his manner relaxed, almost indolent, so that after a moment the Lebanese relaxed his vice-like grip and stepped back towards his desk.

'You are the most expendable member of the team,' he said. 'But killing you would be a waste and, I suspect, a difficult task. You have a right to know certain things, and these I will tell you.'

He sat down and considered the three of them quietly for a moment. The anger was fading, loosening the hard cords of muscle. He took a white linen handkerchief from his pocket and carefully mopped his face, then wiped his hands. Glancing at Slade he gestured towards a decanter of arak before picking up the telephone.

Slade poured the wine and passed it to Raya and Lee whilst Farik spoke rapidly in Arabic. At one point he gave an exclamation of surprise, then asked a series of questions with barely concealed excitement. When he finally replaced the phone he was visibly relieved.

'Which one of you is handy with a knife?'

Slade went still and grunted a brief affirmative.

'It was a brilliant move. The Muslims have already been blamed for the murders, the American Embassy lodged a formal protest half an hour ago. Apparently one of the bodies was so badly mutilated that it hadn't occurred to them that it could be the work of anyone else.' He paused, giving Slade a thoughtful look. 'I suppose that was in your mind at the time?'

Slade gave the briefest of nods, not looking at Lee. 'It seemed to be the thing to do. Who found the bodies?'

'They don't have a record of that. Apparently an American attaché moved in pretty fast and they're holding them at the Embassy. They allowed the police to photograph the mutilated body, but that's all.'

Slade frowned. 'Is that normal?'

Farik gave him a disgusted look. 'Mutilated FBI men aren't

exactly an everyday event, even for Beirut. Who the hell cares what they do, as long as they're convinced the killings were sectarian.'

Lee sipped his wine and looked disinterested. He had wondered how the Embassy would cover the fact that one of the agents had not been killed. Only Max could have prevented an immediate move against Farik, so he was holding off until Lee knew the next phase of the operation. Even now the argument would be raging between Washington and Beirut, and it was only a matter of time before the CIA knew the full extent of C-2's involvement. He put the troublesome thought aside as Farik began to speak.

'What we are involved in is no ordinary crime. For that reason complete security must be maintained until the last phase which, I can tell you now, will take place in two weeks' time. Each of you has his own motives for being here. Miss Dassan, because of her experience as a member of an Israeli commando unit, has specialist knowledge which will be of vital importance in our final objective. She is also an accomplished skydiver and it will be her responsibility to train the attack force.'

He paused and gazed intently at Lee. 'Her motives are altruistic, yours are mercenary. In both cases you will be more than satisfied.'

'You wouldn't like to spell that out in hard cash, would you?' Lee asked coolly. 'I've got very expensive tastes.'

Farik gave him a disdainful look, then glanced at his watch. He sighed, like a man whose patience was almost exhausted, then rose to his feet and nodded towards the loggia.

'Very well, it is almost time. We'll go to my study.'

They followed him across the room, out on to the loggia and along the side of the house to the heavy oak door which he unlocked with two separate keys. Inside, the room was large and cool, the walls lined with books and a few paintings, most of them Dali's but there was one nightmarish scene by Bosch. Beyond the desk which dominated the end of the study was a video-tape deck and a small panel of switches and dials which were clearly linked to a closed circuit television system somewhere in the house. Farik ignored Lee's curious look, sitting down at the desk and opening a drawer from which he took a thin black file.

Slade dropped into a chair and lit a cigarette, watching

Farik with a vaguely puzzled expression. 'What about Keppel and his people?' he asked, finally.

'They're going direct to Dublin,' Farik replied. 'Your little adventure this afternoon made it imprudent for them to rendezvous in Beirut. Fortunately I was able to contact them in time. The three of you will be on the ten o'clock flight to Dublin. From there you will cross by launch to Ravenglass on the north-west coast of Britain.'

Lee sat beside Raya, his manner relaxed, almost indolent, reflecting none of the tensions that were in him. At last he knew their target, but the knowledge gave him little comfort.

Farik looked at Lee and tapped the file before him. 'In here are a series of numbered accounts with a certain Swiss bank. Various amounts have been deposited in these accounts, the smallest of which is a quarter of a million dollars.'

He paused, enjoying their astonishment. 'In the final operation there will be five team leaders. Before they leave they will each receive one of these accounts and, providing they achieve their objectives, the funds will be unlocked by a coded message sent the moment we know that the operation is a success.'

'And the team leaders?' Lee asked, quietly.

'Slade, Miss Dassan, Keppel and his second-in-command. The fifth will be you, Mr Corey . . . providing you fulfil our expectations tomorrow.'

Slade grinned at him. 'Didn't I tell you this was the biggest caper of them all, hot shot?'

'Nothing's that big,' replied Lee. 'If you paid that kind of money at our end then the total take has to be more than ten million.'

Farik gave a contemptuous snort. 'Ten! My dear Corey, the final figure will be at least a hundred million. We are simply the mechanics, the technicians of a plan that will set the world back on its heels. Our masters have already invested some fifty million dollars, and to protect that investment they will take any steps, no matter how extreme, to ensure success of the operation.'

He gazed at them with grim features. 'That includes everyone connected with the plan. If things go wrong, if there is a breath of suspicion against any of us, then they will simply wipe us out and start again.'

'Nice friends you've got,' Lee commented dryly. 'But like

Slade said, you're running out of time.'

Farik nodded. 'True. If the Nevada operation had succeeded you would all now be training for our final objective. Instead we must improvise, and as you know Paxton is the first step towards manufacturing our own atomic bombs. To do that he must have the material.'

He took a map from the file and spread it out on the desk. They moved forward, watching silently as Farik indicated the coastal area of Cumbria.

'Landing by launch at dawn will not present any real problem to you. You will go ashore at Ravenglass where two cars will be waiting. Keppel will have the keys in Dublin. From Ravenglass you drive up to Eskdale, arriving there at approximately ten a.m. You will take rooms at the Bower House, the three of you there for the fishing. Keppel and his men will follow you about an hour later, their cover being that they are walking the fells. In the afternoon Slade will rendezvous with Keppel and together they will make a detailed study of the target. The attack will take place shortly after midnight.'

Lee feigned ignorance, bending to study the map, then glancing at Farik with a puzzled expression. 'There doesn't seem much worth attacking around there.'

The Lebanese laughed softly and stabbed a finger at a point on the coast between Seascale and Ravenglass. 'Windscale. The world's largest plutonium factory, currently processing 2,500 tons of fuel a year. All we need are just twenty-seven kilos of the stuff.'

'And they just let you walk in and take it?' Raya asked with open scepticism.

'No, my dear. They hand it to you.' He beamed at them and took a plan of Windscale from the file. Spreading it out he began to outline the operation. 'Only the British could place the most dangerous material in the world in such a ridiculously insecure area and then, having done that, guard it with a handful of unarmed policemen.'

'Hold on, Calad,' interrupted Slade. 'Last year there was talk of arming those guys.'

'Indeed there was,' agreed Farik. 'But with monumental optimism they keep what weapons they have at the main entrance or in the security office within the restricted area.

The police rely on guard dogs at night, patrolling the main site behind a badly lit fence, and in the restricted zone which contains the plutonium factory and warehouse. The chances of you meeting an armed guard are small, but even if you do he'll have no chance. You will all be equipped with the new American 180 sub-machine gun.'

'The 180!' Lee was impressed. 'How the hell did you get hold of those?'

'You forget we have some very powerful friends. The guns are already in Ireland with the rest of your equipment, and I suggest you get used to them during the trip across the Irish Sea.'

'What's so different about them?' Raya asked.

'Fire power,' Slade answered. 'The 180 is a very special kind of weapon. For starters it fires a stream of .22 calibre bullets at the rate of thirty a second, and because it's recoilless with an advanced night sight it's hard to miss. What makes it impossible is the laser beam hooked into the sight. You just put the red dot on your target and press the trigger.'

'With weapons like that nothing at Windscale can even get close to you,' Farik said, his black eyes gleaming. 'And that's all that matters.'

'Until we want to get out,' said Lee.

Farik smiled and indicated a small black square on the plan. It was in the restricted zone, but some distance from the plutonium factory. 'This is the key to your operation,' he said. 'This is what has been called the atomic dustbin of the world. In these concrete bunkers are tanks containing the deadliest radioactive materials in the universe. Strontium 90, Celium 60, Neptunium, all the hard radiation isotopes that have to be kept in precisely controlled conditions for the next twenty-five thousand years. The British aren't just dumping their own waste in there, they're dumping everyone else's too. And they're vulnerable. My God, are they vulnerable!'

There was silence in the room. Lee glanced at Slade, revolted by the naked hunger in his face. Beside him Raya was staring at the map, her features grim, but determined. With bitter anger Lee realized that Farik's plan could not fail. Where other countries would have guarded such deadly material with crack troops and sophisticated security systems, dear old Britain was bumbling along with a few guard dogs and an assortment of civilian police. Windscale was a sitting duck. And Farik knew it.

'So it's an ultimatum,' Lee said quietly.

'Precisely. Keppel's team head for the tanks which are contained in concrete bunkers. They will place four shaped charges of plastic explosive and connect an electronic detonator. Your group will take care of the dogs and guards, then set up communications with the main security office. The message is simple. They deliver twenty-seven kilos of plutonium from the warehouse, or you blow the charges.'

'And what happens to us if we have to detonate?' Raya asked quietly.

Farik dismissed the possibility with a gesture. 'It will never happen. They know what they're sitting on. If that waste goes critical it will get hot, hotter than anything this side of hell. When that happens no one can stop it. The stuff melts the tanks, melts concrete and rock and starts heading down towards the centre of the earth. Behind it is a radioactive dustcloud that will wipe out half the population of Britain. Not just now, with hard gamma rays, but for the next two decades with leukaemia, bone, skin and lung cancer. Do you think they can risk that? Jesus! They daren't even think about it!'

'Okay,' said Lee. 'So they hand over the plutonium. It's still a long way from home, and I don't fancy handling stuff that hot.'

'Don't worry about that,' Farik replied, taking a photograph from the file. It showed a dull grey billet of metal. 'This is plutonium. It carries no hard radiation, only the soft alpha kind. Anyone could handle it wearing plastic gloves and a breathing mask. But you don't even need that. It will be in half kilo billets, each one sealed in a tin can. The sealing is very carefully checked, so each of you can carry four of them without danger. But you've got to remember one rule, and it's vital.'

Farik rose to his feet and crossed to a cupboard. Opening it, he took out a number of packs of cigarettes. Carrying these back to the desk he placed them in groups of four.

'If you assume each of these packs represents one billet of plutonium weighing half a kilo, then each of you could be carrying four.' He demonstrated by stacking four packs on top of each other. 'This is still safe, even though it's fissionable material. The critical mass for plutonium is 5.5 kilos, so at no time do you ever let that amount come together in one place.'

He gazed at them intently, indicating the various stacks of cigarettes. 'You pile eleven of these in one heap and fission starts by itself. In seconds the plutonium heats up, melts the tin cans, forms a pool of molten metal that can hit four thousand degrees. And that's unhealthy. Most unhealthy.'

He leaned back and considered them for a moment, then nodded as though satisfied with what he saw. 'You leave in one hour. Good luck.'

Chapter 12

They travelled separately on the flight to Dublin. Raya a slim, aloof figure across the aisle from Lee. They had spoken only briefly on the way to the airport and her manner had been crisp and formal, giving him no chance to probe her feelings about the operation itself. Their arrival had been timed to the minute, following a route which had first cut across the city towards the hills in the north and then doubled back to the coast road. Whatever tail had been assigned to them was effectively lost long before they reached the vicinity of the airport.

Lee spent the three-hour flight racking his brain for some kind of solution. Any attempt to reach a phone in Beirut would have been suicide, and from their timetable he was sure he would have even less chance in Ireland. Unless the FBI had been watching the airport, they would be expecting him to leave the following day and would then move in to take the Paxtons. The thought deepened his gloom. Farik was no fool and the death of the FBI agents had put him on his guard. There had been no sign of the Paxtons at the villa and when he mentioned it casually to Samir, the housegirl, she had told him they had left that afternoon. His only hope was that Max had put out a blue index through Interpol, alerting all sources of plutonium. But with the thought came the suspicion that Max would wait, knowing that such a message would alert Farik to the fact that one of his people was a plant. Perm any one from three and he would come up with Corey.

The Boeing 727 touched down at Dublin's Collinstown Airport at 1.15 a.m. in a thin drizzle of rain. The passengers disembarked like grey ghosts, drifting through immigration and customs to stand in forlorn groups around the deserted concourse. Lee went to sit beside Raya who was lethargically reading *Cosmopolitan*. Across the hall Slade had been intercepted by a short, thick-set man in a well-worn raincoat.

'I could think of better weather for crossing the Irish Sea,' Lee said.

She glanced at him and smiled briefly. 'It'll be safer.'

'Maybe.' He lit a cigarette and glanced towards Slade. He was still talking to the man who had to be Irish. 'Now that you're in it for money, what do you do when it's over?'

The hazel eyes regarded him steadily for a moment, then she looked away and gave a small shrug. 'It doesn't matter. I will go back to Israel. The money will go to my people.'

'The Jewish Defence League?'

She shook her head. 'They have money enough. My group are small, badly-equipped and have little influence. Until there is a war again the government would rather forget that we exist.'

'Is that what you want? A new war?'

'Of course not.' She looked surprised. 'But every year our enemies grow more powerful.'

'If Farik uses atomic bombs against the Arabs you'll have it, whether you like it or not.'

'*Ei,*' she said softly, her mouth small with worry. 'But I cannot believe that is part of his plan. If he intended to drop atom bombs, why have I to train you all in skydiving? And why are we so important to his plan? He would need only a crazy pilot.'

'Unless he destroyed the oil,' said Lee slowly. 'How does that grab you?'

'Yes, I have thought of that. But there is so much of it. Even five bombs would do little.'

Further conjecture was prevented by the arrival of Slade with the Irishman. He introduced him as Jerry Meegan and with a cheerful grin he took them out of the terminal building to a battered Mercedes. From the airport they drove south along the coast road, the grey drizzle festooning the land with tendrils of mist that rushed at intervals out of the night.

Meegan kept up a steady chatter, hunched behind the wheel with his sharp, pointed features peering out through the misted windscreen. He was an angular man with nervous hands that had a battered look about them as though they frequently came into contact with large, immovable objects. His eyes were a watery blue, never still, and his hair receded from the forehead into an untidy thatch. He wasted no time in telling them that he was a bomber. He'd used more plastic than an army demolition squad, and when it came to precision he could blow the balls off a grasshopper without it even waking up. 'Begging your pardon, ma'am,' he added, throwing a grin at Raya in the rear of the car.

'How about Keppel and his men?' asked Slade.

'They're all tucked up on board, taking their new guns to pieces. Aahh, they're a happy bunch of fellas . . . even if they don't exactly show it.'

They went through Bray, trailing mist and spray, then turned off the paved road on to a gravel track that led across sodden fields to a line of sand dunes that marked the beginning of the beach. Meegan drove the old Mercedes like a tank, scattering gravel at every bend, then charging across a dune and dipping down to a narrow inlet where a jetty sagged dejectedly against a sleek, powerful motor launch.

Lee collected his bag and moved towards the boat with Raya. Less than ten feet away twin red lasers stabbed at their chests. They froze, recognizing the beams of 180 sub-machine guns.

'Where you from?'

The words came out of the darkness beside the launch, cold and uncompromising. Slade answered with a single word. 'Beirut.'

The lasers flicked off and a moment later lights came on in the cabin of the launch. They climbed on board, passing their bags to shadows waiting on the deck. Meegan was the last to arrive, pushing a heavy suitcase over the side.

'Careful with the case, lads, it'll make one hell of a bang if you drop it.'

Slade was handling it down to the deck. He turned, his face twisted with angry disbelief. 'Are you telling me we had this in the car?'

Meegan chuckled in the darkness. 'Well, I'd have been a bit daft leaving it behind.'

Slade put the case carefully on the deck, his eyes boring into Meegan as he stepped on to the launch. 'You crazy bastard. If that had gone off it would have wrecked everything.'

Meegan grinned at him and picked up the suitcase. 'You're right, Mr Slade, it would indeed. In fact, I might even go so far as to say that not only would it have wrecked the car . . . it would have deposited you in various places from Killarney to Donegal.'

Lee followed Raya into the main cabin, nodding coolly

to the four hard-eyed men who lounged on the settee berths. One of them was tall and blond with the same kind of stillness about him that set Slade apart from other men. He gazed at Raya for a long moment, taking in her lean, healthy body; the arrogance in her eyes when they locked with his. He made the smallest movement of the hand, and Lee saw the youngest member of the group smile slowly. Raya was about to pass him, moving towards the narrow forward cabin. Reaching out he grasped her round the waist and pulled her on to his lap.

'You just relax now. This is fine with me.'

Lee leaned against the bulkhead, aware that the blond man's eyes were fixed on him, waiting for some reaction. He gave none, quietly confident that Raya would need no assistance.

The young man had tightened his grip around her waist, pulling her against him. Raya had not moved, her face devoid of emotion, but as the man turned to grin at his companions her right hand dropped casually to his belt, sliding out the knife held in a scabbard there. She used a minimum of movement so that he was not even aware it had happened until the blade touched his throat. His grin went sour and he quickly tried to pull away.

'Hey, careful. That's razor sharp.'

The knife remained firmly against the side of his throat, the point pricking just below the ear to draw a bead of blood.

'You fancy yourself, do you?' she asked, softly.

He tried to shake his head, then froze as the point dug into his neck and drew another drop of blood. Raya pushed herself to her feet, the knife inches from his face as she glanced at the others.

'I don't play games with children, and I don't fight with fools!' She gazed at the man with contempt, then flipped the knife and caught it by the flat of the blade. 'You touch me again and I'll do things to your face that would make your mother throw up!'

Dropping the knife in his lap she picked up her bag and went through the narrow door into the forward cabin.

Lee gave the blond man, who was obviously Keppel, a mocking grin. 'You satisfied now?'

The man shrugged and rose to his feet. 'You'll be Corey.'

Lee nodded. 'And I suppose you're Keppel.'

He didn't bother to confirm it, gesturing casually to the other men and introducing them as Lorrimer, Hallis and Novak. The young one, still wiping blood from his throat, was Hallis; Lorrimer was thin, gangling, with bad teeth and a nose that looked as though it came from somebody else's face. The eyes were grey and dull, about as memorable as twin pools of muddy water. The third man, Novak, was of a different calibre. He was in his mid-thirties with lean features and black, curly hair. His eyes were dark and shrewd, gleaming with amusement at Keppel's attempt to hide his irritation. He wore a bush jacket, open at the chest to show a small golden crucifix. There was a ragged knife scar on his forearm, and at some time a bullet had glanced off his left temple, leaving a V-shaped scar.

A dull rumble of power came from the rear of the launch, and there was movement above them on the deck. A moment later they were drawing slowly away from the jetty, the sound of the twin diesel engines building gradually to a steady roar. Slade entered, nodding to Keppel and his men, then moving to a quarter berth beside the galley. Crawling into it he stretched out, pausing only to inform them that it looked as though they were in for a rough crossing.

Keppel shrugged and reached into a locker, taking out cans of beer and tossing them to his men. 'We're used to it.'

'That's fine then,' Slade said. 'You can take turns keeping lookout. Meegan's up there now with the skipper, but I wouldn't trust him on a clear day in a paddling pool.'

Novak laughed softly. 'They say he's good with anything that needs a detonator.'

'He's good because he's crazy,' replied Slade. 'He plays with the stuff the way kids play with marbles, only one day it's going to blow up in his face and he won't know a damned thing about it.'

'He'd better know what he's doing at Windscale,' Lee commented grimly. 'If he touches off those waste tanks they'll have to bury us in lead coffins.'

It was not the happiest thought for the day, so Lee left them to wrestle with it, and went up into the forward cabin. Raya was sitting with her knees under her chin, gazing intently at the opposite bulkhead as the waves crashed against the bow, filling the narrow cabin with rhythmic thunder.

Gesturing at the bulkhead which was receiving so much

of her attention, he said: 'What have you got going there? The late late show?'

She spoke without taking her eyes away from it. 'I'm concentrating on being somewhere else.'

'You'll never make it.'

'If I don't I will probably throw up!'

He grinned. 'Imagine you're on a camel.'

Her face went the colour of parchment and she gave him an accusing look. Relenting, he stooped over her in the confined space and firmly turned her round so that her feet pointed towards the stern. Pressing her down on to the berth he straightened her out so that her head was low, rising and falling with the plunging motion of the boat, but by being in the apex of the bow was now escaping the nauseating roll which was increasing as they plunged into heavy sea.

'Stay that way and gradually you'll get used to it.'

She regarded him doubtfully. 'That's hard to believe.'

'It also helps to think about something else.'

'That is what I'm trying to do,' she reminded him.

He bent down and kissed her lightly. 'I know a way that's foolproof.'

Her voice was scornful, but her eyes curious. 'That's a very arrogant assumption.'

'Not from where I'm standing. You're either going to love it, or hate it. But in both cases you're not going to have much time to think about anything else.'

He kissed her then for a long time. At first she lay like a lifeless doll, her lips cold and unresponsive. But then her slender body began to move, pressing gently against him, turning with barely perceptible movements, until she was suddenly soft and pliable, her mouth opening beneath his and tasting of sunshine and pomegranate. When he finally pulled away her eyes came back into focus, no longer curious.

'I'd feel easier if we didn't have those gorillas next door,' she said, quietly.

'You want me to throw them overboard?'

She laughed. 'Could you manage it?'

'I'd leave the big ones for you.'

A thought took the smile away and suddenly she was sad. 'They're not my idea of comrades. They live off death.'

'It's their choice. At least they're professionals. Meegan is the kind of enthusiastic amateur I could do without.'

She nodded. 'His eyes make me nervous.'

'How about mine?' he asked, pulling her gently towards him.

She kissed him briefly, then pushed him away. 'They terrify me. They know too much and say too little, but what they do say has no place on a boat full of ears.'

Lee grinned and lay down on his bunk. After a while her regular breathing told him she was asleep. He thought of Windscale and wondered if it really would be as simple as Farik imagined. Even now he found it hard to believe that tanks with the capacity to lay waste half the countryside of Britain and condemn millions to a lingering death, could be guarded by a mere handful of men.

Corey would have been even more concerned had he known the thoughts that seethed and burned in the mind of Jerry Meegan. Hunched in his raincoat beside the man at the helm, he savoured the savage fever that had grown each day since he had known their destination. He gloated over the images that came and went, fireflies of the mind building fantasies of an entire nation cringeing and weeping as the clouds of doom rolled in from Cumbria. And roll they would, he vowed.

He thought of his younger brother Patrick, and the way he died in Armagh. One moment he was running with laughter on his face, the next he was a broken bloody bundle in the road, moaning to himself like some lost and lonely animal.

There were other images which fed the hatred in Jerry Meegan. There was Sean, who had barely learned to use a gun before the British bullets tore his heart away. And Kathleen, who dressed like a boy in case they didn't have the nerve to shoot. But nerve they had, and the bullets found her as she ran for the border. There was Old McGrath, Will the Sniper, Lattimer, Halliwell and Mrs O'Rourke. All of them gone for Ireland. All of them waiting to be avenged.

Meegan stirred and took the flask of whisky from his pocket. He took a long pull, then passed it to Dolan at the helm. The squat, bearded man who had sailed this course on many a night, took a drink and gestured towards the darker shadow of Keppel on the foredeck.

'He could do with a drop.'

'Let the bastard shiver. They're no different from the British. Dogs at night and pigs in the afternoon!'

Dolan handed back the flask and turned to the helm.

'They're getting you there, Jerry.'

'So they are. It's getting me back that they should be worrying about.'

Dolan gave him a thoughtful look. 'Don't miss your way, Jerry Meegan.'

Meegan laughed, as though the thought amused him. 'If I missed my way on this one, the saints would turn their backs on Ireland!'

Chapter 13

The Bower House Inn is a modest, white-walled hotel in the Cumbrian village of Eskdale, population 450 and not likely to change by anything above single figures in the foreseeable future. Inside are blackened beams and horse brasses, the walls lined with Dickensian prints, the furniture uncompromising oak. The restaurant has long been a haven for gourmets with gargantuan appetites attained by vigorously walking the fells in all kinds of weather.

Lee had not indulged in the local custom, but this had not served to blunt his appetite. He had spent the afternoon fishing the River Esk, catching nothing except sympathetic glances from Raya who had the quaint idea that casting a fly automatically entitled one to a fish. Slade returned from his rendezvous with Keppel shortly before six and together they walked back along the river to the hotel.

Dinner was a leisurely affair, beginning with a delicious salmon mousse and followed by fresh trout cooked in butter and almonds. Keppel ate with his men on the far side of the room, studiously ignoring their table. It was ten o'clock before they finished coffee, Slade announcing that he was going to have an early night, adding in an undertone that the briefing was in half an hour.

Lee took Raya into the bar where they drank cognac and listened to a group of fishermen complaining about the lack of salmon in the rivers this year. A variety of reasons were put forward, one of them being that Windscale was polluting coastal waters with radioactive waste. A recent television programme on the subject, claiming that there was a gradual build-up of radioactivity in seaweed and marine life, had supported this view and the plutonium factory was coming in for a good deal of criticism.

Lee noticed Keppel and his men further along the bar beginning to take an interest in the conversation. A fat, ruddy-faced man with inflatable cheeks was doing most of the talking. He claimed that water used to cool fuel cells from the reactor at Calder Hall, the commercial power station attached to Windscale, had recently begun to leak and for three months this had been kept from the public.

'It's outrageous,' he declared loudly. 'They behave as though we're morons. They only release facts which suit them and if you ask for details all you get is the official run around.'

A bearded man who wore tweeds and smoked an old briar pipe, said that when he tried to get information about the amount of waste held in tanks at Windscale, he had been told that the majority of it was turned into glass which could be safely buried.

'Rubbish,' snorted the ruddy-faced man. 'That process hasn't been perfected yet, and even if it was they could only get rid of the low yield waste. The truth of the matter is that this area is being turned into a nuclear dustbin for half the countries in Europe. God knows how much waste they've got there now, but one thing's certain . . . they're stuck with it for 25,000 years!'

There was a general murmur of agreement and wagging of heads. Keppel edged forward, looking mildly curious. 'That's a long time for nothing to go wrong,' he commented.

'Damned right it is, and where will we be if a bunch of crazy fanatics decide to have a go at the place? I'll tell you where we'll be – in one hell of a mess!'

Lee exchanged a look with Keppel, then turned to the speaker with a sceptical expression. 'Surely there can't be much chance of that? The place must be well guarded?'

An elderly man with thin features who had been silent so far, gave a short, barking laugh. 'Guarded! You'd be hard pressed to guard that place with a company of marine commandos. So what have they got? A handful of police who might be all right for giving out passes, but put them up against a bunch of armed terrorists and they wouldn't stand a chance. Not a bloody chance!'

The red-faced man inflated his cheeks and bellowed approval. 'Absolutely. It was the same with the airports, the IRA bombings in London, even the cricket pitch at Headingly. Nobody does a damned thing until it's too late, and then they spend a fortune on publicity to cover up their own inefficiency. The trouble with this country is that nobody wants to make decisions until it's too late . . . and when it becomes too late for Windscale, it's too late for everyone!'

The bell rang for last orders and Lee caught Keppel's eye along the bar, nodding casually towards the door. They left the hotel and crossed the car park to the annexe where they had all been allocated rooms. Slade was waiting for them, an ordnance map laid out on the bed. Meegan was sitting contentedly in one corner, taping up four cone-shaped charges of plastic explosive and plugging in detonators. Seven gleaming American 180 sub-machine guns were laid out on the other bed, each accompanied by two spare magazines of ammunition.

'Set your watches for ten thirty-one in twenty seconds.'

They studied their watches, Slade counting out the last five seconds. 'Check.' They nodded and then grouped around the map. He indicated Eskdale and began to trace the route they would take to the coast.

'Novak will take one of the cars, Hallis the other, and park them in the station car park. We leave here at midnight, at one-minute intervals, and rendezvous with the cars. From there we go to Calderbridge, then take this road which cuts behind Windscale. The sign says Ponsonby Church and it leads, believe it or not, to within 200 yards of the rear fence.' He indicated a point on the map. 'We go in low across an open field to the fence. Lorrimer, you'll chop through with heavy duty cutters, Novak and Hallis will keep watch. Any sign of trouble and you shoot out the lights along the fence on either side.'

'How about the fence alarm system?' asked Lorrimer.

Slade grinned. 'What alarm system! We got close enough in broad daylight to test the wire. There's no electrical charge in the fence. All you've got to do is cut.'

'We checked out three possible routes,' added Keppel, 'and this one comes out top. All you have to watch for are the dogs. They'll pick up scent and come, and they're Dobermans so they'll be fast. Use your laser sights and take them clean. That way the handler gets the message.'

'How far to the restricted zone?' Lee asked.

Slade produced a sketch of the Windscale works. 'We go through about twenty yards behind this single-storey administration block. We use the building as cover, then cross this road, through the turbines and cooling plant and around the old chimney. From there we'll be able to see the plutonium factory and the first fence of the restricted zone.'

'There are more than one?' asked Raya.

'Two. Each has its own gate and security guard. They'll both be armed, but we'll be moving faster than they can think.'

'They'll still have time to blow the whistle,' Novak pointed out.

Keppel shook his head. 'No way. Hallis, as we go in towards the turbines, you follow the road past the gas-cooled reactor. You'll have to move fast, four minutes maximum, to get within range of the main gate. There's a telephone junction box behind the building. Use your silencer and blast it. By the time they get themselves sorted out we'll be at the silos.'

'Why not just blow the power supply?' suggested Lorrimer.

Slade gave him a disgusted look. 'You don't need a sledgehammer to crack a nut. This is a walk-over – a snap. Keppel and I could do it on our own, except we don't want the rest of you to feel left out.'

'How about the getaway?' Lee asked.

Slade went back to the ordnance map, pointing to the railway line which separated the Windscale works from the sea. 'As soon as they hand over the cans of plutonium we pull back to the railway line. There's a gate located here,' he indicated a point some five hundred yards from the station. 'We cross the line and go down the sea wall. Dolan will come in and pick us up. You got all that?'

They nodded. Novak, who was studying the map and plan of the works, turned to Slade with an incredulous expression. 'It can't really be that easy? Jesus, I've seen sewage plants with more protection!'

Slade laughed. 'A couple of hours from now, when everything's hitting the fan, they'll wish to hell it was a sewage plant.'

Lee was suddenly aware of Meegan, beyond the group in the corner of the room. He was leaning forward, eyes gleaming, his mouth twisted into a malevolent grin. For one brief moment, until the Irishman became conscious of his gaze, he saw the light of madness in his face. Then it was gone, replaced by a disarming grin before he bent over the plastic explosive he was moulding into a cone.

A fine drizzle was falling again when Lee slipped out of the hotel annexe and started down the narrow road towards the station. Slade had been the first to leave and he was under no illusions about the reason. Two hundred yards along the road was a telephone box, glowing like a beacon in the night. Lee walked past it without a glance. Somewhere in the darkness would be Slade, innate caution motivating his actions rather than any specific suspicion that one of his team would attempt to make a phone call. Some fifty yards past the telephone he paused and lit a cigarette, listening to the night. There were no sounds, no moving shadows in the ditch that ran beside the road, but the prickling sensation at the back of his neck convinced him he was right. He was about to walk on when he heard light, rapid footsteps which could only belong to Raya. A moment later she reached him, smiling warmly and slipping her arm through his.

'I wondered if you'd wait,' she said.

'Don't tell me you're afraid of the dark.'

'Terrified. There are so many dangerous characters about these days.'

He tapped the 180 she carried. 'You could be right.'

She laughed softly, turning up her face into the fine rain. 'It's a marvellous night.'

She wore dark slacks and anorak like the rest of them, her hair pushed into a black beret so that she seemed a slim and fragile figure. But the feline grace of her stride belied any weakness, as did the casual menace of the weapon at her side. The drizzle had put a silken sheen on her face so that she glistened in the dim light, more like a lover in the afterglow of passion than a potential killer in the night. He stopped and kissed her, surprised at his own reaction. She nestled against him, her lips brushing his throat.

'Take care tonight, American.'

'If you get any closer there won't be a tonight. We'll end up under a bush somewhere!'

Her warm tongue teased his ear. 'Slade wouldn't like that.'

'Who's Slade?'

She giggled, leaning back in his arms. Suddenly the laughter went out of them and they were thinking of Windscale.

'What do you think of Meegan?' she said, suddenly.

'He bothers me.'

She nodded, her eyes clouded with worry. 'He has the strangest look about him at times. It's as though he's laughing at us all.'

'He's only got to plant the charges. After that he's just a spectator.'

Raya nodded. 'Let's hope so.'

'We go at one-oh-four,' Slade said softly from the darkness.

They were lying in wet grass some twenty feet from the steel mesh fence that circled Windscale. Pools of light at fifty-foot intervals stretched away on either side into the night, beyond them darkened buildings and a glowing jungle of pipes, towers and transformers. Keppel and his men had inched forward to the edge of the light, Lee and Raya holding back with Meegan. The Irishman had said little since they left Eskdale, clutching the heavy pack containing the explosives and refusing all offers of help.

Lee pressed the button of his L.E.D. watch. The seconds flicked away and suddenly it was 1.04. Raya rose simultaneously with him, looking towards the fence. Lorrimer appeared in the light, a silent shadow that slid across the ground then huddled into the steel. They started moving forward, crouching low. Meegan began to follow, other figures rising now in dark shapes around them. There were metallic clicks from the fence, then Lorrimer was through and his red laser beam flicked on three times.

Hallis and Novak ran for the break, ducking through and then sprawling down inside the fence, the stubby 180s covering the north and south approaches. Keppel was next, running forward out of the light towards the administration building. Lee followed, briefly touching the edge of the pool of light, then he was through, crouching with the gun cocked and ready, covering Raya and Meegan. Lorrimer and Novak went after Keppel, fast and silent, whilst Hallis stayed on the edge of the light. Slade appeared, ducking through the opening then lunging into the darkness.

'All right, Hallis. Go for the gate, we give you to 1.09.'

Raya tapped Lee on the arm and gestured. A laser blinked at them from the darker shadow of the single-storey building ahead. They ran forward, covering Meegan who puffed and wheezed with his heavy pack. They reached the building, finding Novak there. He grinned at them, flicked the laser again towards the fence.

'See you inside,' he said, and he was gone.

Slade appeared beside them, glanced at his watch, then

slapped Lee's shoulder. 'Go,' he said. They ran, one on each side of Meegan, across the road and into a forest of transformers and heavy lagged pipes that curled in and out of buildings lost in the grey drizzle. Pools of light were everywhere, from lamps and blazing windows. They moved on, angling towards the tall grey building with corrugated sides which was the plutonium factory. There was a hum of power around them, distant sounds of heavy machinery, the hiss of steam and then the clang of an opening door.

Lee sprawled beside a heavy pipe, pulling Meegan down beside him. A few feet ahead Raya froze against a steel pylon. Light flooded from a door in a building twenty feet ahead. A man came out in a white coverall, descending iron steps. He stopped and took out a packet of cigarettes, putting one in his mouth and lighting it. Lee cursed under his breath, he could be there for five minutes. Motioning Meegan to stay where he was, he inched forward, using the heavy pipe as cover until the technician turned away, then vaulting it and crossing to Raya.

'I'll have to take him,' she whispered. 'There's no other way round.'

'Cover me,' said Lee.

He slipped towards the technician who was leaning against the side of the building, close enough to see the yellow radiation detector on his shoulder. Three steps and he could spare him from a very worrying time. He was on the point of moving when the howl of a dog rose up into the night. It was joined almost immediately by another, this one sounding much closer. The technician turned with a disgusted expression, listening for a moment, then stubbing out his cigarette with a grimace. He climbed the steps to the door, speaking to someone inside.

'Those bloody dogs are at it again, Charlie.'

The reply was lost as the door closed behind him. They moved quickly past the building, then along a narrow passage illuminated at intervals by the light from windows. Raya ran beside him, her face pale and tense. Behind them Meegan came with his pack, pausing frequently to regain his breath. Lee and Raya waited for him at the end of the passage, uncomfortably aware that he was slowing them down to a dangerous degree. Once Keppel broke into the restricted zone they could be permanently cut off. The possibility had certain attractions for Lee, but he suspected that it would have little bearing on the final outcome. Slade would not be stopped, and with such meagre security at the works he would probably switch to an open attack, using the 180s to massacre the guards. It was this reasoning which had so far prevented Lee from dropping back and laying out Meegan, a course which would almost certainly have meant eliminating Raya as well.

The Irishman arrived and sagged against the corner of the building, gasping for breath. Lee reached for the pack containing the explosives. 'I'd better carry that.'

'When I go down – if I go down – you can help yourself to it,' he said fiercely. 'Until then you do what you're paid to do.'

Lee gave him a disgusted look. 'You're so out of condition you need a fucking wheelchair!'

'And if I kick you in the balls, Mr Corey, you'll be needing one too.'

Raya called softly from the shadows, a note of urgency in her voice. He moved quickly to her, looking across an open area to a mass of pipes, cylinders and tanks which extended to a brilliantly-lit steel fence. Above them was one of Windscale's twin towers, legacies of the old reactor which had operated in the mid-fifties.

'Keppel,' she whispered. 'By the big tank.'

He looked towards it, picking out the shadow of Keppel after a moment. He was facing a wide, paved area, the submachine gun held low, waiting. Even as they watched he stepped clear of the tank into the open. There was a snarl from the darkness and a large alsatian raced into view, his long, lean body stretched low as it lunged for him. Keppel raised the gun, pressing a button that activated the laser. It glowed crimson, the pencil-thin beam stabbing out, centring on the dog as it covered the last few yards. There was a brief chatter, almost lost in the hum of power around them, and then the dog was a rolling lifeless bundle. Keppel stepped back into the shadows, moving away towards the fence.

Lee turned to Meegan and gestured at the open ground. 'You go first. Wait by the big tank.'

Meegan nodded, picking up his pack and hurrying away. Lee turned to Raya, noting the taut features and narrow eyes. 'There'll be more dogs now.'

'I know,' she replied. 'The scent of blood will bring them.'

As though in confirmation a long, low howl came out of the darkness, echoing among the tall metal buildings. Meegan was almost at the tank, Lee beginning to scan the surrounding area through the sight of his gun. A horrified gasp from Raya made him turn. Beyond her, already halfway down the space between the buildings, came two Doberman pinschers, their ugly jaws gaping as they hurtled towards them. Even with the shocking realization that Raya was frozen with terror, he was raising the gun and flicking on the laser. The red beam intersected the hairline sight, cutting the night in half and centring on the first of the snarling animals as it leapt at him from a distance of ten feet. He pressed the trigger, feeling the shudder of exploding cartridges, then the dog was cartwheeling into a wall. He stepped in front of Raya and swung the gun, searching for the second, but before he could find it the dog hit him, powerful jaws clamping into his forearm with a blaze of pain. The gun fell from his useless hand as he went over on to his back, the animal landing squarely on his chest, eyes gleaming ferociously as it tore at the arm.

Desperately he tried to get a grip on its throat with his free hand, but the savage contortions of the Doberman made it difficult to obtain a hold. He rolled on his side, chopping at it with an open hand, catching the dog across the throat so that it momentarily relaxed its grip. He broke free, kicking hard with both feet as the Doberman gathered itself for another lunge. The impact threw it clear, and then it shuddered, the snarling rage ending in a strangled cough as Raya's gun blurted out a stream of bullets.

Lee got slowly to his feet, not wanting to look at the arm that burned with pain. Raya gazed at him with pale features, relief mingled with horror. 'Lee, I'm sorry,' she said brokenly. 'It's just dogs. I . . . I'm terrified of them.'

'I'll let you in on a secret,' Lee said dryly. 'I'm not exactly crazy about them myself.'

Slade edged round the supply depot that was the closest cover to the security gate. Beside him Novak crouched with the 180 at his shoulder, finger poised over the laser. A policeman was standing outside the gatehouse, listening with growing concern. The howling of the dogs had stopped, cut off with suspicious finality. He unholstered a revolver and moved towards the phone.

'When he picks up the phone,' murmured Slade.

The policeman lifted the receiver, his eyes roving the brightly-lit area beyond the fence. Nothing moved. He dialled the main gate, then felt a chill of alarm when the line crackled and went dead. He was turning back to the fence when Novak pressed the trigger.

A stream of high velocity .22 bullets tore into the lock of the gate, the small red dot of the laser held steadily on the centre of the mechanism so that thirty bullets a second smashed into a precise area. It took all of three seconds to smash the lock apart, and then there was silence as the gate swung slowly open. The policeman, his mouth dry with fear, crouched by the wall, the gun in his hand. Beyond him, three hundred yards away, was the next guard post and the entrance to the plutonium factory. He debated falling back there, wondering if Smithers could see what had happened. The thoughts froze in his mind as a crimson finger stabbed at him from the darkness, fixing on his chest and moving when he moved. With a shiver of horror he knew that it was somehow connected with the weapon which had destroyed the lock.

'Put your gun on the ground,' a voice said softly. 'Make any attempt to resist and thirty rounds go right in the centre of that little red dot.'

He put down his gun. Dark figures ran into the light, slipping through the gate and moving on towards the factory. One of them, a tall, lean man with a scar running across his cheek, scooped up the revolver. Another man, younger, bound his hands and feet and stuck tape over his mouth. He felt only relief. They wouldn't go to all this trouble if they were going to kill him.

Keppel blew open the second gate from fifty yards, and Novak put a single bullet through the policeman's hand as he reached for his gun. He gripped it with white, shocked features as they moved up to him with the strange, stubby machine guns.

'Where's your radio? Inside?'

He nodded, grimacing as they tied his wrists and feet, ignoring the wound which was beginning to bleed profusely. 'If you go in there without protective clothing, you're as good as dead,' he warned hoarsely.

Keppel smiled grimly and signalled to the men. They took up positions covering the doors to the factory and the gate itself. 'Save your breath, friend. In the first place you're full of shit, and in the second we've got better things to do. Now if you want to talk, tell us where the silos are?'

The policeman could only gaze at him with horrified eyes. Keppel laughed and went into the office, checking the radio transmitter. Slade arrived, glancing at his watch.

'Any sign of the Irish?' Keppel asked.

'On the road now,' Slade replied. 'We're three minutes behind schedule.'

'Who's counting?'

'I am,' Slade reminded him tersely. 'You cover this end with Lorrimer. I'll move on with Novak.'

Keppel shrugged and went to the door. The area between the inner and outer fences of the restricted zone contained a number of buildings, the closest being a tall structure with a number of huge steel flasks used to transport nuclear fuel lined up outside. An overhead crane could travel from this building to a large pond where irradiated fuel elements were stored. Behind it a small group of workers had appeared in the doorway. Keppel tilted the 180, flicking the laser across them. They got the message and hurriedly ducked out of sight.

Meegan went past him, breathing hard, his eyes small and cunning as he nodded to Keppel. 'They'll not be forgetting this one for a long, long time Mister Keppel. Caught proper, with their trousers down and their hands on their little winkles!'

His shrill laughter floated back as he shambled on into the darkness. Keppel turned away, irritated by the sound. Corey and the girl were coming into the light and he saw that the American had a blood-soaked bandage round his arm, the sleeve of his anorak badly torn.

'You okay?' he asked, gesturing at the arm.

'I'll manage. Where's Slade?'

'Up at the silo.' Keppel gestured into the darkness.

Lee and Raya went down the road that curved past the huge six-storey structure that housed the reprocessing complex. The building had few windows, its sides covered with drab grey corrugated iron. Cables snaked out to heavy power terminals and layers of pipes extruded from the centre of the building into a brick filtration plant. The factory hummed and throbbed with power, its fail-safe systems isolated from the harsh realities of the world outside.

They caught up with Meegan as he reached the silo beyond the factory. It was a squat, ugly structure some twenty feet high made of concrete reinforced with steel. Behind the four-foot-thick walls were the double-skinned tanks of stainless steel containing some 700 cubic metres of the deadly liquid waste, the materials so highly radioactive that each tank was crammed with refrigeration pipes to prevent the waste from heating to critical temperatures. Looking at the crude concrete structure, Corey found it hard to believe that this was the world's nuclear dustbin. Inside was enough fisionable material to burn a hole right down to the earth's core, enough high level radiation to contaminate half of Britain.

Meegan stood reverently before the silo, his eyes fixed on the weathered concrete. He reached out, touching it as though half afraid it was some incredible mirage. And then he laughed, his head thrown back in the falling rain, his clenched hands raised towards the sky.

'Jesus!' He cried. 'I love you, Jesus!'

Slade stepped out of the darkness, his mouth thin with anger. 'If you've been at the booze, Meegan, I'll drop you cold!'

Meegan grinned at him and opened his heavy pack. 'Don't you be a-worrying yourself, Mister Slade. I'm just thanking the powers that be for putting me here on such a momentous occasion.'

Slade gave him a thoughtful look, but the Irishman was already beginning to assemble the cone-shaped charges against the wall. He placed the cones precisely two feet apart, connecting the trailing wires to a receiver. When the four pairs of leads were joined to the receiver terminals, he screwed the cover back into place and lifted a wooden box from his pack. He opened it, revealing layers of latex padding in the centre of which was a small black transmitter. He held it casually in his hand, beaming at them, then flicked a switch.

The move was so sudden it took them all unawares. Lee lunged instinctively towards the Irishman, but stopped as he realized there was no explosion. Meegan laughed, an exultant sound, staring at the red light which now glowed on the radio detonator. Slade was very still, waiting.

'Armed and ready,' said Meegan. 'Now all the little devils in hell cannot stop me.'

Slade took a casual step towards him, his eyes flicking a warning at Lee. 'That's great, Meegan. Now I'll take the box of tricks and you give a hand down the road.'

'Oh, you're a fine one with the jokes, Mister Slade. The little box stays with me . . . and if any of your comedians have other ideas I'll blow the lot of you straight into hell!'

Lee gazed at the Irishman with a bitter sense of defeat. His injured arm had begun to stiffen, ruling out any sudden move with the gun. He glanced at Raya, finding her eyes already on him. She was positioned to their left, the 180 held casually in both hands. She could aim and fire in one second, but Meegan could press the button in half that time. They couldn't take the risk and she knew it.

'What are you trying to pull, Meegan?' Slade was asking, adopting a casual stance. 'You know why we're here.'

'Sure I do, but have you any idea what will happen when I press this little button? I'll bring the nation to its knees, I'll have them weeping in the streets, cursing the day they ever set a foot in Ireland!'

'You're full of crap, Meegan,' Lee said quietly. 'You blow that silo and the chances are that Ireland will get the worst of the fallout. Where the hell does that get you?'

He grinned and tapped his nose. 'Feel the rain, smell the wind. It's blowing from the west, not the east.'

Slade made a sharp, angry gesture. 'You're wasting time If blowing that stuff's your bag, then do it. But after we get what we came for . . . after we're on our way.'

Meegan considered him with crafty eyes, but Slade gazed without flinching. After a long, nerve-racking moment he nodded and squatted down against the silo. 'And why not. Let the bastards sweat awhile.'

'Okay,' said Slade, turning away and beckoning to Lee and Raya. 'Stay here and do nothing until we're pulling out. Check?'

'Double check,' agreed Meegan, and gave them a mocking salute.

They moved rapidly down the road to the corner of the plutonium factory where Lee caught up with Slade and pulled him round, the anger erupting in him. 'You crazy bastard! Why didn't you take him when you had the chance?'

Slade regarded him with frozen features. When he spoke his voice was empty, uncaring. 'He knew I might try. This way we get the job done, then worry about the nuts of this world.'

'You know what happens if he blows the silo? Even if we've made the launch there won't be a country that'll have us. They'll hunt us down like mad dogs.'

'Save it,' Slade said coldly. 'If you think you can take him, then go ahead and do it. But when you press the trigger, hot shot, you'd better be sure!'

Slade left them with the warning, striding away round the corner of the factory. The drizzle had turned into a steady downpour, but neither of them noticed. Lee glanced at his watch, astonished to find that only three minutes had elapsed since they first reached the silo.

'He's right, Lee. Even with the perfect head shot you can't be sure there won't be a muscular spasm.'

Lee nodded grimly. 'Yeah. But if we can't get near him no one's going to come up with a better idea.'

Chapter 14

Sergeant Tom Dakin was doing his level best to cope with a throbbing headache. It was undoubtedly caused by tension, although knowing this did nothing at all to ease the pain. He took two more aspirin and gazed moodily out of the window at the front of the reception building. His phones were out of order and his attempt to contact the village police by radio had failed, as he had known it would. Those lads were in bed by now, as were the majority of Windscale's security force.

He turned and walked back to the long counter which, during the day, was a comforting barrier between officialdom and the rest of the world. The room was in shadows, occasional patches of light from the lamps outside touching battered chairs in the waiting area, and speckling the frosted glass partition which hid the rack of weapons and the radio transmitter from the naïve eye of the public. Light also shone through the line of bullet holes in the rear door, a chilling reminder not to try to open it again. At the other end of the room, crouching by the smallest window, was the darker shadow of Constable Purvis.

He was one of the Special Branch men attached to the works, and he held the 9mm sub-machine gun with a certain degree of confidence, although he had not shown much inclination to use it so far. His normal duty consisted of manning the radio and calling the security gates at the factory once every hour. He also kept track of the dog handlers, ensuring that they made regular patrols, and had frequently voiced the opinion that they were only effective against petty thieves and vandals – neither of which were likely to show their noses at Windscale. Tonight he had been proved right. Three of the dogs were dead, the fourth whining miserably in its kennel. The handlers were on the roof of the generator building, together with most of the night shift, unable to get closer to the restricted zone. Their hand weapons were totally ineffective against the advanced sub-machine guns used by the intruders, even if there had been any chance of getting within range.

Tom Dakin sighed and shook his head, wincing as pain lanced up from the base of his skull. Their only hope of getting reinforcements was Constable McKay, but the prospect did not exactly fill him with optimism. McKay had difficulty making a decent pot of tea, so anything as adventurous as running through the night to raise the alarm two miles away was fraught with peril. They had managed to get him out of the reception block through a store room window, instructing him to avoid all strangers and make for Calderbridge. But with all bets riding on young Constable McKay the odds were that he was lying in a ditch somewhere with a sprained ankle.

The radio receiver crackled into life and he moved quickly round the partition. The voice that came from it was bleak and hostile.

'I'm saying this once, so listen good. We've got your waste silo decked out with fifty pounds of plastic rigged to a radio-controlled detonator. The charges are cone-shaped and they'll blow in sequence. You got that? They'll split it wide open.'

Dakin's mouth went dry with fear. He had not had time to think clearly about the purpose of the attack, but had assumed that it was aimed at the plutonium factory. Like everyone else at Windscale, he had come to take the waste silo for granted, conditioned to believe that nothing short of an earthquake could damage it. His knowledge of explosives was only basic, but he did know that a cone-shaped charge was designed to blast inwards, against the surface upon which it was placed.

He switched to transmit and spoke into the microphone, trying to hide the fear in his voice. 'This is Sergeant Dakin. I don't have any authority over the area you are talking about, and I am not permitted to deal with matters which come under the jurisdiction of British Nuclear Fuels.'

'Horse shit!' said the voice. 'You've got ten minutes to deliver twenty-seven kilos of plutonium in half kilo cans. All you have to do is tell the night shift in the factory to carry them out to us at the inner gate. That's ten minutes from now.'

Dakin closed his eyes and took long, deep breaths, hoping to block out the stabbing pains in his head. He sensed the presence of Purvis and looked up at him with tormented features. 'What the hell do we do, Dave? We can't give them that stuff?'

Purvis nodded grimly, looking at his watch. 'McKay won't even be halfway yet. You'll have to stall them.'

'With what? Even if McKay gets there, where are we? It'll take an hour for any kind of force to get here, even using helicopters. And then what? Does that change anything?'

'All right, Sarge! All right!' Purvis rubbed his chin nervously and Dakin saw that his hand was shaking. 'We can't do a thing until the brass get here. Tell him that. Tell him to go fuck himself!'

The constable's voice had gone shrill, his face beginning to gleam with perspiration. Dakin forced himself to be calm, squaring his shoulders and glaring at the younger man.

'Look, Constable, you've been on a course. You know what's in that silo. Can they blow it open?'

Purvis squeezed his eyes shut and started pushing a clenched fist between his teeth.

'Well?'

'Look, you can blow any bloody thing if you've got the right amount of explosive. Jesus, Sarge, what do you think I am? A fucking superintendent! All I know is that they're in a maximum security zone in control of an installation that's classified. All right, we're guarding it – but so far nobody has bothered to tell us what happens if a bunch of nuts blow it up!'

The receiver crackled and the voice echoed in the room. 'You've got nine minutes, Sergeant Dakin. At the end of that time we're taking off and will detonate the moment we're clear of the area.'

'Wait a minute,' Dakin said desperately. 'You don't understand what you're asking. I'm just the night sergeant responsible for security here. I can't authorize the release of plutonium. Good God, man, only the Prime Minister can do that.'

'If the Prime Minister's there, put him on. If he's not, you do his thinking for him. But make it fast, then get on to the factory and tell them the score.'

'They won't listen to me. Why should they?'

'Because they know what they're playing with in there, Sarge. You don't. Tell them we're blowing the silo and you'll think it's Christmas Day. They won't just give us the plutonium, they'll give us the factory as well!'

Dakin was afraid. For twenty-five years he had taken orders and carried out instructions. For ten years he had shouldered responsibility within the narrow sphere of a sergeant's duties. Matters of policy, decisions affecting the daily routine, even the response to requests for information or entry, were all laid down in regulations or covered by general procedure. And there was always the emergency clause, the dire situation which called for immediate action.

Only it did not apply to this. There was the inevitable assumption that a senior officer would be available for consultation, or that sufficient time could be found to communicate with the administration, even the government. In the make-believe world favoured by the United Kingdom Atomic Energy Authority within the comfortable walls of their offices in Risely, Lancashire, terrorists always stormed the main gate in broad daylight with a stick of gelignite in one hand and an old army pistol in the other. They were terrified of guard dogs and suitably respectful of uniformed policemen who, if provoked, would draw a pistol from the armoury and fire deliberately over their heads. They were also lacking in intelligence, incapable of discipline, and when confronted by authority would undoubtedly turn tail and run.

There was no room in their planning for the breed of terrorist who could split an olympic security force wide open, or infiltrate airports, attack army camps. After all, if you closed your eyes and thought about it, they probably didn't even know about a place like Windscale.

Sergeant Dakin wished he'd never seen it. He wished he had stayed with Lancashire Constabulary and settled for the tedious grind of petty complaints and even pettier enquiries. And most of all he wished he was at home with Mildred and the kids, watching Kojak snarling commands and being twice as tough as all the tough guys.

Instead he looked helplessly at Purvis and said: 'I wish to hell the inspector was on tonight.'

'He's not. You are. What do we do?'

He tried to swallow the sickening ball of fear. 'Do you think you can get the bloke outside?'

Purvis's face gleamed like naked bone. 'I suppose. He's got a funny gun. It fires .22 at a hell of a rate. Something new.'

'Yours is 9mm. What are you worried about?'

'Yes,' said Purvis, in a voice that meant anything.

A rush of cool air blew across the room, turning them both towards the door, although logic had already told them it had just been opened by someone. A stocky young man dressed in black with something that looked like a Tommy gun in his hands, was standing inside the door.

'Just put the shooter on the floor, friend,' he said, in a matter-of-fact sort of way.

Dakin read the decision in Purvis before he moved. It began in his face, a thinning of the mouth and a widening of the eyes. It moved, with a kind of shudder, to the hands holding the sub-machine gun. The left gripped it tighter, whitening around the knuckles, and the right slid to the trigger guard, tilting the barrel and swinging it towards the door. There was a sound like tearing cloth, a flicker of light and the smell of cordite, then Purvis dropped his gun and toppled slowly to the floor. Only when he lay in front of Dakin with his arms flung wide, his eyes gazing sightlessly at the ceiling, did he see the gaping wound in his chest and understand that Constable Purvis was dead.

'Now what's it going to be, Sarge?'

'I'll need a phone,' he whispered. 'I'll need a phone to call the factory.'

Chapter 15

Four workers in coveralls and a supervisor in a white coat brought out the cans of plutonium. They were small and nondescript, just rectangular tins with BNFL stencilled on each side. But they were carried with caution and laid two feet apart on the tarmac by the gate. The men made three trips, the supervisor crossing to Slade who was watching with stony features.

'You know this is dangerous, I suppose?' Slade smiled and nodded. 'And there's nothing I can do to change your mind?' Slade continued to smile. 'Then at least make sure that no more than two cans ever come into contact with each other. It's important. If you put them all together . . .'

He stopped as Slade gave him a patronizing look. 'Save your breath. We know about critical mass, nuclear fission and all that jazz.'

The supervisor had sallow features and silvery hair. He stiffened angrily at Slade's words, then spoke with precise contempt. 'No doubt you do know what the words mean, but I very much doubt if you understand them. What you are taking away from here is capable of destroying millions of lives. If any of your men drop one of the billets, puncture the tin or make any one of a dozen simple errors, then you will all be contaminated and there's nothing in the world that can save you.'

'You're scaring me to death,' said Slade.

'I don't give a damn about you, but I do care about all the people who will suffer because of you.'

Slade grinned and tapped him on the chest with the barrel of the 180. 'Then let me tell you something, friend. Next time you mix yourself a batch of poison . . . put a fucking lock on the door!'

The supervisor turned and followed his men back into the factory. Lee stood with Raya and Novak, feeling the tension that gripped them all. Slade beckoned to Lorrimer and Keppel. They drifted over, their eyes still scanning the brightly-lit road. Hallis had appeared in the distance and was approaching at a casual trot.

'We've still got Meegan to deal with,' Slade said quietly. 'And once he knows we've got what we came for he's off the leash.'

'He's sitting up there by the silo,' Lee said, 'watching the road like a hawk. I think he'll press the button if he hears anything suspicious at all.'

'I figured as much,' Slade replied calmly. 'Shooting him was always a lousy idea. I've seen a hundred guys get it, but never seen one drop stone dead.'

'With this gun I can put a burst between his eyes and he'll be dead all right,' said Lorrimer.

Keppel and Novak gazed at him until he grew uncomfortable and started to rub his nose. Slade turned to Lee, his expression sober.

'How about it, Lee? Could you take him with that arm?'

Lee grimaced and shook his head.

'I can.'

They looked at Raya, no one expressing any surprise. She handed her gun to Slade and took off her anorak, removing the belt with the spare magazines from around her waist. She unfastened the top two buttons of her dark blue shirt, then held out her hand to Slade.

'I'll need the knife.'

He gave it to her and they watched as she slipped it inside the waistband of her slacks, positioning it in the small of her back.

'You'd better go,' she said.

Slade nodded and gestured to the men. 'Every man takes four cans. One in each pocket of your anorak, one in each hand. If you have to put them down to use your gun, then make damned sure you put them down gently. Now move it.'

'I'll be staying,' Lee announced firmly.

'She either wins or loses,' Slade said, not without sympathy. 'Staying doesn't alter that.'

'All the same, I stay. We'll catch up with you before you get to the beach.'

Slade didn't like it and said so, but the rest of the men were ready to leave. Reluctantly he handed over Raya's gun and collected four tins of plutonium. They moved off into the night, heading towards the rear of the works. Lee glanced at his watch, reading the glowing digits with a deep sense of frustration. If it hadn't been for Meegan he might have been able to end it here.

He stood in the rain and cursed the complex structures that rose up into the night around him. Only complacency had made this attack feasible, and now the plutonium was on its way to the sea. With bitter anger he recalled the words of an American physicist asked to comment on the increasing availability of plutonium in the world. He had considered the question for a moment, then said:

'I have a dream. It begins with a phone call from the mayor of some large city in the United States. It concerns a letter he has received asking him for some astronomical sum of money. If he refuses to pay, then the author of that letter intends to detonate an atomic bomb somewhere in his city. The letter contains a simple drawing, the basis of which are two pieces of a metal called plutonium and a conventional explosive charge. I would have to tell that mayor to pay the money, no matter how much was asked, then pray that the bomb did not go off.'

Meegan was saturated and the chill night air was biting into his bones, but he didn't mind. He beamed happily at the glowing red light of the transmitter in his hand, caressing it with his forefinger and letting it hover over the small black switch, tensing, teasing the mind. There was movement on the road and he was instantly alert. The slim figure outlined against the lights of the factory was unmistakable.

'It's Raya, Mister Meegan. We're almost ready to go.'

'That's all right then,' he said, watching her closely as she approached and noting that she was unarmed. 'I'll give you time to get to the beach, but once you're in the launch tell my old pal Dolan to go as though all the devils of hell are breathing down his neck.'

Raya stopped before him, slim and lovely in the rain. 'Why not come with us, Mister Meegan. What's the point of blowing yourself away?'

'You wouldn't understand, child,' he said, cupping the detonator in his hand.

'You're sure there's nothing I can say,' she said, looking sad.

'Not a thing, darlin'. What I'm going to do is not just for me, it's for all the poor bastards who died on nights just like this. It's for the arrogant pigs who live in this lovely land and who made it all happen, when less greed and more humility could have melted all the hatred away. It's because Ireland is changing, getting old and ugly, and people don't laugh any more. But tonight I'm going to blow it all to hell and let the wind carry retribution across the land.'

He chuckled softly and stroked the switch on the small black box. Raya leaned towards him, smiling gently. 'I think I understand. You will let us get out to sea?'

He patted her cheek. 'Of course I will. But hurry now.'

She nodded, gazing down at him with tender eyes. 'Will you kiss me before I go, Mister Meegan?'

He laughed delightedly and rose to his feet. 'Darlin', it's a pleasure.'

As he put his arms around her she drove a clenched fist into his testicles with every ounce of strength she could muster. Meegan screamed. Every nerve and sinew stretched tight with the agony that seared through him. The detonator was forgotten, his universe was a pillar of pain that knew no beginning and no end. Even as he began to bend forward, the shrill scream vibrating in his throat, she slid the knife between his ribs and into his heart.

The screaming had stopped for at least a minute before Lee saw the figure of Raya coming out of the darkness. She was sobbing quietly, the detonator in her hand, no longer glowing. He kissed her and she clung to him, her body shaking.

'What else could I do?' she asked, brokenly.

'Not a thing.'

They collected their cans of plutonium and followed the rail line that curved towards the sea. The sergeant and two uniformed policemen were huddled on the road, but they took hands away from revolvers when Raya showed the detonator. Slade had cut the simple padlock that held the gate closed, and it now gaped open to a narrow lane that wound under the main rail line to Barrow. They went through the narrow tunnel to the sea wall, the simplicity of their retreat filling Corey with a bitter anger. In the distance they heard the wail of police cars, rising up into the night. They were coming fast, but their first concern would be dismantling the explosives on the silo.

On the beach Lee took the transmitter from Raya and pulled the cover off, tearing out the wires before tossing it into the sea. The launch was backing water, a light winking at them. He took Raya's hand and together they ran through the breaking waves to scramble aboard.

The low cloud and driving rain made an air search out of the question, but even if there had been time to do so it would have been a futile quest. The launch did twenty knots through heavy sea, heading not for Ireland but the Isle of Man. At three o'clock in the morning they were wading ashore on a deserted beach in Ramsey, squeezing into a large black Mercedes waiting on the promenade. The driver, who glanced only once at the strange tins they placed in every corner of the car, drove like a madman across the island to a private airfield outside Peel. A Cessna was waiting there, ready to take off the moment they were on board. By dawn they were crossing the Bay of Biscay, hugging the waves to avoid being picked up by radar.

They landed at Bilbao at noon, leaving Lorrimer on the plane with the plutonium. After refuelling the pilot took off for the Lebanon, but by that time Lee, Raya and the remainder of the group were checking into the departure lounge for the scheduled flight to Beirut.

It was exactly eight hours since they ran for the beach below Windscale, and according to the radio one of the biggest air, sea and land searches in history was under way.

It was still under way when they landed at Beirut. They adopted the same procedure as before, each member of the group operating independently, ignoring the others. Lee and Raya were the last to leave the terminal building. Slade was watching from a taxi, about to tell his driver to leave, when the plain-clothes men moved in on the couple and hustled them into a car.

'Shit!' said Slade.

'*Pardonnez-moi?*' said the driver.

Slade gave him a filthy look and sank back in his seat. 'Drive, you stupid bastard,' he said.

Chapter 16

'You know what I like about you, Corey? Nothing gets to you. If someone tapped you on the shoulder and said they'd found a way to sink Venice, you'd jump at the chance. You'd buy yourself a pair of flippers and a snorkel and get right down to it.'

Max Weller was in full flow, striding backwards and forwards across the office in Beirut's American Embassy. He paused, stabbing a finger at Lee.

'It's getting so that every time I pick up a paper and read of a robbery or a massacre somewhere, I think: Jesus, are we in on it!'

'Are you all through?'

'Corey, if your personal file ever gets out of the safe in my office my whole god-damn department is through. You've pulled more capers than Al Capone! If they gave you a thousand years you'd still be getting off light!'

He glared at him, blew his nose with a flourish and sat down. 'How's the arm?'

'Lousey. I think I picked a dog that forgot to clean its teeth!'

'You shouldn't even have been there. I put you in to blow the whistle, Lee . . . Not to score home runs.'

'So why wasn't the airport covered when I left? You could have picked me out then.'

Max had the grace to look embarrassed. 'The killing of Bevis got people a little bit screwed up around here. They didn't expect you to leave until the next day.'

'Farik had other ideas. We flew direct to Ireland and from there by launch to Eskdale in Cumbria. The first chance I had to do anything was at Windscale, but by that time Meegan had freaked out and fouled everything up.'

'The Irishman they found dead?'

'Right. Believe me we did everyone a big favour. If he'd blown those silos . . .'

Max winced. 'I don't want to know about it. Just tell me

where the plutonium is and we'll wrap this up right now.'

Lee gave him a pitying look. 'Max, in case it hasn't got through to you yet, this operation is planned to the last detail. It's got more back-up systems than the Apollo launches, and nobody – but nobody – knows what is happening twenty-four hours from now. The plane we flew out in – a Cessna – just dropped some of us at Bilbao, then refuelled and took off. That plutonium could be anywhere in the Middle East by now.'

Max Weller's face went grey and he seemed to get smaller in the big leather chair. He gazed at Lee, willing him to qualify the statement with some small shred of hope. When the words failed to come he swung round in his chair and stared out across the battle-scarred rooftops of Beirut.

'You know Freddy is missing,' he said finally, in an empty voice.

'No!' Lee was concerned. 'When?'

'Yesterday. She acted as liaison with the local police before the raid on Farik's villa. Naturally they found nothing except Farik, who was threatening everyone in sight. She was supposed to report back to the Embassy in the afternoon.'

'Farik?' he asked bleakly.

Max sighed and shook his head. 'We have no proof. This city's still a pretty dangerous place to be, what with the Palestinians and various fringe groups still fighting it out in the suburbs. If it is Farik, he'll make sure he's covered his tracks.'

'Then the sooner I get out of here the better.'

'And if she's talked?'

'Then at least you'll know Farik took her.'

Max steepled his fingers and stared moodily at his desk. Lee could not remember ever seeing him so depressed. He could understand part of it, the fact that C-2 was out of its depth with neither the muscle nor the men to be effective. Ever since the damning Rockefeller Commission on the CIA's subversive activities there had been increasing hostility in Washington to clandestine activities abroad. In spite of the fact that his assignment had begun in Nevada, they were now a long way from home and up against an organization that had apparently limitless resources.

'If it's any consolation, I'm pretty sure the plutonium is somewhere in the Lebanon,' Lee told him finally. 'And wherever it is you'll find the Paxtons.'

'All right,' said Max heavily. 'Let's take it step by step. Farik's fronting for an organization with roots in the States, but with big influence in Europe. It's got the material and the know-how to make a batch of A-bombs, and its motive is money.'

'At least a hundred million.'

'No one's going to part with that sort of money.'

'Check,' said Lee. 'I think the final take is going to be legitimate. You couldn't hide that amount, you couldn't even put it in a hundred suitcases.'

'So what's the target?'

'Oil. Arab oil.'

A cool wind blew in off the mountains and rattled the venetian blinds. The cry of a muezzin floated up from the mosque in Rue Sadat behind the Embassy. Max Weller closed the window, then crossed to a wall map of the Middle East. He gazed at it for a long time before moving back to his desk.

'How?'

Lee shrugged. 'I don't know. You can't destroy a thousand million tons of oil, even with atom bombs. But it has to be that, otherwise why is Raya Dassan so important? She knows that area, she's got connections on the ground. And her next job is to train us in skydiving.'

Weller's head came up sharply. 'A sky drop? . . . Then that can only mean the bombs aren't going to be detonated. Not until you're well clear.' He slapped a fist into his hand, eyes gleaming, walking quickly back to the map. 'It's extortion, on a massive scale, but still extortion.'

Lee was dubious. He had already discounted the possibility. 'I don't buy that.'

Max stabbed a finger at the oil-rich countries around the Arabian Gulf. 'The installations and pipelines in those fields would cost a thousand million to replace. All Farik has to do is place his bombs and hand out the ultimatums. Pay up or blow up.'

'Israel wouldn't be involved in a deal like that, and neither would the CIA.'

'We've checked out the Israelis at ministerial level. They know nothing, and they don't want to know. The agency connection is something we're still tracking down. It's not on file with the Director of Plans, and anything that big would have to originate with him.'

'They got us out of Nevada.'

'You say. They say they know nothing about it. The flight you were on was real enough, a clandestine operation ferrying mercenaries to Africa.'

'Then pick up Mallory and sweat it out of him.'

'They don't have a field operative called Mallory.'

Lee gave him a disgusted look. 'They're covering up and you know it.'

'Maybe.'

'No maybe about it. They fixed the prison break, the passes, the car to Reno. The plane was a charter job, probably leased by one of their dummy airlines. Now for Christ's sake, Max, what more do you want!'

'Proof!' he snarled. 'Right now you're living proof that they're not involved. In case you didn't know, they were in on the cover-up after Bevis died here. Are you with me? They knew Young was alive, so they knew you were a plant. One phone call to Farik and you'd never have got on that plane.'

Lee shook his head in bewilderment. 'Then what the hell is going on?'

'Let's go find out.'

Max took him up to the top floor of the Embassy building, to a suite of offices which looked out over the Corniche to the blue expanse of the Mediterranean. The sign on the door said J. Ferryman, Legal Attaché.

Ferryman was a slim, pocket-sized man in his mid-forties. He wore a grey suit, Ivy-League shirt and tie, and a gold Cartier watch that cost more than Lee earned in a year. His voice was dry and precise, as though he was proposing last year's minutes, but his eyes were chips of silicone that would have looked better in one of Salvador Dali's sculptures. He offered Lee a wary hand and waved at the steel and leather chairs. The office was double-glazed and air-conditioned, and the absence of a secretary only meant that every word was being taped, if not video-taped.

'Before we start, what do you say to clearing the air of a lot of crap that floats around between our respective houses?' He smiled invitingly at Lee and sat down.

Lee gave Max a crooked grin and took a chair. 'Okay. For

starters, you're a bunch of long-nosed bastards who write-off people the way I write-off expenses. You're up to your blood-shot eyeballs in anything dirty this side of the Atlantic, and you've probably had a considerable hand in ripping this particular city apart.'

Max Weller glared at him furiously. 'Corey, for Christ's sake!'

Ferryman waved a languid hand. 'Leave it, Max. We know all about Mr Corey's views.' He smiled at Lee with all the warmth of a viper. 'Our involvement in the Lebanese debacle was negligible. We tried to bring the Muslims and Christians together, tried putting the Palestinians into bed with anyone in town. But they were hell bent on blowing off their toes, so finally we sat back and let them get on with it. Now do you have any other hang-ups?'

'Plenty. They go all the way back to Dallas.'

Ferryman took out a Gauloises and lit it with a gold Dupont. 'That's water under the bridge, Corey. Times have changed, new brooms have been busy.'

'It's not brooms you need, it's detergents.'

'We're all under the microscope these days. Now you've done a fine job, you're into something that we know is very, very big. The question is: Can you take it from here or do you want out?'

'That's not my decision or yours,' Lee said, and looked at Max.

'Lee still thinks your department of dirty tricks have got a finger in somewhere.'

'Maybe they have.'

Max Weller prided himself on playing the best game of poker in Washington, but for a second his mouth was slack and muscles jumped along each side of his jaw. Ferryman sighed and made an open-handed gesture.

'Look, fellas, we don't really know. When you start talking about Texas, the mid-west, you're into fringe groups that are a pain in our ass. I mean it. We use all kinds of kooky numbers and some of them have got to be bent.'

'So what the hell does that mean?' Max demanded angrily.

'It means that I'm on the level. I've checked this out with Washington and we ran a projection on the computer out there. It comes up with a lot of things we don't like. One of them is the Signus Five set-up.'

Max gave him a worried look. 'Isn't that the pressure group backing oil concessions?'

Lee glanced quickly at Max. There had been a reference to an oil pressure group in the file he had shown him. Ferryman was nodding agreement.

'It's a combination of power, money and the kind of mentality that went out with Daniel Boone, but it's still strong in parts of Texas. Signus Five is made up of some of the richest men in the mid-west, men who only need to lift the phone to send a congressman out for coffee. They're fanatical isolationists, believe in a complete American withdrawal from all points east of Boston. For three years now they've been pushing for federal jurisdiction over offshore exploration areas. They want to open up the oil fields of Alaska, drain Texas dry, sink holes all over the Californian coastline, not to mention Cape Cod and Florida.'

He paused and considered them gravely. 'They're hard-nosed and totally secure. I mean that. No way can they be touched.'

'Get to it,' Lee said quietly.

'For the past month they've been buying oil. All over the world they've been leasing tankers, filling up at every field from Venezuela to Bahrein. The interesting thing is that the tankers haven't got destinations yet. They're just cruising around the world . . . an expensive business.'

'Not if you know there's going to be one hell of a shortage of oil in two weeks' time,' Lee said slowly.

Ferryman nodded. 'Right. We'll never pin it on them, of course, they're far too clever for that. Dummy companies, bearer bonds, multi-national leasing corporations that have interchangeable manifests for a hundred tankers. But if we're right, and Farik is fronting for them, we can hit them where it really hurts.'

'The pocket,' Max supplied. 'They must have put out over a hundred million.'

'Ten times,' said Ferryman. 'And they could make as much again.'

There was silence in the room. Such sums of money defeated the mind. You could buy an army for that; buy governments even. Lee's first emotion was anger, but it was almost immediately replaced by a sense of dismay. Nobody risked that kind of money unless they were one hundred per cent certain of success.

'We're missing something,' he said slowly.

Max tilted back his grizzled head and glared at the ceiling. Ferryman watched, his brilliant eyes flicking from one to the other. The air-conditioning had a fault, vibrating every thirty seconds so that the background hum developed metallic hiccups. It was just about the most irritating noise Lee could remember – apart from the girl he took out once who had the nervous habit of fastening and unfastening the catch of her handbag. It sounded just like the safety catch coming off on a Walther PPK. It ruined the evening.

'We all agree that it's oil?' Max asked. They nodded. 'And it's the assumption of your people in Washington that Signus Five are in deep.'

'We put the probability around 65 per cent. There's always the chance that they're a peripheral operation. In exchange for advance warning they put a million in the kitty.'

Lee shook his head. 'That one's out. Farik admits that he's taking orders from the States. His schedule was laid down for him.'

'All right, then,' said Ferryman. 'We go with Signus Five and oil. Your operation grabbed enough plutonium to make five bombs – that's assuming they're going for very basic devices using a fissionable mass of 5.5 kilos. But five bombs could only wipe out major installations in five fields, and the Arabs have resources to put that right in a couple of months.'

'They'd rather pay up than have it happen though,' Max pointed out.

Ferryman disagreed. 'It doesn't go with all these oil tankers. They're gambling that the price of oil is going up – and I mean up. Maybe double to make the whole operation worthwhile.'

'There's one way that happens,' Lee said grimly. 'A new Middle East war with atom bombs going off in Arab territory and Israel getting the blame.'

Ferryman took out a cigarette and looked at it as though it was about to talk to him. The air-conditioning squeaked again and Lee resisted the urge to walk over and kick it.

'We are considering that possibility,' Ferryman murmured, as though the subject was only of passing interest. 'It does have certain attractions.'

'If that was true,' said Max, 'they'd just drop the bombs

from planes with Israeli markings. Instead they're planning a sky drop with Slade's team.'

Ferryman's eyes flicked at Lee who nodded.

'I don't buy any of these things,' he said. 'The bombs are part of the plan and so is oil, but there's something else. Some factor which removes all the risk and is so foolproof that a bunch of wealthy nuts in Texas are ready to throw all their marbles into the ring.'

Max grunted reluctant agreement. Ferryman sighed and ground his cigarette into a crystal ashtray. He gazed at Max and something flickered between them. He turned to Lee, looking as though he'd had a new idea, although it was the same idea he'd had ten minutes ago.

'It seems to me, Mr Corey, that you've got to follow this right through to the bitter end.'

'You could always clean out Farik and his people. Maybe you'd sweat the location of the plutonium out of him.'

'You know better than that.'

'Sure I do. So I go back. When?'

Max rubbed his chin and squinted at his watch. 'Couple of hours.'

'Sooner. If they've got Freddy I don't want to waste any more time.'

Ferryman made an airy gesture. 'That's purely hypothetical. Our concern is the operation. Naturally we have certain resources which you can utilize. A full surveillance squad, direction finder linked to a little bug we'll plant somewhere you won't notice. And the case you brought back is being fixed.'

'Unfix it,' Lee said, his eyes holding Ferryman. 'And do it fast.'

'Just a two-way transmitter and the kind of gas capsules we've found handy in the past.'

'I don't need them and I don't want them. If I go back it's on the same basis as before. No interference. If there's something you need to know, I'll get it to you.'

'Lee, you've got to have a back-up team,' exclaimed Max. 'We've got to keep a check.'

'Then do it without me!' He gazed at them impassively. 'Out of the last team you put on me, Bevis is dead, Young blown, and Freddy missing.'

Max sighed and grimaced at Ferryman. The CIA man didn't

like it at all, but he reached across the wide expanse of desk and pressed an intercom button. 'Jennings? Cancel the suitcase rig. Clean it up and get it to Max Weller on the second floor.'

He switched off without waiting for a reply, his eyes boring into Lee with a mixture of annoyance and contempt. 'Like they say in the movies, Mr Corey, you're the only game in town. But you foul it up and I guarantee you'll never play again!'

Lee rose nonchalantly to his feet and moved towards the door. He paused there and glanced back, giving Ferryman a gentle smile.

'There is one thing you could do, Ferryman.'

'What's that?'

'Fix that bloody air-conditioning!'

'It's running perfectly,' Ferryman said coolly. 'The squeaking is built in. We find it puts people's nerves on edge . . . assuming, of course, that they are the nervous type.'

Chapter 17

They were released shortly after sunset. Raya was brought into the domed entrance hall of the Embassy where Lee was already waiting. Together they were escorted to the door by a minor official who mouthed the diplomatic platitudes as though he imagined they actually believed them. At the doorway the illusion ended as he held out a hand to Raya who gave him a look that would have shrivelled lesser men in their sandals. The official gazed thoughtfully at the darkening sky, then went back into the Embassy.

They turned east along the Corniche, Raya slipping her arm through Lee's and kissing him gently on the ugly bruise that was beginning to blossom over his right cheekbone. The bruise, together with a cut lip, had been Ferryman's idea. With barely concealed satisfaction, he had pointed out that Raya's interrogation would seem far more convincing if she was confronted by a somewhat battered Corey. The CIA man's logic was sound, although his motives left a lot to be desired, so Lee gritted his teeth and allowed an Embassy security man to bounce him off the wall a couple of times.

'Just who the hell do they think they are?' demanded Raya. 'A good lawyer could crucify them over this.'

Lee shrugged. 'First he'd have to prove that we were ever in the Embassy. Somehow I've got a feeling that a lot of people have just developed amnesia.'

'But look what they did to you!'

'I'm the careless type.'

'It's not funny, Lee. Those bastards have no authority in this town.'

He couldn't help smiling at her anger and this only served to infuriate her more. She began to walk away from him with square shoulders. He quickened his pace, catching up with her.

'Just forget it. There's not a thing we can do and you know it.'

She stopped and glared at him. 'Well, at least we could

put a brick through the window.'

He chuckled. 'Oh that's a great idea. Sure you wouldn't like to throw a can of paint as well?'

The anger died and she smiled, touching the bruise on his cheek again. 'What did they want to know?'

'Why we went to Ireland. Naturally I told them that we went to see my dear old mother in County Donegal.'

She giggled. 'And that's when he hit you?'

'No. No, that was when I said that we had to go to Bilbao because she'd eloped with a bull fighter.'

A black Mercedes went past them and pulled into the kerb ahead. Raya was slowing down, her forehead creasing with a new thought.

'It could be dangerous going to the villa,' she said.

'I think we're being checked out right now,' he told her. 'Let's see.'

They crossed the wide boulevard and turned left beside the smoke-streaked walls of the Beirut International. They were in Rue Ayoub, a quiet street lined with elegant apartment buildings. They walked briskly down it to the park on Rue Venus, taking a seat beside sweet-smelling jasmine bushes. The night was humid, droning with mosquitos. After a moment the Mercedes purred into view, turning into Rue Venus and stopping beside the kerb. The engine was switched off, then the lights.

'It could be the Americans?' Raya suggested.

'Too obvious,' said Lee, hiding the tension that was building in him. He was remembering Max's warning. If Freddy had talked, this was just about the way that Slade would go about it. A window in the car whined open and a hand flickered at them from the shadows within.

Raya nudged him. 'They're waving at us.'

He forced a grin. 'So wave back.'

They crossed the road, Lee keeping well apart from the girl, his eyes straining to detect the first sign of menace from the car. Instead he found the sulky features of the blond Dane, Troy.

'Some of us have better things to do with our evenings,' he said, waspishly.

The Dane had no way of knowing how much tension had built up in Lee on the walk across the road. All he knew was that a pair of cold eyes were suddenly an inch from his own, and the palms of his hands were sweating.

'In that case, Sonny, maybe you'd rather walk!'

They climbed into the car and Troy drove them towards the villa in a sullen silence. He stopped twice to make certain they were not being followed, then took the narrow back road along the edge of the cliff to the villa.

Samir opened the door, taking them through the hall and across the lounge to the patio. A buffet was laid out beside the pool and they helped themselves to cold meats and salad. Samir poured glasses of chilled wine and told them that Signor Farik was busy and would see them later. Around the pool, which glowed like velvet in the purple light, were stretched the figures of Keppel, Novak and Hallis. Lee exchanged a look with Raya. She lifted an eyebrow, acknowledging the pointed silence from the group.

They took seats at a table beneath a lantern that hung from the loggia, and began to eat, both of them discovering how famished they were. Between mouthfuls of salted beef and spiced lamb, Raya chattered gaily about the kind of food she enjoyed at home in Israel. It was five minutes before Keppel lounged out of the shadows and leaned on the table, scrutinizing Lee's battered features with studied contempt.

'Whoever did that wasn't trying very hard.'

'He had a handicap,' Lee said, dryly. 'Somebody kept putting a foot in his mouth.'

'So how come they let you out? Both of you?' Keppel turned his suspicious gaze on Raya.

She ignored him and continued to eat.

'Go ask them,' Lee said calmly, and speared a piece of lamb on his fork.

Keppel gripped his wrist, stopping the food short of his mouth. 'I'm asking you.'

Lee sighed and tapped Keppel's hand with his knife, effectively loosening the grip. He rose to his feet and stepped away from the table, aware of the two deeper shadows lurking behind him.

'You know your trouble, Keppel? You've got a bionic mouth. It talks so fast, you can't keep track!'

'All right,' Keppel whispered. 'Explain it to me. Tell me why they pick you up and take you to the Embassy, then let you walk out free as birds a few hours later?'

'Which story do you want? The one where I told them

how we pulled the Windscale job, or the one where I just flash my FBI badge and get the red carpet treatment?'

Keppel moved his hand and moonlight gleamed on the blade of a knife. He took a step forward, but stopped as Raya spoke.

'Unless you're planning to kill me too, I'm going up to my room to collect my gun. Then I'll come back down and blow your head off. That's if Slade and Farik haven't beaten me to it.'

Keppel hesitated, his eyes fixed on Lee. Novak and Hallis stirred restlessly in the shadows. The American smiled. He knew the moment had gone.

'We want to know why,' Keppel said thickly.

'Then ask me,' said Raya, 'because I'm the reason. I have Lebanese papers and some very indiscreet letters supposedly from a minister in the government. They believed them, so they had to let me go.'

'That still doesn't explain Corey's release?'

Lee gave him a look of complete disgust. 'There goes that bionic mouth again! Once they let her go they couldn't hold me, not with Raya telling all kinds of official friends where I was.'

He went back to the table and sat down, leaving Keppel to burn slowly in the dark. After a moment he went into the house and they heard him snarling at Samir, telling her to get him a whisky. Raya was watching Lee over the rim of her glass, her gaze disturbingly intent. As his eyes met hers she smiled and inclined her head towards the lounge.

'I think we've spoiled his evening.'

'Couldn't happen to a more deserving guy. Was it true about the letters?'

She nodded. 'Just a little insurance. All the same, I was surprised to see you waiting for me.'

She was shrewd and far from convinced that it had gone so easily by chance. He gave no sign that he was aware of this, taking a drink of wine and frowning thoughtfully at the pool. After a moment he shrugged and shook his head.

'At the time I was puzzled, but when you think about it there wasn't much else they could do. They ran a bluff, hoping to catch us with the goodies, and when that failed they were on the spot. I'll bet they couldn't wait to see the back of us.'

Her face cleared and she began to relax. 'You're right. Of

course you're right.'

The door to Farik's study at the far end of the loggia opened and Troy stepped out, looking towards the pool and beckoning to Novak and Hallis. They strolled across to him and the Dane spoke quietly for a moment, then returned with them into the study and closed the door. Raya had paid little attention to the incident, but one startling fact had registered with Lee. They had left Troy to put the Mercedes in the garage, and had been out on the loggia ever since. At no time had the Dane entered Farik's study, which meant that there had to be another entrance. But where? And why?

He pictured the study, recalling the walls lined with books, the large desk with its phones and intercom, and the video-tape deck behind it against the wall. At the time he had recognized the control panel as the type used for a closed circuit TV system, but nowhere in the villa had he seen any cameras. The obvious conclusion was that there had to be another room. With mounting excitement he realized that, if Freddy was being held here, it would be in that room.

He leaned back in his chair and contemplated the pool, but in his mind he was visualizing the front of the villa. The ground sloped away from the road with the building wedged into the side of the hill which gradually sloped down to the cliffs. The drive was sunken, leading to the garage which extended along the side of the house at basement level in direct line with Farik's study. It took only a simple calculation to work out that there was a gap between the end of the garage and the rear of the house of at least twenty feet. If this area was, in fact, a concealed room, then it would connect with the study.

'A nickel for them?'

'Not worth it,' he told her, smiling. 'I'm surprised Farik hasn't shown his face by now.'

'He must be plotting with Slade.' She gave him a mischievous grin. 'According to the schedule I'm due to start training you soon. Have you ever jumped out of an aeroplane?'

'It's been a temptation I've managed to resist so far.'

'The first time you'll hate it.'

'And the second?'

'You'll still hate it, but maybe you'll like it a little bit too.'

He grimaced. 'You're such a comfort.'

She smiled and then was serious. 'As far as I know Farik

wants to do the training in the hills. He has some sort of abandoned airstrip up there. This will make it difficult, the cross winds and thermals are not easy for a student. I hope you are a quick learner.'

'That depends on the teacher. How about Slade and the others?'

'All of them have made some jumps, but both Keppel and Novak are experienced skydivers. I am afraid you are the most inexperienced.'

'*You're* afraid? You ought to be over here.'

She rose to her feet, smiling, then spread her feet wide apart and stretched out her arms, tilting her head back. 'This is what you must practise all the time. The star position. It's the way you go off the plane, the position you must hold to control yourself in the air. Gradually, as you get used to the feel of the air pushing against you, you will be able to draw your legs in slightly and bend your arms into the crab position. At that stage you can start moving your body in free fall. It's marvellous, really.'

'Beautiful,' he said, his eyes on her slim, rounded hips.

The blood came and went in her cheeks and she sat down, her eyes briefly on his before glancing away.

'I have not been with a man for a long time, Mr Corey.'

'I'm not at all surprised.'

She glanced at him with quick anger. 'Oh?'

He grinned. 'You're not likely to if you keep calling them mister.'

She blushed and got nervously to her feet. Her normal assurance had deserted her and she hesitated, as though not sure what to do or say next. Lee waited until she glanced at him, then smiled gently.

'I'll bet you're dying to have a bath.'

She nodded, looking relieved. 'Yes. Yes, I am.'

'How long will it take you?'

The question hung between them in the still air. She studied him for a while, like a stranger searching for points of reference, and somewhere she found them. Her eyes softened, became large and luminous. 'Not more than half an hour,' she said.

Lee went into the lounge and found the brandy, pouring some into a crystal goblet. Keppel was stretched out on the sofa, a bottle of whisky beside him, staring pointedly at the ceiling. Lee went out on to the patio and sat beside the pool, sipping brandy and trying to devise an effective plan for getting into Farik's study. He was beginning to wonder how long the two mercenaries would be with Farik when he heard the sound of the Mercedes at the front of the villa. A moment later he picked out its headlights sweeping the sky as it turned along the narrow road leading to the cliffs. He felt a vague uneasiness. It was late and the road led nowhere, except to a picnic area on the top of cliffs beyond Pigeon Rock Bay. Neither Hallis nor Novak were likely to be interested in late-night picnics.

Further speculation was prevented by the appearance of Farik and Slade. There was a strangeness about them both which immediately put Lee on his guard, but just as quickly he sensed that there was no menace in their manner. Slade moved slowly, unsteadily, his face slack and glistening with perspiration. He walked past Lee without giving him a glance, going to the end of the pool and slumping into a chair from which he gazed vacantly into the water. Lee felt a chill of apprehension. Slade was like a man drained of all emotion, and he had once before seen him in that condition.

'I was relieved to hear that you had both been released,' Farik said, taking the seat beside him. 'A few more hours and I would have started things moving.'

'No need,' Lee shrugged it off. 'I think they half-expected to find the plutonium on us.'

Farik smirked with satisfaction. 'And the British think it's in Ireland.'

'It was neat. Impressive. So when do we go for the big one?'

Farik leaned back in his chair, savouring the thought. He was in an exultant mood, his features glowing with an almost religious fervour; a man gripped by powerful emotions that stretched his shrill voice into a vibrating falsetto that grated on the nerves.

'We are so close, American,' he said. 'In one week we will shake the world.' He waved a grandiose hand at the sky, encompassing both east and west. 'The world, Corey. We are about to perform a painless execution of the power politics that spawned the death of this city, the mutilation of my . . . people.'

Lee noted the brief hesitation and wondered just how much of Farik's zeal was motivated by revenge. The Lebanese, as though reading his mind, answered the question for him.

'We are engaged in what is undoubtedly the most perfect combination of political activism and criminal opportunism. You follow? No. No, of course you don't. But soon you will know the targets and see the brilliance of the plan. You could rob a hundred thousand banks and still fail to equal the proceeds of this single venture.' He gave a shrill, cruel laugh. 'It's the ultimate contract, Corey. The doomsday contract.'

Laughter shook his heavy frame, trembled the loose jowls and darkened the skin so that, briefly, he seemed to merge into the night. Only his eyes remained, glittering malevolently like some primeval lizard poised to strike. He was totally unaware of the revulsion in the man beside him.

Farik returned to his study after a few minutes, informing Lee that he and Raya would remain at the villa the following day, but would then go up to the hills in the east to begin training. Keppel's mercenaries would leave that night, but this was merely a precaution to mislead the authorities and the Americans. They would drive steadily all day in the wrong direction, circling back during the night.

'They are not very pleased with the idea,' Farik said, with some amusement.

Lee remained by the pool for a further five minutes, then finished his brandy and went into the house. Once in his room he took a shower and donned dark slacks and shirt. Samir had brought up his bag from the car and he quickly went through it, finding the battered leather toilet case. Taking out the hair brush, he swivelled the ebony top and removed the set of skeleton keys inside. Slipping them into his pocket he went along the corridor to Raya's room. The door swung open at the touch of his hand, the interior lit dimly by a lamp beside the bed.

Raya lay under a sheet, her rich chestnut hair splayed out on the pillow. Her eyes were closed, but she wasn't fooling anyone.

'I knew a girl who kept her eyes closed,' Lee said, in a conversational tone. 'When she finally opened them to say good night . . . it was the wrong guy!'

Raya opened her eyes, trying not to smile. 'Bastard!' she said softly.

He grinned, took off his clothes and slipped under the sheet beside her. 'You're getting to know me better every day.'

She nodded, her gold-flecked eyes suddenly tender. He took her in his arms, kissing her gently at first, but with increasing passion as her warm, slim body curled around him. He entered her slowly, moving with an easy rhythm, letting the tensions in her dissolve until the urgency engulfed them both and she was arching against him, crying out in a voice that shuddered with the intensity of her orgasm.

Afterwards she lay beside him, watching his face and touching his lips with her fingers. She would never be more beautiful, Lee decided. The feline grace which was so much a part of her was enhanced by the satin gleam of her golden skin. Images plucked at the mind, of Raya with a gun in her hand, with the knife gleaming in the lights of Windscale. But he put them aside, aware that her motives were as real and altruistic as his own.

She talked softly of Israel, of a young soldier whom she had first met when she was fifteen. They had become lovers as the shadow of war had darkened the land, unaware that the bloody conflict which would become known as the Yom Kippur was already counting out the minutes and the hours.

'He left one morning so full of life,' she said sadly, 'and when they told me that night that he had been one of the first casualties I could not believe. I kept asking, for days I would not believe. But it was true.'

There were tears on her cheeks and Lee kissed them away. 'And so you had to fight?'

'We all have to fight,' she said sadly. 'To win you must always fight.'

She gazed at him steadily for a moment, and then said: 'Do you know why I told you about Yakov?' He shook his head. 'Because you are the first man who has ever made me feel again the way it was with him.'

'We may not have much time,' Lee said gently.

'Ei.'

She drew sadness around her like a shroud. Lee rose and knelt above her, smiling at the question in her eyes.

'You know this skydiving you were telling me about?' he asked casually.

She nodded, unable to conceal disappointment.

'Well, how about showing me that star position again!'

The gurgle of laughter rose in her throat and she reached eagerly for him.

She was sleeping soundly when Lee checked his watch for the third time, then slid carefully out of the bed. It was 2 a.m. and the villa had been silent for an hour. He dressed quietly, then stood for a moment listening to her breathing. The sheet had slipped down below her small, firm breasts and he watched them rise and fall, moved by her beauty and disturbed by emotions which he knew were futile. Sooner or later, Raya Dassan would find herself on the opposite side of his private war.

'Shalom,' he said softly, and left the room.

Chapter 18

The night was still and cool as Lee stepped on to the loggia and moved through deeper shadows to the study door. Fishing out the skeleton keys he selected a thin steel probe and examined the interior of the first lock. It took less than a minute to identify the mechanism and a moment later he had fitted a skeleton key. It turned easily. The second lock was more difficult. It was the cylindrical type which required precise pressures at three points along the barrel. Working patiently with a right-angled probe, he slowly turned the lock until it finally snicked open.

He entered quickly, closing and locking the door behind him. Crossing to the bookshelves along the right side of the study, he began to examine them carefully. He knew that somewhere along this wall there had to be a concealed entrance to the hidden room. The first series of shelves yielded nothing. An alcove containing a painting by Bosch came next, but the white plaster surface showed no break so he moved on to the final section of bookshelves. After ten minutes he stepped back and considered the entire wall with a baffled expression. There was no door, no hidden catches.

He went back to the alcove and studied it again. He found it finally, a slight depression on the tiled floor that showed more wear than the other tiles. He pressed down on it with his foot and there was a click, then the rear of the alcove swung open. Four carpeted steps led down into a room that contained a large bed flanked by floor-to-ceiling mirrors. There was a remote television camera positioned directly above the bed and another on the wall facing it. He closed the door and switched on the lights, feeling a sense of disappointment at not finding Freddy. He went over the entire room, running his hands through the deep pile of the carpet, checking the bed and the floor beneath it. There was nothing, no sign that it had ever been occupied.

With a final glance around the room he started up the stairs and opened the door into the study. He was about to step through when he heard keys being inserted in the locks. His mouth dried out in the time it took to step back into the room, close the alcove door and switch off the light. Almost immediately he heard the unmistakable voice of Calad Farik, and then the dry, precise English voice of Donald Paxton. The voices went past the alcove door, then Slade spoke sharply almost beside it.

'You just shut your mouth and listen, Paxton.'

Lee crouched on the stairs, listening through the thin wooden door, every nerve tense with the realization of what discovery in this room would mean.

Farik unlocked his drawer and took out a file from which he selected two crude drawings showing a front view and a cross section of a device which Paxton recognized immediately. His face paled and his hand shook as he reached for the drawings.

'We have twenty-seven kilos of plutonium, plus a shielded furnace with remote servos and casting equipment. Your job will be to make five bombs of the gun assembly type.'

'Impossible,' whispered Paxton. 'Melting and casting plutonium is a highly dangerous operation that can only be carried out in a proper laboratory with at least two qualified assistants.'

'Crap,' said Farik coolly. 'One man can do it. You're the man.'

Slade leaned forward, his mouth thin and full of menace. 'You're not listening, old man, and you're not thinking straight either. Or don't you care about your daughter?'

Paxton swung round, eyes burning in gaunt features, his voice shaking with anger. 'You don't know what you're asking me to do. Not even for my daughter.'

'We know,' said Farik. 'We also know this is the simplest atomic bomb yet designed. All you have to do is cast the plutonium and fit it into the casing. You'll have conventional plastic explosives for the centre charge, a barometric detonator and a cobalt steel case.'

Paxton gazed at him in disbelief. 'Cobalt steel? But, good God, man, that makes a dirty bomb!'

Farik was contemptuous. 'Of course it does. Try not to be too stupid, Mr Paxton, or I fear I will lose patience with you completely!'

The nuclear chemist shook his head, the perspiration running down his face in rivulets. He understood the consequences of refusal, but the thought of the havoc the bombs would wreak filled him with horror. 'I can't,' he whispered. 'I really can't.'

Farik was unperturbed. He tapped the drawings in front of him. 'You'll make them. Right now I want you to tell me how long it will take to construct these sections?'

Paxton gazed at him with tight lips. Slade leaned casually towards him and slapped him across the face. A trickle of blood appeared from the corner of his mouth.

'Answer, Paxton, or I'll really work you over.'

'It makes no difference, I will not construct these . . . these abominations!'

'Answer me,' snarled Farik.

Paxton took a deep breath, wiped blood off his chin with a shaking hand. He pulled the drawings towards him and studied them for a moment.

'The implosion bomb would take less time to construct.'

'I know that,' said Farik impatiently. 'But the gun type fits the kind of casing we have to use. Now we understand that there is a central core of plutonium in two sections, and then the outer sphere. The plastic explosive is placed so that it explodes the core into the centre of the sphere and we then have the chain reaction. Is that correct?'

Paxton nodded. 'The cores are easy to make because they have a small mass, but the outer sphere will be close to critical, so melting and casting the plutonium becomes highly dangerous.'

'All right. But how long?'

Paxton was silent until Slade stirred restlessly. Then he shrugged. 'Five days for the spheres, two days for the cores.'

'Good.' Farik was satisfied. 'Tonight you will be taken to the laboratory which has been prepared for you. In seven days I will expect five completely assembled nuclear devices.'

Paxton gave him a baffled look. 'But I have told you I will not make them.'

'So you have.' Farik was very still, his cold gaze dissecting him. 'And as it is a decision only you are able to make it is fair that I should give you a very clear choice.'

Paxton was confused. Farik's manner was supremely confident, as though he had never at any time doubted his ability to compel the Englishman to carry out the work. He turned now to the video-tape unit and pressed switches which began to turn the spools of tape. The screen flickered, then came to life. Paxton went pale and closed his eyes tightly.

'Come now, Mr Paxton,' said Farik, 'this has been prepared especially for you. The woman you see was someone who had transgressed. A pretty young thing, though somewhat stubborn. But all that changed when she was given a certain drug. Being a chemist I'm sure you know all about cantharides and what it does to the sexual organs of a woman.'

Paxton shuddered, opening his eyes and gazing at the screen with tormented eyes. The naked girl writhing helplessly on the bed was no one he knew, but the two men he had seen before. The brutal sexual assault on the girl was conducted with an animal ferocity, her body totally helpless under the massive stimulation of the drug. As the men took her in turns, and then simultaneously, she jerked and moaned in an endless orgasm that had long since turned pleasure into pain. Only her wide, staring eyes revealed the terror of the girl.

The fear and disgust contorted Paxton's features. He turned to Farik, telling him he had seen enough, but the Lebanese only smiled and turned the volume a little higher. Paxton, in spite of his revulsion, was drawn back to the screen. The heavier of the two men was beginning to grunt like some wild animal, his huge hands striking at her. The moans became sobs, strangled cries, and then a long, thin wail of terror as she realized what the man intended to do. The wail became a choking cough as the hands closed on her throat, the thumbs pressing down with brutal force to crush the larynx. It took less than thirty seconds, and then all movement ceased and she was dead.

Slade had watched the recording without expression, but when he turned to gaze at Paxton the Englishman recoiled from the savage hunger in his eyes.

'In seven days' time,' said Farik softly, 'there will be another video-tape, only on that occasion the star of our little movie will be your daughter.'

Paxton swayed unsteadily in his chair, his face grey and dripping with perspiration. He tried to speak, but could not. Farik considered his nails and waited patiently.

'You are animals,' Paxton managed finally. 'You are vile, debased animals. I will make your bombs and do whatever you ask, but in return you must swear that my daughter will not be hurt and that she will be with me during the next seven days.'

'Of course,' beamed the Lebanese. 'We agree and promise that neither of you will be harmed providing you carry out your part of the bargain.'

Paxton nodded stiffly and rose to his feet, moving like a zombie to the door. Farik followed with Slade after switching off the video-tape and television. When the door had closed and the keys turned in the locks, the alcove swung open and Lee walked slowly to the desk. He switched on the equipment and rewound the tape, then sat and watched it run through to the end. Throughout the recording his face was a wooden mask, empty of all emotion. The smaller of the two men was Troy, but the larger man had his back to the camera for most of the time. Only towards the end, when caution left him, did he turn his face slightly to reveal the scar that ran upwards from the corner of his mouth. But Lee had known. In a way he had known since he saw Slade by the pool.

When the tape came to the end he switched the equipment off and sat at the desk with his head in his hands. He didn't move for five minutes or more, and then with difficulty turned to the telephone. A corner of his mind noted that it was a private outside line, but even if it had been connected to the house phones he would not have cared. He dialled the number and waited.

'Put me through to Max Weller. This is code two, blue index.'

He waited, his face gaunt and still.

'We are connecting you,' said a voice. 'One moment.'

It took two minutes, and then Max was on the line, his voice quick and nervous.

'Lee? Do you have the girl?'

'Freddy is dead, Max. I think you'll probably find her in the sea or on the beach along the coast from here. I'm sorry, but it was too late. Always too late.'

'I understand, Lee. It was Farik, of course?'

'He's got the whole thing here on video-tape. Slade and the Dane, Troy, did the . . .' His voice broke and he stopped and took a deep breath. 'They killed her.'

'Then the tape is all we need,' said Max, but his words

were slower and tinged with caution. 'We move in now and clean the bastards out!'

'No. The tape won't implicate Farik, and Slade is already on his way with Paxton. I want them cold, Max. Stone cold. And the way to do that is with the bombs.'

Max was silent for a moment. 'You're getting too involved, Corey. Tell me where Slade is heading with Paxton and we'll put all our people on to it.'

'No idea. Won't have for days at least. It's a laboratory somewhere, but not in Beirut. There are a hundred places in this country that you couldn't even get close to. All the fringe groups hiding out – Muslims, Christians, Palestinians, Syrians . . . Max, forget it.'

He sighed. 'All right, Lee, we'll do it your way. But the second you know where or what the target is, you pull out and blow the whistle. That clear?'

Lee didn't even bother to answer. He put the phone down and sat staring at the blank screen, the images of Freddy pulling at the corners of his mind. The rage engulfed him and he smashed his clenched fist into the desk. Every single fibre screamed out for Slade. Slade dead. Slade put down on the ground with a bullet in his brain, because that was the only thing you could do with a mad dog.

But the next time Lee Corey saw Slade they were five thousand feet above the Sannine Mountains in eastern Lebanon.

Chapter 19

'On the wheel!' shouted Raya, above the roar of the Cessna.

Lorrimer, crouching in the open doorway, pushed out his feet and felt for the step, then grasped the wing strut and pulled himself out. He stood on the wheel of the aircraft, changing feet until his right foot trailed behind him. Wind tore at the yellow jumpsuit he wore, the static line trailing back to the strut it was anchored to inside the cabin. Raya knelt beside the door, looking down, waiting for the drop zone to come into view.

Her hand rose and fell. 'Go!'

Lorrimer jumped back from the wheel, his arms going wide, legs splayed out into the star position. Lee felt the icy ball in his stomach do a couple of quick turns as he watched him fall away, the static line flicking open the pack on his back and pulling out the red and white canopy. And then he was gone and the Cessna was banking, turning into the circuit that would bring it round to the same point again. Slade moved up to the doorway, checking the anchor of his static line, then inching forward until his feet were dangling outside.

Far below a red and white mushroom drifted towards the small yellow cross that had been laid out on the sand in the narrow valley they had chosen as the drop zone. Lee tried taking deep breaths, going over again the brief but explicit instructions they had been given that morning.

Raya and he had been taken from Farik's villa in a battered pick-up shortly after midnight of the second day. It had spent some two hours winding in and out of the back streets of Beirut until the two cars following had begun to lose interest. Then, with split-second timing, a similar truck had slipped out of an alley and they had driven fast for the main Rue de Damas. There the truck had deposited them beside a small Fiat before disappearing into the night.

They drove out of Beirut on the Damascus highway, crossing the El Barouk mountains and branching north at Taalabaya for Zahlé. Dawn was breaking over squat grey hills as they passed through the white-walled town, taking the narrow, rutted track to Qaa er Rim. Novak was waiting for them in the small village beside the mosque, taking the lead in a Land-Rover that spewed a choking cloud of dust until they began to climb up into the Sannine hills.

The camp consisted of a collection of adobe huts, used by a Palestinian force until the Syrian advance had cleaned them out. Now holes gaped in walls and roofs, and sparse grass had begun to grow on smoke-blackened mounds of rubble. It was ideal for their purpose, looking down from the head of a narrow valley where the Palestinians had built a crude, but serviceable, airstrip.

The sun was beginning to put a shimmer of heat in the dry air when they arrived, finding Keppel and the remainder of his men squatting in the shade of the only hut which had escaped serious damage. Their equipment was stacked inside, and as before it was a comprehensive inventory.

A complete battle kit for each member contained fragmentation and CE gas grenades, heavy Colt Commander automatic pistols and the deadly British Stirling sub-machine gun. The jumpsuits had been specially designed to incorporate most of the equipment, the left leg fitted with spring clips so that the Stirling could be clamped there and be immediately available on landing. There were pouches on the thighs for ammunition, even field dressings and drugs, and each yellow suit had a series of coloured bands on the arms which would identify the wearer to the remainder of the group.

Raya began the training immediately, lining them up and shouting out the instructions which they roared back until they were hoarse. Lee was the complete beginner and Raya seemed to take a perverse pleasure in reminding them all of the fact.

'Belly out, American!' she commanded. 'Arms wide, shoulders back, belly out! You're flying – not flopping!'

In her clipped, quaint accent, she quickly demonstrated a quality of leadership which, though surprising, was accepted by them all. Only Hallis proved sullen until she bluntly told him the facts of life.

'How many jumps have you made, Hallis?'

He looked bored. 'About forty.'

'How many free fall?'

He deliberated for a moment until Keppel began to lose

patience with him.

'Cut it out, Hallis,' he said sharply. 'You've never been free fall.'

'Big deal.'

'Yes, it is,' she said in an icy voice. 'In about seven days' time, Mr Hallis, you are going to step out of a plane at a height of eighteen thousand feet. It's cold up there, and it's short on oxygen, and you've got to fly that stupid carcass of yours some two miles across country and open your chute at no more than two thousand feet. Open it higher and you'll be seen, open it lower and you'll die. Now if you think you can do that, just go and sit in the shadow of your ridiculous ego. I couldn't care less.'

She walked away from him and they watched, grinning as the blood burned in his face and he scuffed at the dry earth with his feet. She turned and faced them, shouting out the drill once more. Hallis was suddenly trying harder than anyone.

The heat beat down on them throughout the morning, the thermometer edging its way through 40 degrees and heading for 45. But there was no let-up in the training, and in particular on Lee. Raya singled him out at every stage, pulling his landing technique to shreds and showing him again and again how to lock knees and ankles together and pivot them to take lateral, forward or backward falls. She hammered into him that once he was in the harness of a parachute he could not turn his shoulders, so everything that happened must happen below the waist.

Lee understood her motives. The rest of the group could land and roll, they understood the behaviour of a parachute and the guidance he had yet to master. Nevertheless it was a gruelling four hours during which she drilled into them all the litany of the skydiver.

'One thousand, two thousand, three thousand, four thousand, check canopy!'

At noon they paused for a meal of bread, cheese and fruit. Raya took this opportunity of demonstrating the type of rig they would be using. She held it up on the nylon harness, ticking off the various points.

'This is the American Wedge POD,' she told them. 'It's light, easy to pack, and unlike the majority of parachute packs it doesn't use a sleeve on the canopy. This system has a floating metal ring which controls the crown lines of the parachute as it deploys. It also prevents burning and bunching, and is easily adapted for our first jumps which will be on static line.'

'I know the POD,' said Keppel, 'but I'd feel happier with a conventional sleeve pack. If we're into 25 second delays we'll be doing something like 200 miles per hour when we pull. The sleeve is going to act as a break and there's less risk of a shred.'

'The POD system works,' Raya said firmly. 'I was asked to choose the best equipment for this assignment. Considering the extra weight we'll be carrying, this pack is ideal for our purpose. There are other reasons too. It requires less time to repack the canopy, and it takes either of the canopies we're going to use.'

'I'd just as soon start with a Para-Commander,' said Keppel.

'I understand that.' Raya was sympathetic. 'But we have to train as a team so I'd rather everyone used the standard junior canopy for the next few days. Once everyone has done ten delayed deployments, we'll switch to Para-Commanders.'

She finished telling them about the pack and turned to the canopy itself, a 28ft circle of nylon with large L-shaped panels open at the rear. It would be these panels which provided the guidance, acting as air vents which would push them forward at five miles per hour. By pulling toggles on their harness they could choose the left or right panel, enabling them to turn in any direction.

Afterwards she came and sat beside Lee to eat, her eyes searching his face with some anxiety, not at all sure how he had taken the rough handling of the morning. He gazed at her stonily until her hazel eyes clouded with disappointment, and then he grinned. 'I'll bet you're a heller in the kitchen!'

She laughed with some relief, and kissed him impulsively.

The Cessna circled the valley shortly after one o'clock and touched down on the dusty airstrip. They made their way down to it slowly, sweating profusely under the weight of the rigs they were carrying. Lee recognized the Cessna as the aircraft which had flown them out of the Isle of Man, and made a mental note to cultivate the friendship of the pilot. He was a taciturn German called Gurber who had spoken less than a dozen words on that flight, but apart from Lorrimer he was the only man there who must know where the plutonium had been taken.

Slade emerged from the aircraft with the pilot. He was wearing a yellow jumpsuit and the same POD rig. Raya spoke to him beside the plane, and then they were all climbing in and anchoring their static lines to the reinforced strut in the cabin. The seats had been removed so that they were forced to kneel awkwardly around the open doorway. The pilot revved the engine, then sent the Cessna bouncing along the rutted airstrip. Raya leaned over to Lee, pointing to the chin strap of his crimson crash helmet. He nodded and fumbled with the strap, fastening it tightly beneath his chin. She smiled, gently, knowing what he was feeling. He gave a crooked grin and began trying to remember what it was he had to do when he climbed out on to the wheel.

Slade jumped back from the wheel on Raya's command and fell rapidly away, the red and white panelled canopy streaming out like bright smoke. The Cessna banked and Raya pulled the static line into the cabin, then beckoned to the door. A kind of numbness was settling over him and he was barely conscious of the roar of the aircraft, the constant buffeting as it bounced through the sea of air pockets above the grey hills. He sat in the open doorway and looked down, feeling the nausea rise and a sense of astonishment that he should be here at all.

The aircraft had made a full circuit and far below he could make out the small red and white disc that was Slade, already lined up and drifting in to the drop zone. The sight should have given him comfort. It gave him nothing at all.

'Lee?' Raya shouted above the engine roar. He tried to give her a reassuring grin, but ended up with a grotesque grimace. 'Don't forget. Head right back, belly out.'

He nodded, then she slapped his shoulder and he was lurching out of the cabin, grabbing for the strut and fumbling with his feet for the metal step halfway down the undercarriage. The wind tore at his jumpsuit, hitting him with far more force than he had expected. He looked down, feeling his stomach lurch again as he found only a black rubber wheel between him and the earth five thousand feet below. He steeled himself to step on to it, hoping the pilot had his foot firmly on the brake, then teetered for a moment as he struggled to change feet. But finally he was in position, right foot trailing free, hands gripping the strut above his head, looking into the open cabin where Raya crouched with strained features. She looked down, then back to him. She gave a desperately nervous smile and screamed: 'Go!'

He flung both arms wide and felt his mind freeze as the world went mad. Wind tore at him, he began to slide slowly on to his back, seeing above him the canopy snaking out and knowing he should not be seeing that at all. And then the sky revolved and he was gazing at the grey sea below, slashed with varying shades of brown. He should have been counting the seconds, shouting one thousand and on, but he did nothing at all. In spite of the drill he was acutely aware that, if his main parachute failed, there was virtually no chance of him finding the presence of mind to pull the ripcord of his reserve.

There was a popping above his head as the parachute snapped open, a fluttering of nylon, and with a mild astonishment he saw that he was upright once more, swinging gently some three thousand feet above the hills. He checked the canopy above for any obvious holes, then glanced at the earth below to locate his position. The yellow cross of the dropping zone could be seen clearly at the head of the valley, a wind sock blowing at the apex of the cross. Reaching up the harness he tentatively pulled the right guide string, watching himself revolve slowly to the right. He checked his turn with a tug on the left, then began to calculate his forward speed against the rate of fall.

The air was dry and cool, the exhilaration rising in him as he sank slowly towards the hills in a still, silent world. Far below Slade's parachute collapsed just beside the yellow cross. A mile away the Cessna was banking round for another run. He practised a couple more turns, getting used to the rigidity of the harness now that his full weight was suspended from it. The earth was taking on contours, the valley directly below him. He swung himself round until he was facing away from the wind, reducing his forward speed. The last five hundred feet seemed to take an age . . . and the ground was leaping up at him, smashing into his feet and then the back of his left shoulder as he rolled into the fall.

Slade was standing less than ten feet away, gathering up his parachute. He gave Lee a mocking grin and jabbed a thumb in the air. Lee turned away, still finding it hard to look at the man without revealing his savage revulsion.

Novak, Keppel and Hallis made their jumps, drifting in to the drop zone, the two experienced parachutists showing their prowess by spiralling down to hit the cross dead centre. The Cessna was still climbing by the time the last of them landed, a tiny silver dot in the sky.

'She must be doing a ten second delay,' Keppel said to Lee, shading his eyes as he followed the plane.

A moment later the engine throttled back and a small yellow figure fell away from it. They watched with growing admiration as the figure turned left and right, somersaulted and then spread wide, arms curving back like an eagle as she changed direction above their heads. Keppel was counting out the seconds as she fell, and at twelve the arms swept in, then out again. A second later the parachute streamed out behind her and snapped open. She was less than a thousand feet above the ground, still falling fast, and then Lee saw that she was using a different parachute to the rest of them. It seemed to be missing half its panels, many of the gaps cutting into the crown of the canopy. But she had remarkable control, swinging it left and right, turning into a tight spiral which brought her down to the drop zone, then turning into the wind at the last minute so that she lost all momentum, landing lightly on spread feet and gathering the parachute in her arms as it fell about her.

She moved to Lee, her eyes alight, the smile warmly approving as she solemnly shook his hand. 'Congratulations, *hamudi*,' she said. 'You are now a parachutist.'

The others came over, slapping his back and cracking the usual jokes. Hallis was the last to shake his hand, then paused and looked enquiringly at Raya. 'Why do you call him *hamudi*. Is that some kind of para slang?'

Raya shook her head, smiling. 'No. *Hamudi* means darling.'

Keppel and Novak fell about, even Slade joining in the laughter. She slipped her arm through Lee's, smiling happily at them all.

'Now we repack and jump again. Two, perhaps three jumps before we finish today.'

They managed three. Only Corey and Hallis continued on static line, the others using the ripcord as they fell away from the aircraft. But each jump made Lee more confident of the moment he too would lose the security of an automatic release. His last jump was smooth and controlled, his mind sharp and acutely aware of everything about him. Even as his count reached four thousand his head was tilting back, seeing the canopy streaming far above his shoulders, then snapping open into full deployment.

Raya was delighted with his progress, taking every opportunity to coach him for the first free fall which, she warned him, would be as terrifying as his first actual jump.

'You must snap your arms in fast,' she told him. 'Left arm forward in front of your face, right arm across your chest, gripping the ripcord. It's a one-two movement, both arms flinging out again so that you don't alter your balance and begin to somersault.'

They were lying beside each other in the darkness. Their hut was on the far side of the encampment, the remainder of the men showing no surprise when Raya announced that they would share separate quarters.

'What happens if I just use one arm?' Lee asked.

'You spin. That means you must then go back into a star, correct your spin and try again. You must never deploy a Para-Commander whilst you are spinning.'

'Okay, so it's two arms. Snapping them in fast.'

'Right.'

He snapped both arms round her, rolling so that she was suddenly helpless beneath him.

'I've got just one more question, teacher.'

'What's that?'

'Are you going to call for help if I rape you?'

She considered it in the darkness, then said in a musing voice: 'Only if I really think you need help!'

They were long, exhausting days. Each morning began with a work-out in which they ran a mile in the early heat, practised falls, then sat in a circle around Raya who spoke in her clipped, laconic fashion about the precise control of mind and body they must all master.

Keppel and Novak were already into long delayed drops, showing remarkable accuracy from any height. By the third day Keppel had grudgingly admitted to the Israeli girl that the POD packs they were using had many advantages. He had begun to work independently with Slade who had soon shown a natural ability. By the fourth day they were executing three-man link-ups in the steel blue sky, revolving together, then shooting apart to release their parachutes.

Raya concentrated on Hallis, Lorrimer and Corey, the latter bearing the full brunt of her impatience. They began to use the Cessna alternately with Keppel's group, progressing slowly to a five-second delay. For Lee it was an absorbing experience which, in other circumstances, he would have enjoyed enormously. The exhilaration of a controlled fall, feeling the air surging around him, moving it with hands and feet until he could balance his falling body, was a delight he had begun to share with Raya. After four days he had made thirty-two jumps, ten of them free fall with five-second delays – or in precise terms, thirty-two feet per second, per second, giving a total fall of 1,000 feet before the ripcord was pulled, and at least a further 1,000 feet before the parachute opened.

He was spreading out the junior canopy to begin repacking when Raya came up to him and dropped a new pack at his feet. He glanced at her enquiringly.

'How come?'

'You're ready for the Para-Commander.'

'What about Hallis and Lorrimer?'

She shrugged. 'They're not ready yet. You are.'

He nodded, accepting the decision, although he knew that Hallis would certainly be incensed by the news. The young mercenary made no secret of his dislike for the American, but his companions were under no illusions as to his motives and showed no sympathy. Slade, indeed, took a sadistic pleasure in baiting him. Raya's decision, innocent enough in itself, could prove to be the catalyst for the confrontation he knew must come. In a sense he welcomed it, but at the same time it was a complication he would sooner avoid. In less than three days he would know Farik's plan and be in a position to counter it.

They both buckled on their rigs and walked out to the plane. Hallis and Lorrimer were helping the pilot to refuel, giving Raya a questioning look as she reached the Cessna.

'Lee is checking out a PC on this lift,' she told them. 'You pack your chutes and be ready for the next.'

Lorrimer shrugged, taking it well, but Hallis flushed and moved to her, his mouth thin with anger.

'If he's ready, we're ready.'

'That's for me to decide,' she said icily. 'Lorrimer will get his chance today, but unless you stop pulling your release early you won't even see one.'

Hallis glanced at Lee, his eyes small and deadly. 'Break a leg,' he said. It was the traditional exchange of the parachutist. The only difference was – Hallis meant it.

They climbed into the Cessna and waited for Gurber to finish refuelling. Lee watched Raya check out her equipment, never ceasing to be amazed at her grace and natural beauty. Even in the loose jumpsuit with its flared sleeves and legs, the thick-soled boots and heavy crash helmet, she was magnificent. Their nights together had become a total blending of mind and body. They were conscious only of *now,* of a relationship each instinctively knew was rare and complete. A relationship in which their bodies became instruments delicately tuned to desire, each thought, each movement, finding an answering response which grew and grew until they were no longer aware of time and space. A sensual nirvana which never ceased to astound them, and yet was not at all astounding.

Raya explained it simply. *'We match.'* But for Lee it was at once momentous and tragic. After twelve years he had come to expect no more than a cynical response to the age-old urge. Instead he found himself deeply committed to a relationship which would end disastrously in three days' time. It was a depressing thought, enhanced by the cynicism of his belief that in the tragi-comedy of life destiny had a habit of bringing people together too soon, or too late.

A cool hand touched his cheek and he found her smiling at him gently. 'You think too much, Lee Corey.'

He grinned, shaking off the mood. 'And you talk too much. Turn round and let me check you out.'

She turned her back and he pulled open the nylon flap, checking that the three pins of the ripcord cable were correctly positioned and would slide out easily when she pulled the handle. He sealed the flap, checking the risers and harness, then slapped her on the shoulder. She turned and checked his equipment, pushing his reserve pack slightly higher on his chest so that the altimeter and timer could be clearly seen. After satisfying herself that his equipment was in order she set the timer for ten seconds, tapping the altimeter.

'We'll go out at eight thousand feet and pull at four. You should have deployment at three thousand, which gives you nine seconds to cut away your main chute if you have a malfunction.'

He grinned. 'You're such a comfort.'

She was very serious, indicating the release clips on each shoulder. 'You must cut away from a Para-Commander before going for your reserve.'

'Raya,' he reminded her patiently, 'you have drilled that into me day and night. Especially at night!'

She giggled. 'It was the only way I could get any rest!'

The Cessna took off smoothly and began a long, circular climb to eight thousand feet. Below them the Sannine Mountains became flat and featureless, and to the east the horizon showed the ragged purple ridges of the Chmis Mountains in Syria. Raya was beside the pilot, directing him to the jumping area. When she was satisfied she moved to Lee in the open door.

'The minute you hit the wheel, go,' she shouted. 'I'll be right behind you.'

'You mean I've got company this time?'

She grinned. 'Where thou goest . . .'

The pilot throttled back and he slid out of the door, holding the strut with one hand, pressing the start button on the timer as he stepped on to the wheel and launched himself backwards into the slipstream. Immediately the turbulence tried to turn him, but he was ready for it, closing an arm to stop the roll, pulling his legs together which brought his head and shoulders higher. It took no more than a second, and then he was balanced and could let arms and legs fall into the crab position. Now his hands could feel the slightest change of pressure, pushing down into air that had become sponge rubber. Press to the left, correct for the right. Left arm in, turning left. Two seconds had gone by and he was enjoying himself, a glance at the timer showing that the hand was clicking steadily towards the red zone. The altimeter read only 7,500, but his speed was still accelerating to terminal velocity.

Tilting back his head, he searched the sky for Raya, finding her above and to his right. Even as he watched she closed arms and legs, plummeting like a stone, and then as she drew level with him arms and legs went wide and she was braking, turning, then with complete control sliding towards him in a shallow dive until her arms went wide again and her face was no more than two feet from his own. Behind the goggles her eyes were gleaming with delight, her mouth opening and closing as she shouted something to him, but the words were lost in the wind. Grasping his hands in hers, she kicked and they went into a whirling turn. Lee closed his legs and turned it into a backward somersault, then braking with feet spread wide so that they hung together, looking up at the sky, falling with their backs to the earth. He felt her hands tug, then release his own and he rolled over on to his stomach, glancing at the timer. The finger was about to click into the red. With some reluctance he checked his balance, then drew both hands across his body. The left level with his forehead, the right grasping the ripcord, then flinging them both wide with the ripcord and cable now trailing from his right hand.

On his back the POD burst, flipping open the spring-loaded pilot chute. This was immediately snatched away by the wind, pulling out the main canopy until it trailed sixty feet behind him, braking his plunging fall before snapping open. Then the world was still again, swinging gently beneath his feet.

Raya had delayed her own release until she saw his pack open, so that she was now some five hundred feet below him, turning into the wind. He began a long spiral, losing height rapidly until he was level with her. The manœuvrability of the new parachute was remarkable after the basic canopy he had been using. The guide lines split into four at the top of his harness, giving him control over the complex pattern of open panels in the canopy above. Falling at only fifteen feet per second, he was able to glide and bank in the thermals from the sides of the valley, taking his time positioning himself for the landing. Together they soared over the yellow cross, banking and coming back into the wind.

Lee landed lightly, pulling the guide lines to collapse the canopy, then turning to watch Raya touch down less than six feet away. She came towards him, her smile radiant.

'Wasn't it fantastic?'

He grinned. 'Tell me about it.'

They walked back to the camp, talking enthusiastically about free fall and parachutes, neither of them aware of the black Mercedes until they were walking past it. The laughter died. Calad Farik stood waiting for them, a swarthy man beside him who spoke briefly to Raya in Hebrew.

'Miss Dassan,' Farik said formally. 'It is time for us to talk.'

Chapter 20

Farik's meeting with Raya lasted for the remainder of the afternoon. Keppel took over as jump master, getting in three lifts before the sun began to set. Afterwards Lee helped Gurber to fasten the Cessna down for the night, attempting to draw the man out, but the German pilot was weary and wanted only food and sleep. They walked to the camp together, finding Farik sitting beside an open fire passing round champagne.

Lee gave Raya a questioning look as he sat next to her, but her answering smile was nervous and withdrawn. In contrast, Farik was in an expansive mood, toasting them all and then handing each man an envelope with the jovial benevolence of a self-appointed Santa Claus. Inside the envelope, Lee found the name of a private Swiss bank together with an account number and the code that would enable him to use it.

'Three days, gentlemen,' said Farik. 'Three days and none of you will ever need to work again.'

'Time we knew why and how,' said Keppel, staring into his glass.

Farik hesitated, glancing at Slade and then Raya. He forced a smile. 'It is natural that you're curious, but also natural that I do not satisfy it. That is our strength. Need to know . . . and you do not yet need that knowledge.'

'Tell us about the bombs,' said Keppel stubbornly.

'They are progressing. Paxton is living up to all our expectations and will have them ready for collection the day after tomorrow. That is when you will be briefed. When you collect the bombs.'

'You mean they're close?' Lee asked.

'About two hours from here. There will be no trouble transporting them.'

Keppel drained his glass and helped himself to more from the bottle beside the Lebanese. 'We need to know about these bombs now,' he insisted.

'In good time,' replied Farik.

Hallis leaned unsteadily into the firelight, his face flushed with the unaccustomed effect of champagne. 'You heard him, Farik. Now!'

Farik gave him a contemptuous look, then glanced around the group. 'Do you all feel that way?'

No one appeared ready to answer, so Lee said it for them.

'We feel that dropping with an atom bomb could well turn out to be a one-way ride. This account number tells me nothing, except that if I don't show up there isn't any need to put any money in.'

'Don't be stupid,' Farik said sharply. 'This operation is far too big for anyone to risk anything as crazy as a double-cross. The bombs cannot detonate when you're with them. You must take my word for that.'

'You could tell them why,' suggested Slade.

Farik seemed about to argue, but a look passed between them. The Lebanese sighed and reluctantly began to explain.

'The bombs are designed for a very specific purpose. To carry out that purpose they cannot and must not detonate above the ground.'

He watched the looks of bewilderment on their faces with some satisfaction. 'Oil, gentlemen. Less than a thousand miles from here is one-third of the world's total oil. It is locked in the ground, hundreds – thousands – of feet below the surface, and because of that the Arabs believe it is invulnerable. Attack an oil field – as the Israelis have done – and all you destroy are the installations and perhaps a hundred thousand tons. We are going to threaten the destruction of one hundred thousand million million barrels of oil!'

The impossible figure hung in the still air above them. It was incomprehensible and the Lebanese knew it. He laughed softly, his voice shrill and exultant.

'How?' said Lee, his mind numbed by the enormity of the plan.

'When an atomic device, especially a dirty bomb, is detonated below the ground its radiation is locked in the material surrounding it. Detonate such a bomb in an underground ocean of oil and you irradiate it. You make all the oil radioactive for fifty thousand years. It cannot be used.' He laughed. 'Not without killing everyone from the refinery operator to the petrol attendant.'

'That's fantastic,' said Novak. 'You've got the Arabs over the proverbial barrel.'

'Exactly,' Farik said smoothly. 'Each bomb is in a cylinder which fits the casing of the well head. The fields which you will attack are all using certain wells to pump in water, compensating for the oil they take out. It is simplicity itself to dismantle a section of pipe, insert the bomb, then start the pump to send it down into the oil below.'

'And then what?' asked Keppel.

Farik hesitated only fractionally before explaining that each bomb was armed with a remote detonator. Each country would be required to pay a royalty on every barrel taken from the field. He beamed at them. 'Even if the royalty is only one cent a barrel, it is worth millions of dollars a year!'

Lee knew he was lying, but to expose it would be fatal. Farik and Slade would guess that somehow he had overheard the conversation with Paxton. He glanced at Raya, seeing the fervent glow in her eyes, knowing now what Farik had offered her. There were nowhere near enough of them to infiltrate five major oil fields, but with the help of Israeli commando units on the ground it would be a very different matter. That was Raya's importance. And in exchange for her help Farik had promised absolute peace for Israel. The Arab countries could never risk another war if it meant losing the very oil that sustained them.

Farik left at midnight, spending a further hour with Raya and Slade, but the Israeli who had accompanied him remained by the car and spoke to no one. Later, as she lay in his arms, Lee asked about him.

'His name is Simon. He comes from Haifa with word about my people.'

'So they're involved?'

She nodded, brushing her lips across his chest. 'They will help on the ground.'

'And where will you be?'

'With you.' She gazed up at him, the moonlight that filtered through the ravaged roof glistening on a tear. 'Senor Farik has promised that you will go with the first bomb.'

The sadness in her voice puzzled Lee, and then as he felt the tears on her cheeks he began to understand.

'You mean you're not in the drop?'

'No.' The words were torn from her. 'I have just been told. Tomorrow I must go to Haifa, and then I will drop at night on the first target.' She clung to him, trying to explain. 'It's the most important target, the Ghawar Field in Saudi Arabia. There's no way we can get a commando unit into that area, but one person could stay hidden and then guide you down to the edge of the field. I am sorry, Lee. I wanted so much to make the jump with you.'

Lee kissed her gently and lay on his back, grinning like an idiot in the darkness. There was no way he could tell her, no way he could explain the weight she had lifted from him. When the showdown came, she would be out of it . . . a thousand miles away.

Raya left the following morning, collected by an ancient truck with sagging wooden rails that bulged with melons. It would be a long and dusty ride to Haifa, and as he watched her vanish down the road Lee hoped desperately that Max was having the Israeli border points watched. Raya's presence there would at least warn them to watch for movements out of Israel.

Keppel drove them mercilessly throughout the day, putting both Hallis and Lorrimer into Para-Commanders. The young mercenary was showing increasing signs of nerves, never completing a ten-second delay. Keppel jumped with him twice, threatening to break his arm if he pulled too soon, but to no effect. By the end of the day Hallis was a sullen figure, eating alone and speaking to no one.

On the final day a strange aircraft flew low along the valley. Slade must have been waiting for it, producing a signal flare which he fired as it banked at the head of the valley. It was a large, ungainly aircraft with twin overhead engines, but it landed in a remarkably short distance. Keppel identified it as the British Islander, a medium range transport with all the capacity they would need.

The first person to step out of the aircraft was Mallory, greeting Lee with a laconic grin.

'They tell me you've just about made the team.'

'Just about,' Lee replied carefully. 'Is this a present from Uncle Sam?'

Mallory chuckled. 'Beauty, isn't she? Fresh from the factory and cleared for delivery to Iran.'

'The CIA are really going to miss you,' said Lee dryly. 'With your kind of planning you could start World War Three.'

'That's a crazy idea – but I'll think about it.'

Mallory moved away with Slade, the remainder of them spending the afternoon stripping the seats and doors from the Islander. The pilot who delivered it took off before sunset in the Cessna, leaving Gurber sitting moodily at the controls of the new aircraft like a man who had forgotten what he came for.

Lee strolled back to the camp, his nonchalant manner betraying none of the tension that had been building throughout the day. He knew that somehow he must get word to the Embassy in Beirut, but he was twenty miles from the nearest phone and throughout the week there had been no evidence that Max's men had found the valley.

Mallory revealed the probable reason as they drove along the rutted track towards Qaa er Rim. Lee was in the rear of the Land-Rover with Novak and Keppel, Slade driving with Mallory beside him. The Fiat followed with Hallis and Lorrimer.

'You guys have really got it made,' Mallory told them. 'This whole operation is ticking like a time bomb. Nothing can stop it now.'

'The police won't have given up that easily,' Lee remarked casually. 'Not to mention those spooks who worked me over.'

Mallory shook his head slowly, giving him a disdainful look. 'You still don't get the picture. Okay, you guys are the nub of the operation, but the back-up goes all the way to the States. I read a transcript of your meeting in Beirut a week ago.'

Lee felt the perspiration on the palms of his hands. He watched Mallory's eyes, waiting for the first flicker of menace. To his relief Mallory was continuing in a casual tone, totally unaware of the rigid hand ready to slash for his throat.

'The report came in on telex to Washington, pretty dry stuff with plenty of negatives. But they were obviously getting frustrated out here, so we worked a neat little flanker that's got them all snarled up.'

'What sort of flanker?'

Mallory chuckled. 'You were the key, Corey. We put a dummy set of papers together, then paid a guy more money than he's ever seen to slip across the border into Damascus. He took an Israeli girl with him and a trunkful of goodies like grenades, automatics, that kind of thing. Right now they're both in solitary and no way are the Syrians going to let an American near them.'

'That's neat,' Lee said, covering his bitter disappointment. 'But the guy inside must be losing his marbles to buy that kind of deal.'

Mallory shrugged. 'We'll spring them both. That was part of it. In a couple of days we introduce fresh evidence that will clear them. But right now, in Beirut and Washington, they think you're sweating it out across the border.'

'Thanks,' Lee said dryly. 'I'll send them a postcard.'

They drove for ninety minutes, taking the north road out of Zahlé and branching right to the airport at Rayak. They passed through the town shortly after midnight, and took the main highway to Baalbek. The streets of the ancient city of Heliopolis were deserted, the tall white buildings in darkness. The city had been occupied until recently by the Syrians and many of the elegant buildings in the centre, with their marble columns and sweeping balustrades, bore witness to the ravages of war. In the main square, beside the imposing mosque, Farik's black Mercedes waited for them with Troy behind the wheel. It pulled away from the kerb as they approached, turning west past the hospital and through the maze of wicker panels and mounds of rotting garbage that was the old market place.

The Mercedes led them to a desolate factory on the outskirts of the city, a building with buckled walls and a rusted corrugated iron roof that creaked monotonously in the night wind. Only the barbed wire fence surrounding the place was new, and when Troy flashed the headlights a figure stepped out of the shadows and unlocked the gates. As they went past him to park at the rear of the building, Lee recognized the guard who had been in charge of the Paxtons.

The interior of the factory astonished them all with the possible exception of Slade. An inner shell had been constructed at one end, composed of steel and glass. Through the large centre window they could see gleaming lathes, benches and a modern furnace. Beside the window were the controls of the mechanical arms which extended into the laboratory, enabling the operator to work in safety outside during the actual casting of the molten plutonium.

Farik emerged from a wooden office at the opposite end of the building, amused by their curiosity. He took them to the laboratory window, stabbing a triumphant finger at four gleaming cylinders laid out on one of the benches. Beyond them was the gaunt figure of Paxton, encased in PVC with a large transparent helmet over his head. On his back was an oxygen tank connected to the mask. As they watched he was carefully lowering a sphere of grey metal, flecked with coppery veins, into the fifth cylinder.

'There they are,' Farik said reverently. 'Enough energy to obliterate cities, to vapourize everything between here and Damascus.'

'Gives me the creeps,' said Keppel. 'And how do we handle them without wearing the kind of outfit Paxton is using?'

'That's no problem,' Mallory informed them. 'Once the cylinder is closed there's no radiation hazard. Paxton needs that suit because he's handling the plutonium. You've got to realize that plutonium gives out soft, alpha radiation. Hell, you carried the stuff in cans. Just remember that it's only deadly if it gets into your system.'

Farik nodded confidently. 'It's true. Later I'll personally carry one of them out to the Land-Rover.'

They moved back to the office, where a large map of the Middle East was laid out on a table. Mallory stood beside Farik, content to let him do the talking, but studying each member of the team throughout the briefing. There was a subtle air of authority about him which made Lee suspect that, if he was dissatisfied with any member of the group, he would not hesitate to overrule the Lebanese. In spite of his nonchalant manner and clean-cut features, his eyes were shrewd and full of menace. He was by far the most dangerous person in the room because, unlike Farik or Slade, he had long since replaced emotion with precise and uncompromising logic.

'There are five bombs and five targets,' Farik began, his dark features glistening in the light. 'Each bomb will have a standard parachute set to open automatically at 1,500 feet. Your task will be to guide it down to the target area, using a conventional static line attached to the bomb. According to Miss Dassan you are all capable of doing this and, providing you activate your own parachutes at two thousand feet, you will be close to the bomb at all times.'

He picked up a ruler and indicated five circles drawn on the map. 'These are your targets in order of attack. The

Ghawar Field in Saudi Arabia. The Safaniya Field, also in Saudi Arabia. In Kuwait, the Greater Burgan Field. In Iraq, the Rumaila Field and, finally, the Gach Saran in Iran. As you can see, gentlemen, they are all clustered around the Arabian Gulf so there is no necessity for synchronizing your attack. The moment you are on the ground, head for your drop zone where you will be met by units wearing these.'

He held up a vivid orange triangular badge with a black circle in the centre. He glanced at Corey. 'You will take the first bomb into the Ghawar Field where, for reasons of security, we have decided that only Miss Dassan should be waiting for you. But she will choose an area well clear of the military.' He turned to Hallis. 'Because of this arrangement, you will drop with Corey as back-up. If there's trouble, you protect him at all costs.' Hallis nodded, his eyes flicking at Corey with a gleam of satisfaction.

Farik continued. 'Each of you will be taken to a well pumping water into the oil field. There are many of them, the majority unmanned. You have only to disconnect the service panel beyond the pump, insert your cylinder and get out.'

'I suggest you switch the pump off first,' Mallory commented dryly. 'Otherwise there'll be a hell of a lot of water splashing around.'

There was nervous laughter, then Novak asked: 'How long will it take to be pushed down into the oil?'

'It depends entirely on the field and the water pressure they're using. Most of them are between four and ten thousand feet below ground.'

Lee noticed Farik give the slightest of nods to Slade who immediately leaned forward with a question.

'Suppose there's a slip-up and the bomb detonates?'

'It can't happen above ground,' Farik said smoothly. 'And if it should happen at the depth of the field then you will feel only a slight earth tremor. Many of the wells will crack under pressure, of course, but nothing more than that.'

'No radiation?' Keppel asked.

'None at all.' Farik beamed at them and consulted his watch. 'You have two hours to return to your camp, gentlemen. Take-off is at 4 a.m.'

They filed out of the office to the laboratory where Paxton opened the sealed door and passed a cylinder to each man.

Lee carried his out to the Land-Rover, racking his brain for some way of sabotaging the detonator. But Slade was waiting by the vehicle, supervising the loading and looking as though he did not intend to let them out of his sight for a second. Lee moved back to the factory, slipping into the shadows by the door until the last man, Lorrimer, had emerged with a cylinder. He stepped inside, walking casually towards Mallory and Farik who were in deep conversation.

'Orders, Farik. It's orders from the top.'

'I don't like doing things at short notice.'

'The Paxtons have got to be eliminated. They know everything about your operation. Sooner or later they'll talk.'

Farik sighed, then glanced towards the laboratory and frowned with annoyance when he saw Lee.

'What is it, Corey?'

'Just wanted to check on the drop zone. Will Raya be using a beacon or smoke?'

Farik made an irritable gesture. 'She'll be in radio contact with Slade. He'll explain all that to you during the flight.'

'Oh,' Lee looked apologetic, 'I guess I didn't think of that.'

As he started to turn away Farik resumed his conversation with Mallory.

'I'll tell Troy to do it when the rest of them have left.'

'For Christ's sake, Farik, it's got to be clean and simple. There's no time for that kink! What about Corey?'

Lee was almost out of earshot, so he stopped and lit a cigarette.

'I'd prefer one of Keppel's men,' Farik replied. 'We can't hold Slade up now.'

'Okay, so get Hallis in.'

Lee puffed at his cigarette, then stepped towards the door. He was about to open it when Farik called to him. He turned and waited.

'Corey, tell Hallis that we want him in here, and take his place in the Land-Rover. You can tell Slade that Hallis will follow with Mallory in the Fiat.'

'Right away.'

Lee left the factory, his brain working furiously. There was just a chance that Farik's haste, and his reluctance to carry out his own dirty work, was going to give him the one break he needed. Slade was standing at the rear of the Land-Rover, Keppel's men already inside, when Lee strolled out of the darkness.

'Come on, Corey,' Slade snapped. 'We've got to move!'

''Fraid not,' Lee said coolly. 'Farik wants Hallis and I to stay for a while. We'll be following with Mallory in the Fiat.'

'What kind of crap is that? Farik's not changing things this late.'

Lee shrugged. 'Mallory's idea. He wants the Paxtons taken care of . . . neatly.'

Slade cursed under his breath and moved to the front of the vehicle, telling Hallis to get out. A moment later the engine started up and it moved away towards the gate. Hallis gave Lee a questioning look. 'So what's up?'

'Better see Farik. He's in the factory.'

Hallis grimaced and went towards the door. The Land-Rover was turning out of the gate, accelerating away down the deserted road. Lee clung to the deep shadows beside the factory, waiting until the swarthy Lebanese guard came back from the gate. As the man walked unsuspectingly by he smashed a fist behind his ear, catching the unconscious body before it could hit the ground. He searched quickly for a weapon, finding a Walther P38 and a spare clip of ammunition. Slipping them into a pocket he moved to the factory door, edging it open with nerves stretched tight. He was gambling that Hallis would not bother to mention that Lee was still outside.

Through the narrow slit of the partially open door he could see Mallory and Farik talking to Hallis. As he watched they went into the office, closing the door, leaving Hallis gazing towards the laboratory. He took a pistol from his pocket, a silencer from the other, and began to screw it into the barrel of the gun as he walked across the factory floor. Lee waited until his attention was on Paxton, then slipped inside and ran lightly to the laboratory.

Paxton was gazing at the young mercenary with horrified eyes. He started to say something, a hand outstretched, but Hallis was already raising the gun. There was no time for niceties. Lee stepped into the laboratory, his back to the wall.

'Put it down, Hallis, or I put you down.'

Hallis stood perfectly still for a moment, absorbing the words, then lowered his gun and began to turn. Lee waited, knowing it wouldn't be that easy. Hallis completed the turn, locating Lee, then lunged to one side as he brought up the gun. Lee fired, the bullet taking Hallis just above the heart. He hit the floor, his face slack and bewildered, the eyes focusing briefly, and then with a shudder he was dead. Across the factory the door to the office opened and Farik leaned out.

'You idiot, Hallis,' he screamed. 'I told you to use a silencer!'

Lee remained against the wall, motioning for Paxton to keep out of sight. After a moment he heard the office door close and with some relief moved to the chemist.

'Where's your daughter?'

'They keep her in the old generating room. Down the steps on the opposite side of the factory.'

Lee nodded, remembering that he had seen Troy go down some steps earlier. He was probably with her now.

'Wait outside the factory door. The moment I get her out you both run for the centre of the city. Use side streets, hide if you hear anything at all.'

Paxton was nodding, his face reflecting the torment within him. 'Quickly, please,' he whispered.

The corrugated iron roof creaked and groaned in the night, sawing at the nerve ends as Corey edged along the side of the factory, hugging shadows, eyes fixed on the office. He could see the steps now, leading down into a concrete well with a sagging door at the end. Light shone through the cracks in the door, flickering as though from a lantern. He descended slowly, placing each foot firmly to avoid the slightest whisper of sound. The basement gave off unpleasant odours, amongst them the oily smell of a paraffin lamp. Above him a gust of wind rattled the roof and he froze, his hand on the door, believing for a moment that Farik and Mallory had emerged from the office. He moved again, reaching for the door, then jumped with shock as it opened in his face.

Troy froze in mid-step. It was difficult to tell which of them was more surprised by the abruptness of the confrontation. Lee was the first to move, smashing the Dane back through the door and lunging after him. His gun was useless, a shot would bring Mallory and Farik out of the office, effectively trapping him in the enclosed area of the basement.

He found himself in a narrow room, the floor filthy and the air foul. Two camp beds and a wooden table with a lamp upon it were the only objects in the room. Julia lay curled up on one of the beds, her face frozen in a spasm of fear as Lee hurled himself after Troy. The Dane fell across the empty camp bed, twisting to avoid Lee, then backing away and plucking a knife from a scabbard beneath his shirt. The steel in his hand gave him courage and he stopped backing away, moving it from side to side with rapidly increasing confidence.

'All right, you bastard,' he whispered. 'Come and play.'

Lee stepped to one side, watching him turn, then leaned back as the knife slashed at him. Troy was getting the feel of it now, his eyes coming alight, his mouth curving into a contemptuous sneer. At any moment he was going to realize that all he had to do was shout loud enough and Farik would hear. Lee knew that he had scant seconds in which to act.

He swayed to the right, extending a hand with clumsy slowness, his eyes fixed on the knife as it stabbed at the arm. At the last moment he flicked it aside, then smashed his foot into the Dane's kneecap. The man's eyes bulged and his mouth gaped, the cry of pain starting in his throat, then dying in a gurgle as Lee got a forearm around his neck and gripped the knife hand. They swayed backwards and forwards before the girl's terrified gaze. Lee tried to twist the knife from the Dane's hand, but fear and pain were giving him added strength. In desperation Lee unlocked the arm around Troy's throat, gripping his wrist with both hands. The Dane was already sucking in breath for a shout when Lee forced his arm down, pushing him forward on to the angled blade of the knife. It sank deep into the Dane's abdomen and a second later his shrill scream of agony was echoing up the stairs and around the empty factory walls. It was unmistakably the cry of a dying man.

The office door burst open and Farik ran out, bellowing for Hallis. Behind him Mallory already had a gun in his hand, reaching for the light switch and plunging the factory into darkness.

Lee crouched at the bottom of the steps, hearing the tense whispers from the two men. Farik still wanted to believe that Hallis had killed Julia, but Mallory was too old a hand for that. In the room behind him the harsh breathing of the Dane suddenly stopped and the only sound was the stifled sobbing of the girl.

Corey mounted the steps to the factory floor, feeling for

the wall and moving silently along it until he was well clear of the light from the basement. Footsteps ran across the concrete floor, then someone stumbled and cursed softly. There was no mistaking Farik's shrill falsetto. Lee smiled, settling back to wait. The Lebanese was moving away towards the laboratory, looking for cover rather than quarry. Corey held the Walther P38 in both hands, straining his ears for Mallory, knowing he was the dangerous one. The hunter.

'Okay, you bastard. Who are you? Not Slade, or Keppel. Lorrimer's too thick, so it's either Novak or Corey?'

The CIA man's voice whispered around the walls, seeming to come from nowhere and everywhere. Lee gave up trying to place it, realizing he was using an old trick. By holding a board or piece of metal in front of his face he was throwing his voice at different walls, making it impossible to locate him with any accuracy.

'I personally checked out Novak through the mercenary bureau in Amsterdam, so I know he's not a plant. It has to be you, Lee Corey. And you have to be with the Feds.'

Lee had to admire his logic, and he had to keep him talking. He had narrowed the voice down to the area around the office and that meant Mallory was hoping to get some idea of his position before switching the lights back on. He held the P38 tightly, ready for the blinding flash of light, wishing he had the PPK version that could put a stream of bullets through the wooden walls of the office.

'Why don't we talk, Corey? We're on the same side if you'd start to listen . . . Have you any idea what it will mean to destroy Arab power in the west? I'm telling you, the CIA and the President are one hundred per cent behind this caper.'

'Crap, Mallory,' Corey said, turning his face to the wall and whispering so that the words hung in the air. 'In the first place the CIA don't know a thing about it, and in the second they don't know a thing about you. You're operating for Signus Five, for hard cash, and my guess is that you worked your way into the CIA as a mid-west field operator.'

There was a long silence. Lee smiled grimly, imagining the shock Mallory must be feeling at the mention of Signus Five.

'Okay, so it's cash,' Mallory said finally. 'You can still settle for that. Five million in any country in the world. I guarantee it.'

'Save it, Mallory.' Lee had the pistol lined up on the area

of the office, sure now that he was crouching in the doorway.

'Give it a thought,' the voice insisted softly. 'There's only one alternative. Even if you get me, they won't rest until you're in little pieces.'

Even as he said the last word the lights exploded throughout the factory, dazzling him, but as the black figure flickered in the office door he fired by instinct, placing a stream of spaced shots across the doorway. Mallory was on one knee, balancing a Mauser automatic across his left wrist as he swung it in an arc across the floor. It took fractionally more than one second to find his target, and in that moment the first bullet had smashed into his shoulder, turning him into the path of the second bullet which hit the jaw, ricocheting off shattered bone up through the cortex into the centre of the brain. Lee was still firing blind when Mallory hit the floor.

Changing the magazine in the P38, Lee moved cautiously along the wall, searching the shadows around the shell of the laboratory for some sign of Farik. The building was still, silent. He was halfway along the factory wall when he saw the shoes. They were Farik's, close to the door which was ajar. With bitter frustration he realized the Lebanese had slipped out during the talking. Apart from the problems that would cause when he tried to leave, he dare not let Farik warn Slade. He ran to the door, flattening himself beside it to look out. Almost as he did so he felt the warning prickle of fear, subconscious alarms going off as he realized his analysis was false. Farik would not leave. He had more to lose than anyone.

'If one muscle moves, Mr Corey, you are dead.'

The voice came from the laboratory. Lee didn't need to look to know that Farik would be standing there with a gun.

'Open the hand and let the gun fall,' he instructed.

'It's cocked.'

'Then we'll have to hope it doesn't go off and blow a hole in you.'

Lee let the gun fall to the floor, then turned slowly to face the Lebanese. He was stepping out of the laboratory, gesturing with his gun.

'In here. Keep your hands up and be careful, putting a bullet in you is going to be such a pleasure.'

He went into the laboratory, walking straight ahead until Farik told him to stop. He was beside the small blast furnace and against a steel work bench.

'Put your hands behind your back,' said Farik, his voice thick with emotions that brought a cold sweat of fear to Lee's face. For a moment he debated ending it now, turning and lunging at the gun. He rejected the thought and put his hands behind his back, allowing Farik to slip a wire noose around them, jerking it tight. He swung Lee round to face him, the eyes glowing with sadistic delight.

'Bastard!' he hissed, slamming a fist into his stomach.

Lee doubled up, gasping, and would have fallen had not Farik looped the end of the wire over a metal bracket, pulling it tight to stretch up his arms. Supremely confident now, the Lebanese went to the furnace and pulled out a thick steel tube connected by rubber hose to oxy-acetylene cylinders. It reminded Lee of a thermic lance and a numbness began to settle over his mind as he realized what Farik intended to do.

He took his time, glancing frequently at Lee's pale features, enjoying the fear he found there. Finally he was ready, flicking his lighter in front of the tube which spurted out a blue-white lance of flame. The shrill laughter echoed around the room, then slowly he advanced towards him.

Lee was only dimly aware of the large steel claws which seemed to swoop down from the heavens, clamping on Farik's shoulder and his neck. Cogs moved and cables tightened, closing steel fingers that crushed bone and flesh, then lifted the screaming Lebanese high above the laboratory floor.

Outside the glass window Paxton operated the robot arms with an almost scientific detachment. Only the eyes burned with hatred as he watched the figure writhe and scream, heard bones snap, saw the blood falling like crimson rain. Finally, without the slightest expression of pity, he jerked the controls in his right hand and the steel claws contracted around Farik's neck, snapping it like a match stick.

He unhooked the wire and freed Corey's hands, never looking once at the figure above them. They went out of the laboratory, Julia rushing to him from the basement steps.

Lee spoke to him briefly, then ran for the Mercedes. He doubted if Paxton would be able to find a phone at this hour, and even if he did the chance of getting prompt action through Beirut was doubtful. In less than ninety minutes the Islander would leave, and there was no way he could let it leave without him.

Chapter 21

The last five miles along the rutted track which twisted its way into the Sannine Mountains was a hair-raising drive, even by Lee Corey's standards. The Mercedes slid and jolted around bends that doubled and redoubled into the night. Boulders came and went, craters pounded the suspension, but his only hope of reaching the plane in time was by pushing the car to the limit. During the drive to Zahlé he had considered the possibility of driving to Beirut, waking the Embassy staff and alerting each of the threatened oil fields to the danger. The chances were that the Arab security forces would have reacted in time, but the real problem was Slade.

If no one arrived from Baalbeck his suspicions would be aroused. And when a man like Slade became suspicious there was no way of guessing what he would do. Certainly if Lee was in his position he would postpone the attack, move the aircraft and bombs to a new location, then find Farik or Mallory. The moment Slade discovered that they were both dead he would devise some new plan and carry it out.

It was a risk Lee dare not take. Not as long as Slade was in possession of five fully armed atomic bombs.

The car roared over the last rise, headlights sweeping across the valley below, then began descending to the line of glowing oil lamps marking the runway, flickering like fireflies in the night. As he reached the floor of the valley and bounced over rock-strewn gullies and mounds of shale, he could hear the roar of the Islander's engines. A light flashed at him from the fuselage door and he breathed a sigh of relief, slewing the car round in a sliding stop, then running for the plane.

'What the hell is your game, Corey?' Slade demanded, his face tight with anger. 'We should have taken off five minutes ago.'

'We had trouble,' Lee gasped. 'Farik thought you might hold off so he told me to take the Mercedes.'

'What kind of trouble?'

'The stupid kind,' he said, climbing into the Islander. 'That idiot Troy let the girl get away while Hallis and I were dealing with the old man. You know what it's like in the dark round here. They were still hunting for her when I left.'

Slade's eyes bored into him, searching for some thread of duplicity. Lee gazed back until finally he cursed softly and began to move towards the pilot's cabin.

'My kit on board?'

Slade paused and pointed out the equipment beside the five gleaming cylinders. Lee sat down, feeling the tension begin to dissolve. Keppel came and sat beside him, his jumpsuit festooned with grenades, clips of ammunition and a wicked-looking knife clipped to the top of his reserve parachute.

'You say Hallis stayed?'

Lee nodded. 'You should have seen Farik. He was like a madman, screaming at all of us. Mallory and Troy covered the rear of the factory, Farik and that stupid guard searching along the fence. He was going to send Hallis and me along the road in case she tried to reach the town, and then he realized that Slade might cancel.'

'It was getting that way,' Keppel admitted. Then with reluctant approval. 'I guess if it was between you and Hallis, there wasn't much of a contest.'

'That's right,' Lee said calmly, remembering how the mercenary had turned, telegraphing his move, trying for an impossible shot.

Gurber opened the throttles of the Islander's twin Avco Lycoming engines and it began to lumber along the runway, lifting away in a remarkably short space of time, to start a long, low climb out of the valley and over the Sannines towards Syria. Lee stripped off his clothes and donned the jumpsuit together with the thick-soled para boots. He hoisted the rig on to his back, buckling each section until there was no movement in the POD. He clipped on the reserve chute, placed four grenades in loops at his waist, slipped the Colt Commander into the pouch on his right thigh and spare magazines for the pistol and the sub-machine gun on his left. Picking up the 9mm Stirling he checked it thoroughly, recalling the last time he had held the deadly British weapon as part of a terrorist attack on Rome's Leonardo da Vinci Airport*. There had been no way out of that situation either.

Slade returned from the cockpit and hunched down beside

* *The Connector*, Collins, 1975

Lee on the floor. There was an uneasiness about him, as though some sixth sense was gnawing at his instincts.

'Did Farik say anything else to you?'

Lee thought about it. 'No. He was foaming at the mouth most of the time, screaming about what he was going to do to Troy if he didn't find the girl.'

'But the situation didn't make him consider delaying the drop?'

'No way, Slade. That's why he sent me. He was afraid you'd hold off if no one arrived.'

Slade pulled the knife out of his scabbard on his reserve chute, idly playing with the tip, turning it in his hands so that it gleamed coldly in the cabin lights.

'Yeah, he'd think that all right.' Suddenly he relaxed and gave Lee a crooked grin. 'You go in on your own then, hot shot. Make it good.'

'Like an apple in a barrel. Raya's sharp. She'll have it all weighed up on the ground.'

'Right. She'll be using a two-way radio and a reflector. We'll home in on her signal, at a maximum height, then you go when she uncovers the reflector. You'll probably see it before you jump, but even so you'll pick it out easily enough.'

Lee nodded. 'What height do I drop?'

'Eighteen thousand feet. We'll be on oxygen in the cabin so you better take one long deep breath before you go.'

'That's the best idea you've had all day.'

Slade grinned. 'At least you'll keep your mouth shut for a change. If you open it above ten thousand feet you'll be in trouble.'

Lee gave him a tight-lipped smile and stretched his legs out across the cabin floor. Facing him were the five cylinders, each numbered in order of drop. They were about three feet long, quite small in circumference to allow an easy passage down the thousands of feet of pipe. Inside the barometric detonators would be set for the depth of the oil field it was destined for: Gawar, 5,900; Rumaila, 10,000; Greater Burgan 4,000. He sat and studied them, working out how they came apart.

There was a barely discernible line halfway along the nearest cylinder which looked promising. He bent forward, re-tying the lace on his boots, getting close enough to the cylinders to be certain. They were obviously in two sections which screwed together. In one section would be the outer sphere of plutonium. In the other, the plastic explosive and detonator placed behind the core of plutonium, ready to blast it into the outer sphere. Dismantling it would not be difficult, but reaching the detonator without touching the plutonium was the kind of problem he would rather be without.

Novak, Lorrimer and Keppel had started a game of three-card brag at the forward end of the cabin, getting as far away from the open doorway as possible. Slade had rejoined the pilot, so Lee carefully shifted his position until he was no more than a short dive from the door. If the Paxtons had got through to the Embassy, then Max would be doing his utmost to lay on a fighter interception. If that happened he wanted to be through that door in zero seconds.

The first pale light of dawn was touching jagged mountain ridges less than a thousand feet below. They would be well into Syria by now, so they were almost certainly the Nasrani Mountains. He glanced at his watch. Almost five o'clock. By daylight they would be over Iraq, hugging the mountain ranges to avoid radar. He leaned back and closed his eyes, trying to formulate a plan. After an hour he was forced to admit that any attempt to take over the aircraft would be suicidal. Even though Keppel and his men were absorbed in their cards, Lee was under no illusions as to what the outcome would be if he faced them with a gun.

The Islander followed the low mountain ranges from Syria into Iraq, dropping into valleys and hopping a thousand ridges, rising with the land into the Mountains of Shammar. There were no fighter patrols, and what radar existed in the sparsely populated region was aimed at Israel. With increasing concern, Lee watched the parched landscape flow past, the steel blue sky featureless and empty. Paxton knew where they were heading and when, yet there was no indication of any search by the Saudi Arabian Air Force.

At that precise moment Donald Paxton was desperately trying to persuade a bored Lebanese policeman that he was not a spy, not a criminal, not an illegal entrant.

'For God's sake, man,' he said bitterly. 'Just call the American Embassy in Beirut.'

'Then you are American?'

'No, I've told you, my daughter and I are British. But the

Americans will explain.'

'The American Embassy has no jurisdiction over British subjects, if you *are* British, of course.'

'All right, all right, call the British Embassy.'

The policeman sipped black Turkish coffee and studied the form he had laboriously filled out. Paxton fumed. On the other side of the office Julia Paxton sat dejectedly, thinking of Lee Corey.

'They will not take calls before eight o'clock. Perhaps we will do it then.'

Paxton closed his eyes and visualized his favourite equation. He had been trying to get through to him for almost an hour, after wasting two hours with a constable who could not speak English and answered every question with the word 'Passaport'. He took a deep breath and tried again.

'If you will just let me use the telephone. One call. That's all I ask.'

The Lebanese studied the ceiling, the floor, the smoke-stained fingers of his right hand, and said: 'You have the money to pay for this call?'

'No. But you *will* be repaid.'

The policeman smiled, sure of his ground. 'It is not possible. If you cannot pay for the telephone it must be paid for by the police. If it is a police call it is official, and such a call I could not authorize. Only the commissioner could give such an authorization.'

Donald Paxton mopped the perspiration from his face and controlled a powerful urge to strike the man. 'When will he be here?'

The Lebanese consulted the four walls and the ceiling, then shrugged. 'Perhaps eight thirty. Perhaps nine.'

At eight thirty the Islander was climbing steadily, a silver speck above the desert, and Lee Corey finally accepted that there was going to be no interception. There was only one course left open to him, but it had to be taken with split-second timing.

The card game had ended. Keppel and his men sat with still features, watching the Arabian Gulf crawl over the horizon. The atmosphere was thin and cold. Each breath seemed to take forever. The cylinders of oxygen were passed around with increasing frequency as they began to approach eighteen thousand feet. Slade appeared, signalling to Lee. He rose and sat by the doorway, feeling the leaden ball of fear, wishing there could be some other way. The earth was a featureless plain of sand twisting around the brilliant turquoise eye of the Gulf.

Slade crouched beside him, watching the desert far below. Keppel and Novak carried the cylinder marked No. 1 to the edge of the door, arranging the twenty feet of static line in loops beside it before passing the end to Lee. He gripped it in his left hand, pulling down his goggles and checking the harness. The parachute that would support the bomb was a small reserve pack, clipped to the side of the cylinder. Keppel knelt beside it and armed the 'Sentinel' automatic release which was already set for 1,500 feet. At that height a spring-loaded pin would detonate the small explosive charge, releasing the parachute.

Slade was speaking into the two-way radio, bending forward in the doorway. Lee took a deep breath from the oxygen cylinder, pushing back the dizziness, trying not to think of Raya on the ground below. It had to be precise, he told himself. If he was a fraction of a second too soon or too late he would fail and the Doomsday Contract would be fulfilled. The awesome responsibility was draining the strength from his limbs. He felt light-headed, no longer conscious of arms or legs. Then Slade was turning to him, bellowing in his ear, and suddenly every nerve was firing signals. The adrenalin began to flow.

'Any second now,' shouted Slade. 'The moment you see the flash of the reflector, you go.'

He nodded, steeling himself to move slowly. His right hand slipped down to his waist, unhooked a fragmentation grenade and brought it across his body to his left hand. He pulled the pin, holding the detonator arm tightly, moving it back to his right side. No one noticed, everyone was gazing down at the desert below. A brilliant light flashed. Keppel pushed the cylinder through the open door and Slade roared: 'Go!'

Lee fell forwards, waiting until he had almost cleared Slade's crouching figure, then flinging the grenade back down the body of the aircraft. And then he was out, spreading arms and legs wide, twisting in the howling slipstream, his brain splitting images and freezing them. Images of Slade glancing at his hand a second before the grenade left it. They had seen.

In the Islander the grenade bounced along the floor, its detonator firing with a crack. Keppel and Slade watched it roll the length of the plane, then turned as one for the doorway, diving out without pause or hesitation. Behind them Novak was a split second slower, then he too launched himself out of the aircraft. Lorrimer was halfway down the cabin, watching Corey leave and trying to hide his tension, when the grenade flew past him, hitting the floor and bouncing away down the aircraft. With numbed disbelief he watched it strike the forward bulkhead, then roll against a cylinder of oxygen. The disbelief became horror and he glanced towards the doorway in time to see Keppel and Slade dive out, followed almost immediately by Novak. He began to run for the door, his tight harness and heavy packs dragging at each step. The fear rose like bile in his throat and he began a long howl of anguish. He was one step from the sky when the grenade exploded. The blast ripped open the fuselage, tore into the cockpit and disintegrated the controls before Gurber's uncomprehending eyes, blasted Lorrimer out through the doorway where he whirled and twisted like a rag doll. He felt no pain, was unaware of the dozen fatal wounds in his body. The last thing he saw was three figures far below, swooping towards a fourth figure that had to be Corey.

The moment Lee had stabilized his fall, he released the static line attaching him to the bomb and angled his body, turning over on his back. Keppel and Slade were already in the sky, Novak following in a clean dive. He noted the fact without surprise, more concerned with the effect of the grenade. He doubted that the explosion would trigger the atom bombs, then wondered if he would see the flash if it did. A second later the aircraft blew apart a thousand feet above him and began to fall slowly towards the desert. A great weight lifted from his mind and he began to concentrate on staying alive.

Keppel and Slade were closest to him, no more than two hundred feet above. He watched them falling with perfect control, Keppel closing arms and legs, increasing his velocity, then flinging them wide again. Only now he had the Stirling sub-machine gun in his hands, holding it against his chest with elbows pushed out to keep him stable. Slade followed suit, then beyond them Novak fired the first burst.

Corey watched with a detached admiration at the way he

held the weapon against his chest, the stubby barrel giving out tiny white flashes as it spat a stream of 9mm bullets towards him. They were rapidly reaching terminal velocity of 180 mph, Keppel and Slade kicking with their feet, twisting shoulders and hips to bring them directly above him. It was time to make life difficult for them.

He swept in his right arm, closed his legs and flipped over on to his stomach, spreading wide into a star, then kicking with his feet to turn at right angles. The thin air howled around his body, his mouth tightly closed to hold the oxygen in his lungs. Below the earth was still a hazy sea of sand, but a brilliant light was flashing at him some four miles ahead. He wondered if Raya was able to see him yet, then decided that she could not. There was a crackling past his ear and with a shock he realized that someone had managed a burst that close. He moved again, banking and soaring away to the left. He balanced, then grabbed the Stirling from his leg, feeling his body start to somersault, every muscle straining to correct. The spinning turn stopped and he was on his back again, finding with a shock that Keppel was no more than fifty feet away.

Keppel's expert knowledge of skydiving was giving him much greater mobility, and this was also true of Novak. Even as Lee picked him out some four hundred feet above, the mercenary arched his body into a perfect aerodynamic form and dived like a golden arrow, accelerating through the TV barrier to well over 200 mph. Lee waited for him, cocking the Stirling and pulling it hard against his chest. Novak would have to brake and position himself before he could fire.

Slade fired another burst, realizing that Novak was taking a dangerous gamble, but the air was getting thicker, screaming in his ears, pulling at the machine gun so that his shots went wide. Novak spread wide, gun clenched in one hand, grenade in the other. Ten feet below him Lee pressed the trigger, feeling the recoilless weapon shudder gently in his hands, sweeping it across the yellow figure above. The bullets ripped into Novak, killing him instantly, then his hand opened and the grenade floated free, bobbing about but keeping pace with the dead mercenary. Lee saw the detonator puff smoke and recognized the danger, closing his arms to dive forward, kicking with his left foot to bank away. Above him Keppel and Slade were also moving, turning left and right away from the grenade below.

Two seconds later it detonated, shredding the lifeless body of Novak, filling the air briefly with scarlet rain which glistened in the sun and then, like some grotesque mirage, evaporated into a small pink cloud that took its place in the sky. Lee checked his fall, glancing at his altimeter and noting that he was now at ten thousand feet.

It was still no more than twelve seconds since they had left the plane.

Keppel was away to his right, Slade some four hundred feet above. He decided to ignore the latter, concentrating on Keppel who was already positioning himself for attack. He fired a burst, then turned and moved at right angles to him. The air was thicker now, beating at him with pneumatic fists, pummelling legs and arms and threatening to tear the weapon from his hands. He opened his mouth, sucking in a deep breath, feeling the welcome oxygen clear his head. He was turning slowly, the menacing figure of Keppel drifting across his eyeline, hanging crab-like in the sky with the stubby barrel of the Stirling tracking and holding him. It fired a steady burst and the air popped all around him, one of the bullets glancing off his helmet with an impact that raked the muscles of his neck.

He turned and dived, but Keppel was ready for the move, tracking him with ease, following each desperate manœuvre with tenacious skill.

Together they wheeled against the steel blue dome, Slade content to follow them down, awaiting the outcome of the duel. They rose and fell, banked and turned, soared to and away from each other like exotic birds of prey. The guns fired but the sound was lost in the constant scream of air. Their bodies twisted, executed impossible turns, but Keppel still clung to his quarry as they raced for the earth below.

Lee checked his altimeter, felt a chill of fear as he saw the needle moving rapidly towards two thousand. Below, the desert was no longer a featureless plain. He could see the ribbons of oil pipes, the wells that stretched away on either side towards the gulf. Keppel was waiting for him to go for his ripcord, knowing that the first one down had the advantage. He would delay to the last possible moment.

The altimeter needle was on two thousand, into the red danger zone. He steeled himself for the pull, eyes fixed on

Keppel as he came in crabbing, gun held steady. It fired, spitting light, and he felt a numbing blow on his leg that sent him spinning madly across the sky. Lee closed arms and legs, flung them wide, corrected, then snatched for the ripcord. Any malfunction now and there would be no hope of deploying the reserve. He felt the POD rip open on his back, the pressure increasing on thighs and shoulders as the streaming parachute began to break his fall. And then, with the desert leaping at him, the canopy snapped open above his head and he was swinging gently in a silence that seemed deafening.

Keppel's Para-Commander was snapping open some two hundred feet below and to one side. Immediately he began to turn and slope away, trying to get clear and on the ground. Lee took careful aim, then pressed the trigger until the magazine was empty, watching the bullets plucking at the canopy below, shredding panels, cutting lines. He had no way of knowing if Keppel was hit. The weakened crown of the canopy suddenly gave way, ripping open, sending Keppel plummeting towards the sand some four hundred feet below. He gathered momentum as he went, the canopy collapsing into a tattered bundle that fluttered uselessly above his head.

Lee watched without emotion until the tiny figure crashed into the desert, then he began to look for Slade. He found him finally, a thousand feet above, driving his parachute south to put him well clear when he landed. In the shimmering haze of the desert to the north there was an oily mushroom of smoke and a distant concussion as the Islander crashed. He noted with relief that it was well clear of coast and oil field. Clearing the radioactive plutonium from the desert would be a major operation that would take months, perhaps years.

He turned slowly, searching for wind direction, feeling his rate of descent decrease. Then the sand was drifting up at him and he was touching down, collapsing immediately as his left leg buckled beneath him.

Releasing the harness he let it blow away, examining the bullet hole in his thigh which was steadily oozing blood. The bone appeared to be intact, but it was doubtful if it would bear his weight. Two hundred yards away a small white canopy collapsed around a glittering cylinder. He began to crawl towards it, then paused and fitted a fresh magazine in the Stirling. He was cocking the gun when some sixth sense made him glance up. Slade was swooping down, suspended beneath his Para-Commander, guiding it straight at him. Instead of landing out of range, he had turned back, using Lee's landing to disguise his actions.

The Stirling began to fire when he was still a hundred yards away, detonating a ragged line across the desert. Lee hurled himself to one side, pain stabbing through his injured leg. Bullets were exploding all around him as he lifted the barrel of the sub-machine gun. Slade had gauged his approach perfectly. He was swooping out of the sun at a decreasing angle which would, in seconds, have put him above and behind Corey's back. It was a desperate gamble, providing him with a clear line of fire, but equally setting him up as an easy target. Even as Lee turned he was pulling at the guide lines, swinging into the gentle breeze which briefly gave him lift.

Lee waited, his Stirling tracking the swaying figure which was moving in a wide arc around him. Needles of light flickered from the gun in Slade's hands and the sand exploded around Lee. He was only dimly conscious of the stinging sand, of the echoes that shattered the silence, his gaze riveted on the figure that swooped like a golden hawk. Slade fired again, the burst of 9mm blasting a line of holes across the desert which ended a foot from his face. Lee ignored them. He was remembering Freddy, the way she had looked, the terror in her eyes.

Slade was banking again, less than fifty feet from the ground, manipulating the guide lines with casual skill to bring him round for the final approach. Lee allowed him to complete his turn, then pressed the trigger. The Stirling chattered, sending a stream of bullets to meet the figure that swooped towards him. Slade was powerless to avoid them, managing only one desperate burst at the elusive figure below before the bullets tore into him. Lee watched dispassionately as the descending figure jerked in the air like some macabre puppet, only taking his finger off the trigger when Slade was drifting over his head.

He passed no more than ten feet above him, the Stirling clenched in frozen fingers, the head sunk low to gaze blindly into infinity. A trail of blood fell across the desert, ending like an exclamation mark where the body crumpled into the sand.

Lee put his weapon aside and began to slit open the leg

of his jumpsuit. The crunch of feet on sand made him glance round, his stomach tightening with miserable alarm as he saw the gun in her hands. It was the moment he had dreaded. Raya had come, as he knew she would, and he searched her face for some flicker of compassion. All he found was revulsion.

'You!' she said bitterly, as though still unable to comprehend it. 'All the time it was you. A spy!'

He shook his head wearily. 'Just a policeman, Raya. Doing what he has to do.'

'This!' She spat the words at him, gesturing at the body of Slade, to the bloody bundle that was Keppel a hundred yards away. 'You've destroyed everything we worked for.'

He nodded calmly, wondering how many seconds he had left. The Uzi in her hands was steady, her gaze unwavering. Only her bewilderment held him back from infinity.

'Who do you mean by we, Raya?' he asked quietly. 'Farik, Slade and Mallory? Or your own people?'

'It is the same,' she said scornfully.

He shook his head. 'Wrong. You were conned. This was not for Israel, it was for money. Neither your government, nor the Mossad, knew anything about this. Your cell in Haifa was used, just as you were.'

Her full lips curled with contempt. 'There is no point in lying.'

'Exactly. I know you intend to pull that trigger, so go ahead. But afterwards do me a favour. Open that cylinder over there and look at the detonator. You'll find a simple barometer which will close a firing circuit when it reaches 6,000 feet below sea level. There's no fancy remote control, there couldn't be that far below ground.'

She looked uncertain, her eyes boring into him. 'There has to be a remote control.'

'Only if they were planning to hold a gun to the heads of the Arabs. But that was never part of the plan. Their way was very simple. Detonate the bombs and clean up in every oil market in the world. It's got nothing to do with politics. Only money.'

'I don't believe you,' she said, but the words were etched with doubt.'

'Then go ahead and shoot.'

The words hung between them and he watched the hardness

come into her face. She was less than ten feet away and with a curiously detached interest he watched her finger whiten on the trigger. The heat of the sun became a cold wind, the light itself fading like a lamp running out of oil. She was suddenly a distant figure, slim and lovely, and tears glistened on her cheeks as she pressed the trigger.

With a mild astonishment he heard the shots crack the air above his head. Then there was silence and the sky was bright again. Raya sank slowly to the sand, the sobs torn from her in deep, shuddering breaths. He waited until the spasms were over, then crawled painfully to her.

'You and your people were involved because they needed a scapegoat. Who else would destroy Arab oil fields with atom bombs?'

'To destroy the oil would end Arab power,' she said, with some uncertainty.

He shook his head firmly. 'No way. Sure, they would lose a lot of their wealth, but they own a sizeable chunk of Europe already. There would still be Arab oil, twice – maybe three times – as expensive. The people behind Farik have been buying up oil for months, selling currencies in the west, speculating on the stock markets. God knows how much they would have made. Only one thing is certain . . . Israel would get the blame.'

'*Ei,*' she nodded, her young face lined and sad. 'It would have been another war of attrition. It would be the end.'

He kissed her gently and she clung to him.

'What now?'

'Well, if you're not too busy I could do with a tourniquet. Then we just sit around and hope that my people are saying nice things to the Saudis.'

She looked at his shattered leg and tears welled up into her eyes again.

'To think I could have killed you.'

He grinned. 'You mean you weren't trying?'

'Trying!' she spluttered. 'Do you really think I could have missed?'

'Then why did you?'

She gazed at him solemnly, then touched his face with a gentle hand.

'It was too much to bear. I would have felt each bullet every day of my life, *hamudi.*'

Chapter 22

'Maybe you should retire,' Max was saying, perched on the side of the hospital bed in Al Qatif. 'I can think of one or two useful jobs you could do.'

'Tell me about them,' Lee said dryly.

'Liaison officer with the meteorological department. They have an opening at the North Pole.'

'It's a thought. You think I'd get the job?'

'I can guarantee it,' Max said fervently. 'In fact, Congress sat all night debating whether to have you decorated or deported.'

'How did the voting go?'

'Lee, why in hell couldn't you have let us handle it from Beirut? It would have been clean, sterile, a snap. The plane could have been shot down by Arab fighters for violating their air space. End of story.'

'I had to be sure. Suppose they'd missed?'

Max groaned and looked up at the ceiling. 'You didn't have to tell the Saudi Arabians that the girl was working for us. She's Jewish, for Christ's sake!'

'So is Henry Kissinger.'

'Lee, I've got so many knives in my back I feel like Rasputin.'

Lee beamed at him. 'You just broke my dream!'

The door opened and a nurse came in accompanied by two orderlies. She smiled at Lee with limpid eyes, not even looking at Max.

'The ambulance is here to take you to the airport, Mr Corey.'

Max frowned and glanced at his watch. 'There must be a mistake. It's not due until this afternoon.'

The nurse looked puzzled. Lee tapped his forehead with a finger and rolled his eyes. She began to smile again and gestured to an orderly who rolled the invalid chair forward. They had lifted Lee into the chair and covered him with a blanket before Max had worked it out.

'Just a moment,' he said. 'Is this thc plane to take Mr Corey to Washington?'

'No, sir,' said the nurse. 'It is a charter flight to Zurich.'

'The mountain air will do me good,' Lee said conversationally. 'And as the Arabs were so grateful it was the very least they could do.'

'Out of the question,' snapped Max as they rolled him towards the door. 'You're due in Washington tomorrow morning.'

Lee nodded to the attendant who continued rolling the chair out into the corridor. Max followed, talking all the way to the ambulance. The gist of his message, punctuated with growing frequency by colourful expletives, was that a comprehensive report was needed to avoid a congressional enquiry. That the department's insurance plan did not cover hospitalization in Swiss clinics. That if he didn't obey orders he was fired.

Lee threw him a mocking grin and rolled up into the ambulance.

'Say hello to Ferryman and his buddies.'

'Corey,' Max grated in his most devastating tone. 'You've got two weeks. Not a day more.'

'Listen, you miserable bastard! A leg like this takes months.'

'So I'll send you crutches!'

They closed the ambulance door, leaving Max fuming in the road. What added insult to injury was the fact that Lee Corey had kissed the nurse waiting for him in the ambulance. She had been tall, slim, distinctly attractive with hazel eyes and wild, chestnut hair.